MW00510454

Tobias Jenkinson was born and raised in North London, attended school only when forced to do so. Upon leaving school, he took employment in various unskilled positions of gardener, compressor operator, milkman and lager mate. Upon meeting his wife of fifty-two years, he joined the Royal Air Force and had a very successful career of twenty-two years as an avionic technician. Post his air force days, he became an aircraft technical contractor working for various air forces and manufactures as a technician and instructor in both Europe and the Middle East, where he found he had a lot of time on his hands and took an interest in writing and here ten years later is the first of the resultant output.

Tobias Jenkinson

CODENAME NEMESIS

AUSTIN MACAULEY PUBLISHERS™

LONDON * CAMBRIDGE * NEW YORK * SHARJAH

Copyright © Tobias Jenkinson (2021)

The right of Tobias Jenkinson to be identified as author of this work has been asserted by the author in accordance with section 77 and 78 of the Copyright, Designs and Patents Act 1988.

All rights reserved. No part of this publication may be reproduced, stored in a retrieval system, or transmitted in any form or by any means, electronic, mechanical, photocopying, recording, or otherwise, without the prior permission of the publishers.

Any person who commits any unauthorised act in relation to this publication may be liable to criminal prosecution and civil claims for damages.

This is a work of fiction. Names, characters, businesses, places, events, locales, and incidents are either the products of the author's imagination or used in a fictitious manner. Any resemblance to actual persons, living or dead, or actual events is purely coincidental.

A CIP catalogue record for this title is available from the British Library.

ISBN 9781528980791 (Paperback)
ISBN 9781398409019 (ePub e-book)

www.austinmacauley.com

First Published (2021)
Austin Macauley Publishers Ltd
25 Canada Square
Canary Wharf
London
E14 5LQ

I would like to thank my wife, Gerrie, for her encouragement and tolerance.

When the criminal underworld become so powerful, they are able to corrupt the forces of law and order that oppose them and in so doing will be untouchable by those forces, and then the country will head into anarchy, the general population will be left with no recourse but to accept the situation and suffer the consequences.

Before the situation exists, it is the time to call in NEMESIS, the upholder of balance and justice. But who will be the pawns she can use? They have to be unknown but all seeing. The FBI, Special Branch, Interpol and such are limited; they must support the law and act within it for the benefit of the whole population, but because of these limitations and visibility, the organised criminal world can defeat them.

The section is unknown, its operatives contracted as and when needed and licenced to use the tools of the underworld to re-establish balance. John Wilcox and Dylan Williams are two of these soldiers of Nemesis.

Prologue

The Thales WK450 Watchkeeper Surveillance drone pursued its quiet, stealthy programmed flight, through the inky black night sky. Flying high above the dark mountainous terrain of Afghanistan, it was invisible to any earth-based watcher, and neither could the quiet, almost silent, Winkle engine be heard, so to all who were not part of its operation, it wasn't there. But it was there, and although it could not be seen, or heard, it could see very clearly what there was to be seen.

Although the drone had no understanding of what it saw, the images it did see were sent in a continuous stream to its base, where the operational watchers would understand what was seen, and they in turn would send messages to those who needed to know what had been seen and had the power to react.

This night, the watchkeeper had seen and was still seeing ten men, as they moved through the silent night without causing any disturbance. Having left their vehicle some five miles behind and walked the remaining distance to the village that was the object of their nights' endeavours, may have been a little excessive but necessary. Any sound travelled well in these mountains, and it was important they arrived unannounced; by travelling on foot, they could be sure their approach to the village would not be heard.

Four of the team of Taliban fighters were each carrying an RPG launcher and five grenades, whilst each of the other six was carrying their AK-47 Kalashnikov rifles and five more bombs each. The objective of this night's raid was to cause a large amount of destruction and fifty RPG bombs would be sure to do that, and hopefully convince the population of the village to sever their connection with the British forces and obey the rules laid down by the general counsel of the Taliban.

The team was about two hundred yards from the villages' central market when the leader signalled six of the men to stop and crouch down, while himself and the other three men with RPGs remained standing and prepared their weapons, ready to fire.

The silence of the night was suddenly torn apart, and as a single shot rang out, the Taliban leader collapsed; the rifle round had hit him in the centre of the forehead, and he was dead before his body touched the ground. A second shot followed the first in quick succession, the shock of the first shot had delayed the reactions of the second standing man; this delay caused him to be the second to die. An onlooker would have had difficulty in identifying the sound of the second shot, for simultaneously, as one, ten SA 80 rifles on fully automatic fire brought deadly thunder to the scene. The six remaining Taliban fighters returned fire, as they ran forward to pick up the fallen RPG, but having no leader to co-ordinate their actions, their defence was disorganised and ineffective. As it was, it would have made no difference if their leader had still been alive, for they were in the open and the British soldiers were in sheltered positions; the in-balance was too great, and the men were quick to realise it. In a crouching zigzag run, they tried to escape, but the controlled fire from the British troops was deadly; only one man managed to get as far as three hundred yards before the crack from the single-shot M24 sniper rifle could be heard once more, and he too fell.

The firing ceased of its own accord, some thirty or so seconds after it had started, concluding, as it had started, with the final single shot. For a time, the post-firefight silence was or at least seemed total, then, as hearing returned, the soldiers, still at their posts, could hear the first sounds of movement. The civilians were, cautiously, coming from their houses to see who were the victors and who the vanquished; they'd no doubt as to who the protagonists were. There were only ever the two sides, but they were pleased to see the British squaddies, now slowly advancing on the unmoving prostrate Taliban.

There was a sense of relaxation and cheer amongst the villagers, now they would not have to worry who, from the population of the village, would live and who would die; it wasn't unknown for every man, woman and child to be slaughtered if the Taliban survived.

"Nice shot Williams," the troop commander said to the one man who stood separate from the rest of the troop. Dylan Williams had reloaded his M24 sniper rifle while continuing to study the surroundings. His had been the lead post, some twenty yards in front of the rest of the troops, who had waited for his shot, the sound that would signal the start of the action, and that shot would say the first of the enemy was down, and as it was Williams firing, the man down could be assumed to be dead.

The troop collected the bodies into a group ready for the medical team, who would come to tidy up in the morning. None of the Taliban fighters had survived, and generally, it wouldn't have made much difference if they had just been wounded; the troop had no medic with them so could offer no more than basic first aid. If a wounded man received any treatment that night, it would only have been rudimentary, and if the injury had been more than superficial, he would have been expected to die anyway.

For his part, Corporal Williams when he had decided there was no chance of any more fighters appearing, finally came off of the alert. Cradling his rifle, he took one more look around finishing with a look at the now lightening sky; he couldn't see the watchkeeper, but he knew it was there; he gave a silent thank you to this unseen entity then returned to the rest of the troop.

Come the morning, the relief troops arrived, and the story of the night's action was passed, both officially, troop commander to troop commander, this being the story that would be put in writing for later discussion, and unofficially, squaddie to squaddie, the two stories rarely agreed with each other, but who cared, then it was all in the troop carrier and back to camp for a good day's sleep.

Part 1

Chapter 1

Henry Filamont showed no reaction to receiving the scrap of paper from the man sitting next to him at the diner's counter who had very circumspectly slipped to him; he only slipped it into his pocket, along with the change he had received from the waitress, then he stood and left the diner to return to his office.

The man had sat down soon after Henry; he was not someone Henry actually knew, but he'd seen him in the diner from time to time, when they'd acknowledge each other and maybe pass some comments about the poor showing of the Kansas City Chiefs, their local football team. The man spoke in a loud brash voice, and Henry would more or less agree with him but in more measured tones.

When the time had come to pay for his lunch, he'd called over the waitress, passed some bills, and as he'd collected his change and brought his hand back, it touched the paper. Now the man next to him turned to Henry and pointing to the results page of the paper, and almost in a whisper, as if talking to himself, and without looking at Henry said, "Don't read it till you're away from here, and don't react."

Henry had been a policeman for a long time; he knew when he was being given a tip, and by someone on the other side of the law; he didn't need the warning. The man was now back talking in his loud voice to the customer on the other side of him.

With the paper burning a hole in his pocket, Henry walked back to the federal building, where he worked in the Federal Bureau of Narcotics.

Ω

Henry, born and brought up in the downtown area of Dallas, had been only ten years old when he had seen one of his school friends shot and killed, by a drug-crazed no count. His friend had only been a bystander, but the junkie was out of control and out of his mind, probably because of the impure drugs the pusher was supplying. From that moment, Henry was determined he would be a policeman and help to get the drug addicts, and dealers, off the streets.

Henry had left college with very good grades, good enough to have given him a successful and interesting life with a good income in almost any profession he might choose, but his ambition to join the police was still as strong as ever. He declined the opportunity to go on to university, and instead, he applied, was accepted and joined the Dallas city police.

It turned out that he was a natural at the job. He had the ability to get to know people, the good and the bad, and he was very observant, always aware of his surroundings. Henry had known the streets of Dallas from childhood but patrolling those same streets, from a position of responsibility, showed him a side of his home city he'd never even imagined, the necessity to increase his knowledge quickly became an imperative. Whilst learning the ins and outs of policing, he never lost his aversion to the drug scene and always kept his ear to the ground. Any information, no matter how unimportant that came his way, he would pass to the narcotics squad.

Once he had qualified for the position of detective, he became part of the same narcotics squad and his willingness to tread the streets, even in his own time, continued to improve his arrest record and make him a bit of a celebrity in the precinct, a rising star even. But as the saying goes, what goes up must come down; the fact he was getting the arrests, meant others were not. Eventually, malicious rumours were heard; nothing solid, just mutterings, such as whether he was working with the drug gangs. No matter what the truth was, if you throw enough shit at the wall, some of it is going to stick.

After these insinuations had been going on for some time, it started to affect his work. He could see that even though he had the support of his captain, sooner or later he wasn't going to be wanted around the precinct; already there were enough people who didn't want to work with him; he decided it was time to move on before he was pushed. If he was going to stay true to his ambition, there was only one place for him to go; he applied for a position with the FBI and was accepted.

Henry enjoyed his training and finished Quantico with a merited pass and was assigned to the city of Philadelphia, once again on the Narcotics Team.

The following year, although he was content in his new post, his success seemed too slow. He made fewer busts; he told himself it was because he didn't know the streets and set about righting this by wandering in his spare time, in the same way as he had at the beginning of his police career.

It took a full year before he realised the real problem, which was that he should now be working in a much higher-level of detection, but instead, he was still trying to do the police work he'd done as a policeman. It had always been the job of local police to handle the routine work, making the small-time busts, and passing on intelligence, this was how it had been for Henry in that role.

Now Henry's job was to look for, and bust, the big guys, the organised gangs, the ones who worked interstate and international. With this new understanding, he had reassigned his whole outlook, instead of walking the streets, he spent more time reading reports and interviewing suspects and witnesses; he now thought of his working life as though he had been playing checkers but now had moved on to chess, and once again, he started to enjoy the challenge he had set himself.

Henry had never married; he realised he was a workaholic and dedicated to his work; he would never be able to give to a marriage what he should. He sometimes, mainly when he attended parties given by his friends, thought he might like the family life but soon realised he was more than content as things were.

One day in spring, a day that had started slowly for Henry, some routine paperwork and a check on the computer to see if anything was breaking in the rest of the police world, he found nothing of interest. It was past 10:00 when Captain Reynolds of the state police knocked on the door.

"Hello, Mike," Henry greeted him; they'd known each other since Henry had taken up post, they both did the same job, Mike for the state and Henry for the nation. "It's been a long time. I've a feeling that no matter how glad I am to see you, I'm going to regret it, but I'll ask anyway, what can I do for you?"

"You make it sound like I only show up when there's a problem," Mike said, feigning hurt, "you really know how to hurt a man."

"Come on now," Henry replied, keeping up with the usual banter they normally shared, "if we were in the bar, it would be social, but you dragging yourself all the way across to my office, that means work, for me."

"Yes, well that may, or may not be true, but I'm sure you would do the same for me. Anyway, back to business, we have located a crack lab, and we're ready to take it down, but we've just found out that they've been selling out of state, so that makes it federal, so we're going to need you along to represent the government's interests, if that is, you haven't got anything planned for this evening, but don't worry, we'll do all the work, as usual."

"Listen here, the next time you guys get to do some work I want to be there; it's always good to see the unusual. Where's this lab then and when are you going to close it?"

"It's here in the city. And I want to go in tonight. The word is they normally start up at about 10:00, so I'm planning to hit them at 11:00; is that good for you?"

"Yeah, I was only planning to sleep anyway; let's have the meeting point address."

The team for the evening included four men from the city police, four state troopers and Henry. The meeting point was a street one away from the building that was being used as a Crack Lab, and Mike Reynolds allocated the dispositions. At 5:11, they took up their places, then at precisely eleven o'clock, two officers swung the eighty-pound post hammer and opened the door.

It being a large building, there was a scramble as the drug makers tried to escape; in the melee, a shot rang out followed by two more. The second two had sounded different to the first so was probably a police response to the first; the three shots were enough to make the other villains surrender; they were drug makers not killers, and a few years for in prison for making and supplying was nothing, but if someone got shot it could be life.

Only one person was injured, the one who had fired the first shot, so an ambulance was called, and unfortunately along with it came the press. Henry found this out as he was leaving. He didn't like the press, especially the photographers; it was hard to be undercover if your face is all over the papers, but what was, was, so they got the picture and he left the scene, not knowing the direction his investigations would take, all because of that picture.

Chapter 2

Gerry Norman was not a big man in terms of body attributes, but he did have a powerful character and had had since he was a child. From that early age, his schoolmates and others on his block thought of him as a bit slow, and a touch on the dim side, but they never teased or annoyed him in any way, when they were around him they were very careful because of the way he alluded menace; basically, he scared them.

Gerry's school days were a lonely time; he spent most of it by himself; he attended school but didn't really learn. By the age of fourteen, he had managed to pass out of school by simply not going, so took no qualifications with him. His parents by this time had also had enough of him; he didn't attend school, and he constantly wandered the streets; they gave him the option of either changing his ways or clearing out of their house; he took the latter option.

Finding work proved to be impossible; no one wanted him; they'd say either he was too young, or he lacked the necessary qualifications, but the truth was he still engendered fear, even in hard-bitten employers, so he remained an outsider; a bad smell that everyone wanted gone.

Unable to find work and with no one to help him, it was no surprise when Gerry drifted into crime, only small-time, shoplifting, taking things that others had left unattended, examining the inside of open garages or sheds, petty things, things he could easily sell or things he needed like clothing or food. It was one of his garage 'inspections' that finally gave Gerry a career path.

One day, as he wandered the back entries and alleyways, he found the door of a garage not quite closed; he could see no one around so decided to take a look. Inside there wasn't much of interest to be found, but before he could leave, with the few things he thought he could use, the owner arrived and caught him.

Unlike Gerry, Arne Shultz was big of body, had a lively mind, and he had the same air of menace that had so blighted Gerry's life. Gerry had every reason to be worried, and when he picked himself up off the garage floor, the place that

Arne's punch had put him, he was worried, but he stood ready to defend himself. Without much hope of doing so, Arne smiled.

"That little tap," he said, "was what you deserve, not for being in my garage but for getting caught. Now then, son, who are you?"

"Why? What's it to you, going to turn me in to the cops?" was Gerry's belligerent reply.

"Don't be cheeky now or I'll give you another clip, so what's your name?"

After some hesitation, Gerry finally said, "Gerry Norman," still not relaxing his defiant stance.

"Okay, Gerry, my name's Arne; what's your story, and why are you in my garage?"

Gerry didn't really have a story; he'd never thought to have one, never needed one, so had trouble answering. This guy didn't look hostile but boy could he hit, not the sort to annoy. Finally, he made up his mind.

"I ain't got no story, 'cept no one wants to give me no work so I have to help myself. I came in here to see if there was anything I could use, but you've got less here than I've already got."

"Yeah," Arne said, "I thought so, actually, I like your style, son; you got caught but you're still prepared to stand your ground. You fancy a cup of coffee?"

Gerry was thrown, why's this guy acting friendly? Okay, he hasn't lost anything, but he's no reason not to just kick the shit out of me and give me to the cops.

"Why," he asked suspiciously, "what have I got for you?"

Arne smiled. "You might possibly be useful to me, and I think I can be useful to you, so do you want to find out?" Arne gestured to the door. Gerry thought a bit longer but decided he had nothing to lose and accompanied Arne into his house.

Arne made coffee, and they sat and talked, at least Gerry talked; he'd never had any sort of confidant, even his parents never used to listen to him. Arne was a good listener, and once Gerry had started, he couldn't stop, all the injustice he'd suffered, always being an outsider, not wanted for games in school or work even at the lowest level, having to make his own way, it all came out, and Arne let it flow.

Once Gerry had finished, Arne made more coffee then looked at Gerry for a long time; Gerry started to get agitated, but finally, Arne said, "You, son, have a problem, in that you scare people."

"You don't need to tell me that," Gerry responded.

"Hear me out," Arne stopped him. "I say you've got a problem, but it can be turned into talent; you could use it to your benefit."

"And just how can I do that?"

"Well, you're living in a criminal world, a world where if you scare people enough, they'll pay you to go away, and just like me, you don't have to do anything to scare people; you're a natural." Gerry was beginning to show interest. "I could use you to help me, to collect from people who might not want to pay and need a little persuading. We'd have to build you up a bit first; you still need to look the part, even if you do scare the shit out of people with just a look. If you're with me, I'll teach you how to work out and fight, and you'll have to learn to shoot a gun, what do you say?"

"If I'm getting you right," Gerry clarified, "you run a protection racket and think I can be trained to do the same, is that right?"

Arne again gave his slow smile. "I knew you were bright, that's exactly right, but it's not my racket; it belongs to someone much more important, but yes, I do run it, and I'm always on the lookout for new talent." Gerry took a little time to think.

"Will I be working for you or for the man?"

"For me, at least until I'm sure you're properly trained."

"And what's in it for me?"

"Well, to start with, you've got nowhere to live, so you can move in here, and I'll feed you and give you a bit to spend. Then when I think you're ready, you'll get to work and get a part of the take." To Gerry, it was a no brainer. At the moment, he had nothing, not even a place to live, so rent and keep would be good and spending money made it better.

"Okay, I'm in, can I start now?"

"Now that's what I like to hear, someone who can make up his mind, okay, you're on the books. Do you want to go collect some things?"

"What I've got you can see; there's nothing else and no one else."

Ω

19

Life became a lot more complicated than Gerry had expected; to start with, he had to go to the gym, every day, and Arne made sure he did. When he objected, a clip from Arne would show him the error of his ways. He had to go to the shooting range once a week, to learn how to threaten with and shoot a gun.

He would accompany Arne on his rounds and obey the rule of not talking; all he was expected to do was stand and look menacing, something he didn't have to train for. The whole of what they did was criminal, and Gerry knew it. He hadn't learned much in his life, but right and wrong had been hammered into him, but with the way, everyone had treated him, all his life, allowed him to put the moral argument aside. On the upside, this was the first time in his life he had a purpose and a mentor who understood.

It took two years for Gerry to become the man Arne wanted him to be, and allowing him to do 'the round' by himself; the clients knew who he was and didn't give him any trouble, so now, apart from his keep, he had money in the bank and respect in the streets.

It was two months later when Gerry's life took its next turn. It was an ordinary day; he was doing his round making the collections as usual. As he approached the general store, run by Mr Davies, he saw two men loitering outside the shop; the men, one big and the other not so big, were obviously waiting for something, and as he drew near, it became obvious that he was what they were waiting for. Gerry had already called at a few of his clients so was carrying a fairly large amount of cash; it was looking as if this might be the robbery Arne had warned him was possible, but when he reached the shop, the larger of the two men smiled and asked if he was Mr Davies' insurance man. This didn't in anyway disarm Gerry, and it was pretty clear they knew exactly who he was. "That's me," he confirmed, in a tone that said so don't annoy me.

"Fine," the big man said. "I've got a message from my boss; he says there has been a rearrangement here, and we are to take over the cover for the whole of this street, so if you'll care to just move along, we'll get on with the business."

Gerry could see what was happening; another gang was trying to move in on his territory, this couldn't be allowed; it was something else Arne had warned him about. He could back off and get the man to solve the problem, but that wouldn't be good for Gerry; he was supposed to take care of his area, whatever the problem.

"I'll need a little more information first. I know my boss will ask me," he said. "Could we take this discussion somewhere a little less public? We don't want everyone to be listening in, do we?" He indicated an alley that went behind the shops; the big man acquiesced, and they moved off the street and out of sight, the younger man leading. As soon as they had turned into the alley, the big man turned and swung a full roundhouse punch at Gerry, but he had been ready for it, and he easily avoided the punch then launched his own hard jab into the man's solar plexus, this did connect and he staggered back. Gerry turned to the younger man who had now turned and looked unsure of whether to get involved. "Stay out of it," Gerry warned, then looked back to the large man who now had decided Gerry was not going to be a pushover; he'd decided to change tactics and was reaching into his coat.

The man was wearing a large Crombie overcoat, which hampered his attempts to reach his gun. Gerry, on the other hand, had on a light leather 'Bomber' jacket, his Colt .38 was out in a second, and without hesitation, he shot the big man in the face. Arne had told Gerry to always carry the snub-nosed .38 with the filed off foresight, rather than a big colt or such like; he could now see the wisdom of his words.

As the big man fell, Gerry heard a noise to the side of him, swinging around he saw the younger man had now decided to join the fight; the noise had been the sound of his jacket being undone, so that he could draw the big .44 magnum from his shoulder holster. The gun had just cleared the jacket when Gerry shot him.

Looking around and seeing no one was taking notice of the gunfight, Gerry put his gun away and walked to the far end of the alley, out onto the street and headed for home. As he crossed the river bridge, he carefully wiped the .38 and then casually dropped it in the river.

Arne was pleased when Gerry related the morning's events. *The boy had come good*, he thought, but he realised he couldn't put him out on collections again, someone seeing him might put two and two together and call the cops, and the other mob would be looking for him, so he decided it was time to introduce him to the boss and make him a full member of the gang.

Chapter 3

Phillip Marcosie was head of the Philadelphia syndicate, by dint of having taken over from his father when the old man had retired. 'The Syndicate' was originally known by various names; the government called it organised crime. The general population used 'Mafia', a name brought over from Italy and Sicily in the early 1900s, but as the world changed, the gangs became more business-like, and the old names became too synonymous with the shoot-em-up gangsters of the 1920s.

The various criminal groups across America chose to change to more acceptable, discreet names. When Phillip took over from his father, he decided the name syndicate was much more respectable, and the old terms, such as 'Godfather' or 'soldiers' or 'made men', all became a thing of the past. The names now were chairman, directors, agents and such like.

The names had changed, but the business never did; any crime, drugs, prostitution, gambling, robbery, just about anything continued apace, and in the Philadelphia and Kansas areas of Missouri, a lot of that crime happened by the arrangement or agreement of Phillip Marcosie and his directors.

Gerry stood respectfully in front of the massive desk; it was the only item in the office that was impressive; the bookcase chairs and other fittings were very much run of the mill, but the desk, that was something very different. It made Mr Marcosie look small in comparison, but nobody would ever voice such an idea. Maybe he might have been slight of build, but Mr Marcosie could never be thought of as small.

Arne Shultz had introduced Gerry to Mr Marcosie, explained his background and training, and related the events leading up to this presentation.

Phillip Marcosie always allowed his section bosses to select their own workforce, as Arne had with Gerry, but he reserved the right to decide if a man should or should not become a member of the syndicate. When someone suggested a person be made a member, he would always want to know that the man had proved himself that he was willing and able to carry out the tasks he was set. When Arne Shultz, a man he had great faith in, explained how Gerry, on the street and unaccompanied, had shot two men who were trying to muscle in on syndicate business, he had to see him immediately.

"Gerry," Marcosie said, "it seems you're the right sort of man for us, exactly what we need in the syndicate; you've shown how resourceful you can be, and how you have the interests of our company at your heart. Tell me, would you like to join us as a full member? It could be very good for you, as I'm sure it would be for us."

Gerry hesitated a few seconds, not from indecision but to make sure Mr Marcosie had finished speaking, then replied, "Yes, sir, I would feel it a great honour to do so, and I very much appreciate your offer, but would I be still able to work with Arne? I mean he's taught me so much, and I will always feel I owe him a lot."

"Very well said, young Gerry; it's good when a man knows where his obligations lay, but no, Arne here is responsible for the collection of the payments due to us, but at present, it wouldn't be safe for you to tread those same streets, remember, both the police and the other group will be looking for you. I do however have a position ready-made for you in the drugs section. Tony Boscono has recently lost his assistant, and I'm sure you would be able to fit in there, would that suit you?"

"I'm sure I could fit in anywhere you think suitable; it's a pity I won't be working with Arne any more, but I realise you are right. I have made a few enemies now."

"Good, that's settled, Arne here will, I'm sure, be pleased to introduce you to Tony." This last was a dismissal although Gerry didn't realise it. Arne on the other hand did, saying goodbye to Mr Marcosie and giving a touch on Gerry's arm, got him doing likewise, and they both left.

Ω

Tony Boscono was not the sort of person that endeared himself to Gerry, or for that matter to anyone else, and in fact, he couldn't care less about it. He stood five foot eight but weighed maybe two hundred and fifty pounds, and all of it was fat; he wobbled when he moved and was always in a sweat, even in the snow. He had a brash loud voice and was forever shouting at everyone around him.

Gerry couldn't work out why anyone would employ Tony, but Arne pointed out that there wasn't anything Tony didn't know about drugs, where to get the raw material, how to make it into what the street wanted, and most of all, how to sell them; he was a very valuable man.

Gerry was not keen on working with drugs, but this was his life now so he would have to make the best of it; it wouldn't be looked on in a favourable light if he asked for out, so he did his best to learn as Tony took him through the system.

The system was straightforward; the raw product was brought into the country, mainly in ordinary cargo ships, cocaine from South America and opium from the Middle East. Then they were brought into the state by semi-rig drivers who worked out of the docks. The drivers delivered them to other semi-rigs, which in fact were mobile laboratories; they processed the raw into sellable drugs that were passed to the pushers that supplied the junkies. Of course, artificial drugs like amphetamines and crack were totally created in the laboratories.

Gerry never had had anything to do with drugs; he'd seen plenty of junkies either spaced out or shambling along, twitching, looking for their next fix, or for some money to pay for it. Now he saw it from the other side; Tony showed him how much money was made; the initial financial outlay was multiplied by many thousand times by the time it was sold.

"The basic powder," Tony said, "would kill the junkies if we sold it like that, so we cut it, that is we mix it with talc, maybe ten to one. Then we sell it to the pushers, who will do the same, so increasing their percentage, therefore the junkie gets something like a hundredth of what they think they're getting, that is if the pusher is honest; some of them cut it even more, but it's still enough to get them high and to keep them hooked.

"When the junkies are new to it, they'll probably cut it themselves, so to start with, they get a modest high on next to nothing, but as the dependency bites and they get really hooked, then they use it as it comes. And now they need to buy more to satisfy their need; they'll pay all they can to get it, neat, isn't it?" It felt quite sickening to Gerry, but it was the junkie's choice; they created the need themselves; the syndicate was only supplying what was wanted or needed so who was he to worry?"

Week followed week and Gerry found he was more of a delivery driver than a drug dealer; he would collect the product from the semi lab, wherever it might be parked that particular day, then distribute it to the pushers, and collect the price Tony told him to collect. Sometimes, he might have to get a bit rough with the pushers, especially if they wanted credit, credit was a no-no, unless Tony said so and that would be only if Tony wanted to hook the man in on something else. It was a good rule, as when a pusher needed credit, it would probably be because he was using his supplies on himself, and if that was the case, it wouldn't be long before he became useless to the syndicate; credit was never given to junkies. Gerry had been working drugs for nearly six months when it was brought home to him exactly what the real effect of drugs was.

This day he had made his last delivery and stopped to pass the time with the pusher, a non-user who seemed a reasonable sort, but someone who was new to him. While they were talking a young girl came up and asked to buy, the pusher wanted to see the money, but she had none. "Go get some," the pusher told her.

"But I got no work; I'm right out," she replied.

"Not my problem, but here," He took a card from his pocket, wrote in it and passed it to the girl. "Go there and be nice, and then you can come back and get your fix." The girl left.

"How old do you think she is?" Gerry asked in an offhand way.

"Oh, she passed thirteen three weeks ago; I gave her a discount as a birthday present."

"So, she's hooked?"

"Yeah, but I've sent her to a pimp I know; he'll get her work then she'll be able to have her fix."

"Thirteen, a junkie and now a hooker, a poor start to life."

"Oh, she's nothing special; I've hooked then as low as nine." By now, Gerry knew that by hooked the pusher was telling him he'd given the youngsters drugs, either free or very cheap, until they we're hooked on the stuff. "There's plenty of work for youngsters like that, plenty of old men who can only get it up for tender chicken." Gerry was sickened, not only the thought of the suffering of the girls but of the attitude of the pushers who ensnared them.

The next day while reading the paper outside his regular coffee shop Gerry saw a picture of the body of a young girl that had been found in an alleyway downtown. One look at the picture was enough for him to know it was the young junkie the pusher had sent to a pimp. The girl's injuries were consistent with a brutal sexual attack so the article said. Gerry could read no more; he was happy to accept adults becoming junkies and suffering what goes with it, but the thought of young girls, and probably boys, suffering such, before they had had a chance to learn the dangers, was not acceptable to him. But he wasn't foolish enough to think he could change anything, and he knew he was just as locked in as the junkies. There was no way he could walk out on the syndicate; he belonged to it body and soul.

Over the next couple of weeks as he made his delivery to the pushers, the thought of the girl would come to him, and he would wonder if this pusher or that pusher was ensnaring the young. The thoughts became overpowering and came to a peak when a pusher asked for credit. Gerry couldn't control himself; he let go at the man, and by the time he had finished, the man needed an ambulance.

"I can't go on like this," Gerry finally admitted to himself. "I've got to do something to control these scums, either that or get out of it, but that's not an option, maybe if I ran, maybe abroad somewhere but that wouldn't do anything to stop them, and what would I do abroad? No, I'm stuck, either I run and let the kids look after themselves or I close my eyes and ignore it."

He was having this debate with himself outside his usual coffee shop, and although he could hardly see the print on his paper with his mind in such a turmoil, he did catch one item. The article told that the police, with FBI support, had found and closed a crack lab. The picture was of the FBI narcotics squad, as they were leading away two men.

It wasn't the article that attracted Gerry's attention, but the picture that went with it. Gerry stared at the picture; he knew one of the squad's members, the FBI man out front, that is he didn't know the man, but he did recognise him. They used the same diner; they'd often had lunch sitting right next to each other, and he'd never known the guy was a fed. Gerry didn't know anything else about the man; it wasn't as if they had spoken to each other; in fact, they had only ever nodded hello or passed a few comments to each other about football, but the paper did know him.

The article gave a full portrait of Henry Filamont, including statements from people who had worked with him; he seemed to be an upright guy, and more importantly to Gerry, an honest one. He knew for certain there were a lot in the police force that weren't. If he was as straight as the paper said, now might be a good time to talk to him, but if he did so, he would have to be very, very, careful.

Chapter 4

When Henry was finally sitting at his desk, he took out the note; it was written on a plain piece of paper; he unfolded it and read.

I work for the Marcosie syndicate on the drug's side. I'm not happy in the way they work, and I'm prepared to talk to you 'and only you' if you meet me at the train depot in the carpark at 10:00 tonight. I'm in a dark blue ford, 'come alone'.

An inside man in the Marcosie set up, Henry thought, *is it a joke*? Henry could hardly believe it, he'd had his lunch alongside a person he would dearly have loved to know all this time but didn't know it, and it seems he wants to talk.

He re-read the letter; it seemed straight forward; it could be a trap, but it didn't look like it, and he could recognise the man so he'd be able to track him if it was a hoax, but he would have to be careful and check out the meet thoroughly. There was plenty of people who would like to remove him from the scene as much as he would love to remove them. There was no way he could not go to the meeting; this could be the thing he had been waiting for.

The Marcosie syndicate was a very tight organisation. Henry had never heard of anyone from the inside ever talking about anything; there had been a few unexplained bodies of Marcosie soldiers. But to get a break into the Marcosie narcotics department, it could be like all his birthdays rolled into one. Of course, it would be dangerous for him to go alone and against bureau rules, but he had to go.

Taking a piece of paper off his desk pad, he wrote down all he knew about this man including a full description, and where he knew him from, then placing it in an envelope, he placed it in his desk draw. *That's it*, he thought, *if it's a trap, someone should be able to track it and find the man.*

Ω

Gerry was more frightened than he had been for the whole of his life; he knew that if the boss found out he was even meeting with the Feds, he would be dead, and it wouldn't be quick. In the unlit carpark, his dark blue ford was almost hidden, with just enough light for it to be seen, if you knew it was there, or if you were looking for it.

He'd been in place for nearly an hour, watching, seeing people and cars come and go; there were some cars that stayed, but he could see there was no one in them, and there was no one loitering around trying to be casual. He was ready to start up and go at the first sign of something out of place, but he saw nothing so he stayed.

Henry arrived only a minute before 10:00; he parked to the rear of the carpark and switched off. Getting out of his car, he cast a look around the area; he saw the ford parked in the shadow but gave it no attention. When he was satisfied, there was nobody around; he slowly walked over to the ford, his hands clearly visible and his walk casual, giving no sign of aggression, this was the first possible contact into the Marcosie syndicate, and he certainly didn't want to scare him off. As he reached the car, the door opened in invitation, and Henry got in.

"Are we alone?" the man in the car asked.

"We are from my side," Henry responded, "are you sure of your side?"

"Yeah, we're clear. I read the article on you in the paper; it says you're clean, one of the good guys, is that true?" The question was presented in an 'it had better be' fashion, and the sense of menace the man exuded suggested it was best it was true.

"If you mean, am I paid by the likes of Marcosie, then I'm not, and I never have been. What is true is that all my working life has been dedicated to taking down the organised drug business."

"Okay, so if I give you anything, will anyone be able to trace it back to me? And I mean anyone, like who you might pass it on to."

"I don't know your name, okay, but by chance, I know where you eat, so if I really tried hard, I probably could find out, but I don't intend to do so. If you've got something for me, I don't have to tell anyone where I got it, that's the way we work, but of course, it's got to be provable or it's no good. I can't operate on hearsay."

"Right, I'll accept that, but remember if they find, out I'm dead."

"Yeah, I know how it works, but let me know why you're prepared to talk?"

Now the point had been reached, it was put up or shut up time. Gerry once again felt the twinge of fear, then he thought of the dead girl; he had to do it.

"Okay," he said, "I'm going to take this from the beginning, so you'll know where I'm coming from." Henry nodded in understanding; he knew the man was having a fight with himself, so let him do it his own way.

Gerry related his life, from being an outcast, to getting caught by Arne then joining the Marcosie syndicate, finally how he got into the drugs business, concluding with the story of the young girl and the pusher.

"So that's it, I'm not willing to be a part of that sick crowd. I'm not the clean-living type. If the drugs had been only about adults who had lost it, I wouldn't be talking to you now, but I don't hurt children, but what I do want is to bring the sick shits down."

"A fair story," Henry said. "You're not on your own; I've heard similar many times. You need something and along comes someone to give it to you, and by the time you realise it's not what you really want, it's too late. They've got you, and if it's young kids, they don't know the real price.

"If you work for me on the inside and give me useful information, then when it gets too much to keep on going, I can pull you out and give you a new life, if that's what you want?"

"Okay, that's good to know but that's in the future. I can handle things for now, providing you keep your end clean," Gerry responded. "For now, I'm going to take a chance, and we'll see if I'm still alive in the future." Taking an envelope from his pocket, he passed it to Henry. "That's everything I've got on the Marcosie drug scene so far, don't hit them all at once or they'll know it's an inside job."

"Okay, I know how to play it, and it'll be some time before I even start, but is the pusher who sold the girl in here?" Gerry assured him he was. "That'll give me a place to start, him and his pimp and hopefully the trick who killed her. Now, how can I contact you?"

"Only by post," Gerry said emphatically. "I've opened a post box in the name of Mike the Menace." He gave the rest of the box details. "If and when I've got something for you, I'll leave a message at the diner, so that's it, we'll only talk again if I really have to or if were having lunch at the same time."

"Okay, Mike, if I want something special, it'll be the post box, if you have something, it's the diner, bye now." Henry got out of the car, and it immediately moved off; he walked back to his own car in a meditative frame of mind, this is more than he had even hoped for, he would now have to see if it was real.

Chapter 5

"The cops have arrested one of our pushers," the anguish in Tony Boscono's voice told all who heard that he was amazed at the happening. "And I don't get it, we've paid the cops to leave our people alone, something's gone wrong somewhere." Tony was talking generally to those in the room, but Gerry Norman felt as though he was talking directly to him. Gerry felt pleased; the fed had proved true; he'd left it three days before acting and now that sick shit was off the street; it made him feel good for the first time in a long time, but he had to be careful not to show it.

"Which one have they grabbed?" he asked, although he was pretty sure he knew.

"Oh, that weirdo who works down on Chestnut Street; he's one of yours," Tony now addressed himself straight at Gerry. "You must have seen him recently, was he okay ? Or has he been trying too much of the product?"

"He was okay last week. I sold him his usual, but come to think of it, he was a bit loose with his mouth, boasting about hooking younger kids, maybe someone was listening."

"I always said he was crazy." Tony tapped his head to clarify his point. "Well, they've got him, him and another one of his weird friends; they're charging him with accessory to murder, so we're probably better off without him, but we will have to find someone else to cover that area. Have you got anyone in mind?"

"No, I thought he was solid down there. I'll have to start looking around, see if he's left anyone who can step up; I'll think on it."

"Well, do so, and do it soon, no" – Tony became thoughtful – "better leave it two or three weeks in case the cops are making a thing of it, find out if there are any new cops down there, maybe it's some rookie who doesn't know the game, yes, best not put anyone in place till I get back."

"You going somewhere then?" Gerry asked casually.

"Of course," Tony answered, with a tone that said Gerry should have known, "yes, you haven't been here long enough to know. The reason we're so successful at producing heroin is that each year I go to Afghanistan and buy the crop from some villagers up in the mountains, so each year I get a holiday over there."

"It doesn't sound the sort of place for a holiday," Gerry said.

"I don't do holidays so I wouldn't know if it's good or not, at least I get a rest from all of you" – he indicated all in the room – "so that would have to be treated as a holiday. Oh, and by the way, we're having a barbecue on Sunday at my place, so the wife says you're all invited, that means I expect to see you all, okay?" The look on Tony's face said he was accepting no objections; they all agreed they'd be there.

Gerry didn't like barbecues; in fact, he didn't like socialising in general, but to the six of them that worked in the drugs section, an invite from Tony was an order. So as demanded, at two o'clock Sunday afternoon, he duly presented himself at Tony's house, made small talk with his wife, drank a few beers and ate a couple of burgers. There was a large crowd so it was easy for Gerry to fade into the background and sit quietly until others started to leave, then he could getaway.

It was getting on to 5:00 and Gerry was thinking the party must finish soon, when Tony, with a deep frown on his face, stood up and clutched his chest. Gerry had never witnessed a heart attack before, but this must have been a really bad one, for Tony's mouth moved but no words came out, then with a look of sheer pain on his face, he collapsed. By the time someone who knew something about first aid got to him, Tony was dead.

Being a witness to the demise of Tony Boscono left Gerry feeling nothing, and the only thought in his head as he left was that *this would cause a lot of problems for the syndicate; it was a happy thought.*

The next day on his own initiative, Gerry called the syndicate secretary's office to ask what was going to happen now that Tony had died; the assistant to Sonny Minelli, the secretary, told him it would be sorted out when the secretary got back from holiday, so Gerry was to keep things running till then. Gerry didn't have any idea how to run the drugs setup, but he did his best.

Ω

A week later on Monday lunchtime, Henry again found himself sitting next to Gerry, as he hadn't seen Gerry in the diner for over a week, he assumed it was no accident, and he was right. Gerry wasn't being brash in the way he was last time they met at the diner, but he did make occasional loud comments on articles he found in the paper he was reading. Once he had finished his burger, he got up to leave, and as if an afterthought, he passed his paper across to Henry. "Here," he said, "there's an article in there on page ten; it's all about the dangers of eating lunch, then going back to work." With that and a loud laugh, he left, leaving his paper for Henry, who made sure to take it with him when he also left; he was sure there would be something of interest to read in it.

Ω

So, their drug buyer wouldn't be making any purchases this year, or any other year, this was going to cause a bit of a problem for Marcosie Henry thought. According to Mike the mechanic, this Tony was the only one to go buying, and Henry spent a long day over how he could use this information.

It was good to know how the syndicate got its base drugs and that could now be stopped, but he wanted more; there must be more, but he would have to find it.

Putting the Tony Boscono matter aside, Henry gave time to what else Mike the Mach had for him. There wasn't much, apart from the pushers being hassled and another syndicate trying to take over. The other lot weren't yet making a bid out in the open; they obviously weren't ready to take on Marcosie in a full gang war, only grabbing customers here and there, really just business as usual.

It was late when Henry put away his notes and went home. After eating the meal, he'd picked up on the way, he sat and tried to watch some TV, but he was too tired to concentrate on the images, so turned off and went to bed.

The working of the brain is not fully understood, even by the scientists who study it; in fact, it's hardly understood at all, but what is known, is that the subconscious never stops working. When asleep, it's the consciousness that takes a rest. Henry had learned this small fact long ago but had never thought of it, but this night, once the consciousness had switched off and let the subconscious do some real homework, it told him the answer to his problem; it was simple and obvious and would cost very little.

33

When he awoke in the morning, the subconscious passed to the conscious what it had worked out overnight, the answer was laid bare in Henry's mind, and he couldn't understand why he hadn't seen it the day before. He got to his office early and again reread the notes from Mike the Mach; it was all there.

The death of Tony Boscono would by now be known to all the Missouri criminal organisations, and they would know that Marcosie was going to have to find someone else to go get his supplies, so if any of them could interrupt the mission, Marcosie sooner or later would run out of the product. The idea that Henry's brain had worked out was to do the intercepting the buying trip himself, but the good part would be to put the blame on one of the other gangs, and maybe start a gang war, which only the law could win, but how? He wrote a note to Mike the Mach, asking who would go for the opium and when, then posted it and waited.

Ω

It was another three weeks until Sonny Minelli showed up. Gerry had done all right as a stand in so Sonny decided to leave him doing it.

"But I can't do the buy in Afghanistan," he told Sonny, "That was Tony's and only Tony's."

"Yeah," Sonny agreed, "but that's okay. I've got someone else to do that, an outsider but I'll be going as well so you don't have to worry about that."

Chapter 6

Abdullah Mohammad Abbas had been traveling all day, from his remote mountain village in northern Afghanistan to Kabul. His old TATA truck that had been new in the 1950s, now showed every one of the injuries and general wear and tear that constant use, on the tracks and unmade roads of the mountain regions, had caused and had left it in very poor condition, with a set of operating characteristics that had to be well known only someone fully experienced in its ways, could possibly manage to drive it for more than a few miles. Abdullah was very used to ways of the truck and with a bit of cursing and a lot of kicking was able to get it to where he needed to go, usually.

Being the headman of the village, it was Abdullah's task to deal with any administrative tasks that came along. He was required to arbitrate on disputes, chastise and even punish wrong doers, officiate at formal occasions, marriages and such like. It was an unpaid responsibility and at times bothersome, but it did give a feeling of importance and wisdom, when he was consulted on any and every matter that effected the village. When he was called to attend a council of all the villages in the valley and being asked to represent their collective interests, his feeling of importance could not be matched. It was on behalf of the council that he was now traveling to Kabul.

For years past, when it became time to sell the village's crops, the buyer would know and arrange to come and barter a price; he always gave a fair price, even though it would take a day's argument before everyone accepted it was. This year though he had not been in contact, it was assumed by the village elders that it must be he was not going to buy this year, for he'd previously always arrived almost to the day when the crop was ready. It was an annoyance to all the villages, for it meant the sale would be late; it wasn't the disaster some of the more depressing villagers thought; it would only mean a delay, but not a great one. There were always buyers for the year's opium crop, especially from

America, so one would be found, and the man who would find a new buyer for them lived in Kabul, so Abdullah must go to Kabul.

Ω

Keith Bowman was the American Embassy meeter and greeter and general factotum for the embassy in Kabul. He was generally thought of as a permanent fixture, for he had been in post for quite some time; in fact, it was nearly ten years, this was much longer than usual for embassy staff, but whenever the time for his next posting came, he always requested to do another tour of duty.

The first time he did so there was some surprise, but as there was never anyone else wanting the post, with the land being mainly mountainous dessert, and with a constant threat of terrorist atrocities, this was hardly surprising, so the administration was happy to leave him there in post for another tour of duty.

It wasn't the love of the country that made Keith want to stay, it was because he had another, unofficial, position, that of contact man for a homeland crime syndicate, and with the responsibility for arranging the buying of the opium that was produced each year, by the mountain villages.

From the time he left university and entered the diplomatic service, Keith's choices of occupation were out of his hands, if they had ever been in them. Being the son of a Mafiosi, the organisation had paid for his education, and it was taken for granted he would pay back, by following in the way of his father and doing what the organisation wanted. Keith had no problem with living the duplicitous life; he earned good money from both employers, and in a few years, he would be able to settle down, maybe get married and perhaps set himself up in a nice little business.

At present, Keith was having a quiet time; there were no visitors to be entertained on behalf of the embassy and no explosive outrages to be examined for American involvement, so when Abdullah Abbas rang his business mobile and requested a meeting, he was free to arrange to meet him within the hour.

They chose a small discreet coffee shop on Taimani Street, in the Shahri-now District, a place they both knew well. It being a part of his embassy duties to be involved in anything that might have an American interest, if he was seen with a local Afghani, it wouldn't cause any particular interest, so there was no reason for the meeting to be secret, but as the dealings with Abdullah would be a part of his non-official work, it was something he preferred to keep a little clandestine.

The meeting, as with all meetings in the Arabic world, had to start with the obligatory pleasantries, starting with health. 'How are you, I hope I find you well?' 'I am very well, thank you, and I hope you are also well?' 'I am thank you and how is your family, etc.' These pleasantries would go on for maybe twenty or thirty minutes covering all aspects of each other's lives; it was something that was of critical importance to the Arab mind but found to be a strain on the Western mind, and of course, it was accompanied by numerous cups of tea, but eventually when each considered the formalities were completed, the subject of the meeting could be stated.

"The man who buys our crop has not been in touch," Abdullah said. "He usually shows great respect by being very punctual, but not this year and the harvest is almost complete. Of course, we all hope he is well and not been laid low causing him to miss the visit; we would be very sad to hear of such a thing, but the harvest is nearly in, and we will need a new buyer very soon."

The information was new to Keith; he didn't have any direct dealings with the actual purchases and was very careful to make sure of that, but he was the organiser, the man who put one party in touch with the other and would usually be informed if there was to be a change in who the parties were to be.

"This is very serious," he told Abdullah, with an appropriate worried frown on his face, not that he considered it that serious. "I have not been informed of any problems. I must contact America and find out what the problem is, but you mustn't worry. I am sure there will be a simple explanation and will solve it and will do so this very day, and when I have, I will inform you straight away. Are you returning to your village today?"

"No, I have a brother living in Dahoi-Bala, and I will be staying with him and his family until this matter is finished."

"That is good," Keith said, "then I will contact you there tomorrow or the next day." With that and after the parting pleasantries, they parted, and Keith returned to the embassy.

As soon as he was in his office, Keith took out his laptop and compiled an e-mail; it was in a code that only he and the person who would receive it would know but would not look suspicious to the American intelligence agencies, who listened in to all electronic messages.

The e-mail laid out the problem as Abdullah had told it to him and requested an explanation and new arrangements. When the send button was pressed, the message did not go directly to the US but through a number of different servers, situated around the world, and by the time it entered the United States, the point of origin would not have been able to be detected.

Keith's e-mail finally ended its travels in the e-mail inbox of Simon (Sonny) Minelli, who was the secretary of the Kansas syndicate. Sonny had a background similar to that of Keith, the son of a member of the syndicate, that had paid for him to go through university, where he studied business finance, administration and law, qualifying with good degrees, then joining the administration of the syndicate, where his abilities soon moved him up to the secretary's position.

Ω

Phillip Marcosie, a very neat and tidy man, was always very regimented in his dress and disposition when he arrived at his office. He always looked every part the managing director of a large successful company, even carrying a very expensive embossed leather briefcase, not that he needed to carry one, it could easily have been carried by one of the two assistants that accompanied him, that is the two assistants who accompanied him almost everywhere, and ensured he didn't meet or have to listen to anyone he didn't want too. He always expected to be treated with formality, he would freely hand out criticism if any employee failed to stand when addressing him.

On this day, when Phillip arrived, he found Sonny Minelli awaiting him.

"What's this?" Phillip asked surprised to see Sonny so early. "Has the organisation collapsed?"

"No," Sonny replied, "we're still on the up at present" – a smile on his face – "just a minor hiccup with getting the product from Afghanistan. It seems Tony Boscono has failed to arrange the collection this year, and the farmers are getting worried."

"I'm not surprised he hasn't organised it. Tony died three weeks ago; he had a big heart attack; you didn't know?"

"No, I've been in the Bahamas on holiday for the last month, and no one's told me. Poor Tony, how's his wife taking it?" Sonny was genuine in his concern; he'd liked Tony and his family.

38

"Oh, you know what these women are like, all the family crowded around and all saying what a good guy he was. I went to the wake, had a few beers and got away as soon as I could. Anyway, enough of that, so it seems his team is letting things slip, have we got anyone else in that section who could take over for now?"

Sonny thought for a moment. "No, they're all pretty run of the mill; there is the man you put in there some months ago. Tony was training him up; he thought he might become his deputy in a year or two, but no, he's not ready to go buying yet."

"That's a pity, have we got anyone else, or will we have to farm this out to someone else? Do we know anyone who might be worth considering?"

"There's only one I can think of off the top of my head," Sonny said, thoughtfully, "if you remember, we were thinking of taking Anthony James, the guy who runs a small-time operation out at Osage City. He could probably do it; he's been running his outfit for some time now."

Phillip gave it some thought. "Yes, I remember; he's running a tight ship out there, doesn't ask for favours, always shows respect, and doesn't interfere with our other projects." Phillip went quiet for a minute or so. "Okay, if you think he's worth a try, go for it. I tell you what, I'm having a party on Friday, get him to come along, and we'll take a look at him."

Sonny made a note. "And in the meantime, what shall I tell the farmers?"

"Ah, come on, Sonny, you can handle that, can't you?"

"Sure, I'll get on to Bowman, and he can tell them it's a go as usual, and we'll let them know the who when they tell me the when."

Chapter 7

Anthony James, a large man, both in height, at six feet four inches, and in bulk, at twenty-two stone, a smart, quick thinker, who had made and run a successful although limited business of crime. Tony, as he liked to be called, providing it was in a respectful way, liked to tell others that he was a self-made man, and to a large extent, he was, but it had been his father who had taught him, encouraged him and inadvertently financed him, the rest, he had done for himself.

Marco Spinelli, Tony's father, had been a small-time petty thief, who had never amounted to be enough of a criminal to be a problem to the police. They knew him well enough and had arrested him on numerous occasions, but he was slippery and normally managed to avoid being charged, and although he had spent some time behind bars, it was only for short periods.

The New York crime mobs also had the same attitude as the police towards Marco, and for the same reasons, he was just too unimportant to cause them any problems, so generally, they and just about everyone else ignored him, which was the way Marco liked it. As long as he was making enough to get by on, he was happy.

Marco's wife Maria and son Antonio, both knew well Marco's choice of employment and expected every day to hear he had been arrested and jailed, or worse had fell afoul of one or other of the gangs that ran New York, but it rarely happened, if it did, they'd check how long the sentence would be, then continue with their lives. Maria worked part-time as a hairdresser, while Tony, officially still at school, would stand-in for his father in providing income for the home when he was otherwise detained; he wasn't as good as Marco of course, but he managed.

The family's lives changed completely on a day that started as normal, with breakfast as a family, something Maria insisted on, then they went off to their various activities. On Marco's part, this entailed walking around the city streets looking for a mark he might be able to relieve of some valuable, then having done so would head for the bookies for a few hours, by way of the pawnbrokers if his gain had been something to sell.

The man, Marco's eagle eye caught sight of, looked a bit casual to be walking these streets, a big man, no one he knew, as far as he knew, but what attracted Marco, like a bee to honey, was the large briefcase the man had with him. Luggage was one of Marco's specialties; people were so careless with it; they would put it down anywhere, without thinking there would be someone who might pick it up. Not knowing the man or what might be in the case made no difference to Marco; it looked to be of good quality leather, so even if there was nothing inside although from the way the man was carrying it said there was; he could pawn it and make a few bucks.

Marco followed the man for a full five minutes, until he stopped at a newsstand, here the man, as expected, put down his briefcase whilst he got some change out, to pay for his paper and cigars. If Marco could ever be said to be gifted, it was in the speed with which he could acquire an unattended bag. The man had hardly let go of the case and reached into his pocket, before Marco had picked it up, and as if by magic had disappeared into the crowd, and it was only seconds later he had turned a corner, and he and the case were completely gone.

Marco took the case home and opened it; he didn't even have to force it as it was unlocked, but as he did, he nearly had had a heart attack with the shock of seeing. It was full of money, big money, fifties and hundreds; the bills were not new and stacked and banded as if they had come, or were going to the bank, just crammed in any which way. Marco let out a prayer of thanks and started to count.

One hundred and twenty thousand dollars. For someone who, on a good day, only expected to make fifty or a hundred, it was a king's ransom. Marco spent the next hour planning how he could spend that much money, but then, as always, reality came around and brought him up short.

Who the hell walked around New York with a case full of money? he asked himself. *And in such a casual way, was the man stupid? There were probably more pickpockets and opportunist thieves in New York than anywhere else in the world. I should know, if you had to carry valuables in a case, you chained it to your wrist, didn't you? Or better still travelled in a car or at least had two heavies to escort you.*

Marco took a more careful look through the case and took out a notebook; he had seen it when he had first opened the case but had ignored it; he didn't want it to interfere with his counting. The book contained a long list of names and numbers; he could recognise some of the names; they were local businessmen.

Marco had never been the brightest or sharpest person working the streets, but it only took him a few seconds to make the connection that he had taken the case off of a protection money collector. Effectively, he'd robbed the mob. No wonder the man could walk around without worrying; no one would dream of doing more than saying good morning, taking the bag was a death sentence. His next thought was that he was looking death in the face.

How the hell was he going to get out of this, his mind was racing, maybe if he gave it back as soon as possible, yeah and seriously apologised, or better still say he found it and knew it had to be theirs so brought it to them, maybe then they would forget about it.

No, that wouldn't work; they wouldn't believe him. Let's face it, he was a light-fingered thief, exactly the type who would have taken it, no, they wouldn't believe it, even if it was true, you didn't take anything off of the mob without paying, and he had nothing to pay with, even if you give it back, you wouldn't get a free pass.

If he took it back and they were in a very good mood, and he was having a very lucky day, they would only break his legs and give him some hospital time, no, again, they were never in that good a mood, and Marco Spinelli was not known to be that lucky, and he didn't even have Medicare.

So, he couldn't give it back, but someone might have seen him; there's always someone, and sooner or later, they would find him, then they would have to make an example of him. Thinking about it, Marco could sense his days were numbered.

When she got home from work, Marco told Maria about the case, like him she had first thought of the spend-ability of the money, then the problems the money would cause, then they both agonised over their position.

By morning, the only conclusion they had reached was that they couldn't remain in New York, the mob, whichever one it was, would already be looking for whoever had taken the case. They were sure to find someone who saw Marco with a briefcase, someone who, even if they hadn't actually seen him take it, knew Marco never carried a briefcase. The only chance for Marco and his family was to skip town, to get away as fast and as far as they could before they were found.

The decision made, they explained the situation to Antonio, a bright lad for his age, who took it in his stride, as most teenagers would, and agreed they should go. The family packed all they could carry and headed for the train station; they checked the departures and took the first train out, this happened to be heading west into the heart of the country.

On the long trip, they had to, as a family, think out as to what they were going to do with the money. Marco and Maria got lost in a fantasy of the spending they could do, but Tony had a bit more brains than his parents and had other ideas.

"Look," he told them, "if we spend it, it'll only last for a few weeks or months, then we're back to the old life and that would mean going back to a city with all the time worrying about the mob. What we've got to do is invest it, put it into something so it'll make more money, and we can then live well for life." Although Tony was only fifteen years old, his parents were not the sort to ignore him and listened to what he said.

"And what sort of business can we run?" Marco asked. "What do we know about anything? I've never held down a job long enough to know how a company runs."

"He's right," Maria confirmed, "we've always been small-time crooks, nothing more." She had become depressed at the idea the money couldn't be spent but understood what Tony was saying.

"Now there you're both wrong," Tony said with a slight smile on his face, "we all know about something." His smile became brighter when he saw the consternation on their faces. "We all know about crime; we've been involved in it all of our lives, think about it, how difficult is loan sharking? Or dealing drugs, or running a couple of girls on the street, this is what we've studied all our lives." The discussion continued on and off for the whole of the journey, and by the end, it had been agreed Tony's way was the way to go. All idea of spending the money disappeared, and now they were going to use it as seed money, in their underworld business.

They had made no plan as to where they could settle, only took the first train out, then made two changes at random, and after three days eventually arrived at the small town of Osage in Kansas, Missouri.

Osage was somewhere very different from New York; it was not the sort of place where the Spinelli family would normally have been found, not their style at all; it was smaller than any precinct of the big apple, so it seemed the right place for them to settle. They changed their family name to James and became Mike, Mary, and Anthony James.

The first thing they had to do was to establish themselves as a normal family. Mike found a job driving a delivery van, and Mary returned to hairdressing. Tony went back to school; he now had a reason to learn, knowing he would be the one to run the business once they got it started and would never be able to leave it to his parents. They were just not up to it, so the family settled in.

Things finally started to look good for Mike and family. Now Mike had a job he found easy, and surprisingly, enjoyed; he wasn't always looking over his shoulder ready to run, or keeping his eyes open for something to steal. Now, he had a business to run, at least Tony allowed Marco to think he was running it.

Loan sharking, as Tony had suggested, was an easy way to start. In the course of his work, Marco got to know a lot of people, with many of them always looking for some money to get by on, and with very high interest rates, it made a good return. Tony, on the other hand, made a contact with a drug supplier and started pushing drugs. No matter how large or small a town, there was always a market for drugs, especially in high school, the market Tony started with, and drugs made an extremely high profit.

The family prospered; they even became wealthy enough to buy into some legitimate businesses, which gave them a good way to launder the profits from their illegitimate activities.

All looked set for the family James, to have a very comfortable life, that was, until Marco made the biggest, and last, mistake of his life. At the height of the football season, along with some of his friends, he decided to take a weekend trip into New York, to watch the Yankees play. He considered he was safe enough, no one would remember him or the briefcase incident after all this time. He was wrong and was recognised.

He made a run for it, but a few years of soft living meant he was not as fast as he used to be, and one of the pursuers shot at him. The shot hit him, as was intended not in a vital part, that would have been unfortunate, for he wouldn't have been able to tell them where the money was if they'd killed him, so they had intended to wound him and had succeeded. But because of the hard interrogation he then received, the filth in the ally where they carried out the interrogation, and the time gap, before he was taken for medical treatment, blood poisoning had set in, and he died.

This ending wasn't good for Marco, but it was a very lucky break that he wasn't carrying any identification, so the mob was still unable to find the family and demand the money back. It was also fortuitous that after the Yankees game, Marco had become separated from his friends, this didn't bother them unduly; they just assumed he had found some action elsewhere and caught their train and went home without him.

Tony and his mother, on the other hand, were pretty sure what had happened, so although they made a reasonable pretence of trying to find Marco, they did not pursue the investigations too hard and preferred to suffer the indignity of having everyone assume the missing James senior had left for pastures new.

Ω

Anthony was eighteen years old when his father disappeared, maybe a bit young to be running a business, and a business that included both legitimate and illegitimate enterprises at that. Tony, however, didn't really have to take over from his father; after all, its conception and daily operation had been his from the start. He was strong enough and able enough, with enough contacts to see off any others who made an attempt to take over the business, and he was even able to keep the business growing.

One of the lessons he'd learned, even before they had left New York, was always to be careful not to get greedy; he took great efforts to never tread on the toes of the neighbouring city mobs and syndicates. If he started upsetting them, then he would have to be prepared to start a war, and his organisation just didn't have the muscle, but he had shown that he was prepared to defend his territory if necessary and that was enough.

Because of the great care, he took, to avoid annoying the local underworld, it gave Tony some concern the day he received an invitation to attend a party at the home of the local syndicate boss, Phillip Marcosie. Of course, he knew who Marcosie was and the local power he controlled, compared to which Tony's operation was insignificant.

The invite was not a request, no matter how pretty the card was; it was an order to attend. He couldn't turn it down, even if it took him into a place where he didn't want to go but go he must, and as it was, it turned out to be a very nice evening.

Tony was welcomed by Marcosie and his wife and made to feel relaxed and comfortable. Mrs Marcosie spent a fair amount of time with him wanting to know about his personnel life, gently admonishing him for not yet being married, a man of business needed a wife she told him. He was introduced to a lot of people, some he knew and some that were known to him; he realised if he got the recommendation of Phillip Marcosie, all these contacts could possibly be of great help in way of future business.

It wasn't long before Tony could see he was being examined; it looked as though some of those gathered wanted to get to know him, and by the end of the evening, he was feeling very content in that he hadn't made any mistakes. As he was leaving, Mr Marcosie, he couldn't think of him in any less formal terms, no matter how often he had been told to call him Phillip, had asked him to visit his office the next day as there was a job he would like to put his way. Yes, of course, he could call, this could be a big opening for Tony, at least he hoped so.

Tony didn't have any worries when he turned up at 9:00 the following day; the secretary welcomed him warmly and took him through to the office. It was a very large office, maybe five hundred square feet, with a ten by eight desk over by the window and two large sofas with two easy chairs on the opposite side.

Four men were gathered in the room when Tony arrived; they all greeted him but didn't introduce themselves; they hadn't been at the party the night before, and he only knew them by hearsay, so they might like him, in theory, but not that much, yet. Marcosie invited Tony to sit and have coffee; a jug and cups were laid out ready on the coffee table, for five minutes they passed some pleasant small talk. Marcosie then took control.

"Tony," he said, "we've been watching you." Tony felt worried, and as if seeing Tony's concern, Marcosie re-assured him, "Don't worry, it's nothing bad; we just like to know who we're dealing with, and I assure you all the reports have been good; we're very pleased with what we've seen. You're very good at running your business; you're not too ruthless and this makes you popular, even with your, clients." Tony relaxed some. "And," the boss continued, "more importantly, you show respect and don't poach on anyone else's territory, so that makes you popular with us." He indicated the other men with a wave of his hand; they all nodded in agreement. "So now, we've got a problem, and we think you can solve it for us." He gave a questioning look at Tony.

"I'm sure I would be only too happy to help in any way I can," Tony quickly replied, he couldn't say much else, "but you must remember I'm only a small operation with limited facilities and manpower."

The boss smiled. "Yes, we know all that, but it's good to hear you say it; it takes a big man to admit he's not the tops in business. You see, that shows the honesty I said you have, but this job would only need some of your time; we have all the facilities and planning that will be needed." Tony was suspicious but made sure not to let it show.

"What we want is for you to go and sort of supervise some business for us. You see, just at the moment it would be inadvisable for us and our senior associates to go away; there are people who would take advantage if we took our finger off the pulse if you know what I mean." He gave a questioning look at Tony who gave a knowing nod of the head, even though he didn't understand. "No, the job would only be a matter of watching others and seeing things go smoothly; however, it would involve you going to Asia for a day or two, could you do that?" Again, Tony acquiesced he knew where about Asia was but that was all.

"Okay, let's summarise," he said this to the room in general, "at some date soon, Tony here will go with Sonny Minelli to Kabul, where they will collect the money and meet a Piet Botha, he will look after you, a sort of security and guide, he'll take you to the village to collect the product. Then this Piet will take both of you, and the product, to Gwadar, that's in Pakistan, where you will put it on the boat. That's it, then you both come home. You're clear with that are you, Tony?" Tony nodded. "Okay, thanks for coming in, Tony; we'll let you know when we have the final dates." It was a dismissal and Tony took it as such.

As he drove home, Tony's thoughts were mixed; this could be the big break if it all went well; he couldn't see why they didn't have someone inside their own organisation, but that was neither here nor there, but it could be his death knell if it went wrong. Either way, he could not have said no. "Where's this Kabul place?" he asked himself, and he'd have to look it up when he got home.

Chapter 8

Sir James Campbell was the head of 'The section'. A short, stocky man with a gruff manner and a chipped way of speaking, a no nonsense character that had been formed, by twenty years in the Royal Navy, from midshipman to Commodore, ten years in the metropolitan police, and another ten years in the special branch, plus a couple of years with MI5 before taking over 'The Section'.

'The Section' had never really been formed; it could be said to have developed. It had started as an idea, a sort of debating subject between Sir James and other people who were concerned with security, plus a few politicians and civil servants, in all the sort of people who had to deal with the country's safety.

The discussions eventually coalesced into the need for a clandestine investigative organisation, set to handle the dark, organised side of crime, and it would operate somewhere between the police and special branch on one hand and the MI sections and military on the other. The sort of no-man's land where the intelligent, influential and organised criminals and general malcontents and subversives operated.

It soon became clear that although the official security services could investigate and prove who the problem individuals were, they were never able to get a case brought to trial, not for want of trying but when they did have a case and tried to prosecute, it died, witnesses would disappear or be found to have died, files and evidence would be lost, and judges would throw out cases on the slightest pretext or would mislead the jury, but it would be nothing that couldn't be explained, so the criminals were left to continue as they wished.

Eventually in cases, where influence was being used, to defeat the legal system, it was realised that a more direct approach was needed and a more direct action unit was needed, and 'The Section' was formed.

Operating in secrecy and across multiple ministries, their remit was never written down, so that any case against a person or organisation that was unable to be solved legally, by the everyday security agencies, cases that the only possible acceptable solution would be illegal, became theirs. Probably what the Americans would call a 'black Ops' department, but the British couldn't be so theatrical, so it remained 'The Section', a simple but confusing name, which was exactly what was intended.

One of the points from the original discussions about forming a department like 'The Section' was that it must be secret. The past had shown that any department could be infiltrated if it were known to exist, so when it was actually brought into existence, it had to be hidden in amongst the other security departments of the bludgeoning civil service.

The existence of The Section was known to very few, in any of the ministries that supported it, those that did would never be able to find it; it was an office that was somewhere, but if you went somewhere to find it, then it would be somewhere else. No one ever visited, and if something was needed to be sent or received, then it would come through other, more transparent, departments, and PO boxes.

This concealment hadn't been easy. Funding, the principal worry of all government departments, had to come from more than one department if it were not to become visible, likewise, equipment and facilities would have shown the existence of 'The Section' if it purchased on its own, so had to be requisitioned when needed, but it would have to be by the use of ministerial authorisation, so that it could not be declined, even if the minister concerned didn't know who was requiring it or why. Eventually, 'The Section' became a reality and even the untouchable criminals began to disappear.

Ω

Sir James Campbell had been selected to head up 'The Section' by no less than the prime minister; he'd needed someone who had the strength of character to make the decisions that the Section would need to be made. Because of his extreme tenacity, his devotion to the country and the up keep of good law and order, and his appreciation that sometimes you had to fight fire with fire, these attributes made him a natural for the job.

Sir James did not believe in wasting time or words; he usually came across as officious and almost rude, but it was just his way. He didn't differentiate; it was made clear to everyone from the prime minister down, the gospel according to Sir James was the only gospel and all would adhere to it. He would not accept interference in 'The Section' or with its personnel. If his manpower erred, they would get the rough end of his tongue at the very least, but if they were in trouble with 'outsiders', he would support them against all, although he liked to think they didn't know that, which of course they did.

The man power of 'The Section' was selected by Sir James personally, they came from many other agencies, such as police, the MI's, military police, even some members of the criminal fraternity, the main thing they all had in common was an unsurpassed excellence in their abilities to investigate and a willingness to step outside the law they were upholding.

There were only ten people who were a direct part of the Section, these were the investigators; it was their job to find out all that could be found out about a subject, only when they could prove a subject's position was causing a security problem was the case presented to Sir James, then it would again be examined to ensure no legal means could be used, then Sir James would present the case to the prime minister, who decided whether a sanction would be issued.

To avoid having a large workforce, the investigators would select 'contractors' to actually carry out the operations, if they couldn't manage by themselves, or needed special skills, these specialists knew nothing of the Section, only that it was official and paid well. They would receive their orders from the investigator they knew and no one else, if they needed anything, it would be delivered to them, and if they had something to send, it would be collected.

The Section, of course, didn't work office hours; the only stable staff in the office were Sir James and Jennifer. Jenny Dolton was Sir James's personnel secretary and general factotum, and often, when Sir James was going off at a tangent, his lead holder, everyone else was expected to do their own administration.

It was accepted that the Section's staff were conscientious. If they had work to do, either in or out of the office, they were expected to do it, and would do it as quickly as possible and without bothering to seek permission, that would be wasting time. If they were not working a case, they could take off any time they wished with no more than a word with Jenny; of course, they were always in touch and expected to drop whatever they were doing and return to the office, office meaning the case they were working rather than a building. If a case required them, it wasn't necessary to record time off, and whatever time someone had off, they would definitely make up for when they were working.

Sir James was invariably the first to arrive at the office each morning and would be the last to leave, which left everyone else, who hadn't found a reason to be elsewhere, undecided as to when it was a safe time to arrive or leave. This particular morning, from behind his desk, he observed Jenny arrive and called her on the intercom. Jenny, as often before, acted as though she hadn't heard him, she was used to Sir James's promptness, so continued to take off her coat and hang it up before responding to the call.

"Yes, Sir James," she said, not bothering to say good morning, that wouldn't be appreciated; it would be wasting time.

"When Mr Wilcox finally decides to put in an appearance, send him to my office."

"Yes, Sir James." He could have added 'immediately' to the request but didn't, that would be taken for granted, always.

John Wilcox was always late, that is, he always arrived after everyone else; there was a good reason for this, it is that he lived out of London, therefore had to face the train trip in. Sir James knew this and understood, but still he liked to make a thing of it. He considered it 'kept him on his toes', not that it mattered what time he arrived.

John Wilcox, a tall thin man, often known as 'the grey man', by his colleagues, because of his ability to disappear, literally, he was in-descript to a point where people failed to notice him. Someone could be talking to him, he would take a step aside into a passing crowd and the person would not be able to find him, even if someone did notice him, they would soon forget, and when asked to describe him, very few could do so. With a cheerful outward going disposition, people took to him with ease; he could enter a situation, be accepted, become a part of the situation, and then be gone, leaving people wondering who that was. A product of the Royal Military Police and MI6, he had been considered suitable for 'The Section', in a large part, because of this chameleon ability.

The happy-go-lucky persona, that he generally showed to the world, would disappear in an instant. If the situation required it, he could be ruthless; he had the training, ability and mentality to kill or maim if the situation demanded, or if that was the purpose of his task, and after the action, he could return to his usual pleasant self and never think about his actions, again a talent that endeared him to the section.

Like most of the members of 'The Section', Wilcox was unmarried; the nature of the work and the time spent in other parts of the country, and world, made a standard home-life impossible. It also tended to make someone more careful to the extent of limiting their performance, that is why his love life had always been a matter of short but pleasant interludes.

This morning John had intended to do no more than put up his feet on the desk and read the paper, not much different to what he would usually do if in the office, but as they say all plans are subject to change, and this morning's change occurred when Jenny, having heard his arrival, put her head out of her office door.

"John," she called, "boss's office." There was a smile on her face as she said it.

John thought it over, as far as he knew, he hadn't done anything wrong, or failed to do something he should have, so it must be a job; there hadn't been anything in the news that might have caused work for 'The Section', so he'd have to go in blind. He looked at the others in the room, took a deep breath and stepped into Sir James's office; he didn't knock as that wasn't expected, and it would have wasted time.

"Good morning, Sir James," he tried and got a hard stare for his trouble.

"I saw the minister yesterday." Good old Sir James don't bother with any preamble Wilcox thought; he would have liked to know which of the three ministers it was that Sir James had seen, as The Section answered to three different ministries, but he didn't think it would be very sensible to ask. "He has been presented with something that has to be cleared up; it's not really our work, but the politicos have made it so, therefore, as you're not busy" – Sir James liked to get his little digs in – "I've got a job for you." Sir James continued, "Or to be precise, the Americans have asked the minister to do a job for them; he's given it to me, and I'm giving it to you." Sir James did like to be precise. "You've got an appointment at ten o'clock this morning at their embassy; you're meeting a Henry Filamont, go see him, find out what the job is, don't commit us to anything and make sure to find out who's paying, then come back and tell me." By 'tell me', he did actually mean talk to him, a lot of the things carried out by the section were better not written down.

Sir James lowered his head and returned to the file he had been reading. Wilcox knew he had been dismissed, even if nothing had been said, so he left, apart from an unwelcome greeting, he had said precisely nothing and didn't even have a file he could read, oh well.

Ω

Wilcox had the time, so he decided to walk to the appointment. Grosvenor Square, situated in the affluent west end of London, is in fact both a circle, formed by a pleasant little park with impressive trees and ponds, and a square formed by the majestic buildings some of which date back some one hundred to one hundred and fifty years to the heyday of the British Empire. The south side of the square is dominated by the much younger building that is the American Embassy.

While walking to the embassy, Wilcox mused over what the Americans could need The Section for. It was very difficult to guess because of the variety and type of work they did, but the Americans had a lot more agencies than the poor old UK, so why would they need us. Officially, The Section was a part of the home office, so could work at home. But there again, it was an arm of the foreign office, so could take on work abroad. Then again, it was supported by the police, and finally it, was a part of the ministry of defence, so could work on military matters, yet even knowing all the fields they could work in, still didn't help in the question of what the Yanks wanted with The Section.

At exactly ten o'clock, Wilcox presented himself to the body scanner that was found inside the door of the US Embassy. He was found to be of no direct threat to the well-being of this small part of America and was allowed to proceed as far as the reception desk, where he stated his business. A phone call was made, and a few minutes later, Henry Filamont appeared and escorted Wilcox to his office. Wilcox had no idea as to what Filamont's position was, but as there was no sign hanging on the door, he assumed it would be some sort of security section, maybe the 'Black Ops' department he'd just been thinking of.

They had exchanged small talk on the way up to the office, so once the door was closed, Filamont got down to business.

"Do you know anything about the illegal drugs business?" he asked.

"Not too much," Wilcox replied. "I know the names and effects of most drugs and where they come from and have a good idea of how they're distributed, but that's all."

"Well, that's more than most people know. I ask because a particular type of drug is what this is about, well, not only but it's where we need your help. This is a bit of an unusual task, under normal circumstances it's something we could do in house, but this time, there is a complication." Filamont had an almost humiliated look about him. Wilcox sat back and gave him time.

"I'll start at the beginning. I've been trying to break the narcotics arm of a mid-west crime syndicate for years, but it's a very close-knit unit and until now I've had no luck, that's until now, or actually two weeks ago, when I got a break. I've been contacted by an insider who has given me good information that's started a ball rolling.

"He's been able to tell me how the syndicate gets its heroin, or rather, how it gets the raw opium from which it makes it. It turns out that one of the syndicate members goes to Afghanistan every year and buys the whole crop from one valley and ships it home, are you with me so far?" Wilcox confirmed he was. "With this information, I could stop this year's shipment, but either one of the other gangs would buy it up instead, or we could kill the buyer, and that would cause a war amongst the syndicates."

"So, you want us to shoot someone," Wilcox interjected, showing he still wasn't quite with what Filamont was after.

"Right, we need someone to be killed, really, he's just a nasty little small time crook, a gangster, I suppose you'd call him, in himself a small time hood, of no interest to anyone, but he's going to Afghanistan to represent a large and dangerous syndicate, his death, in itself, if executed correctly, could cause a large hole to be created in that syndicate and hopefully cause the gang war I mentioned, from which the only winner would be Uncle Sam."

"Okay," Wilcox put in to try and help, "as you say, you could 'normally' handle the problem, so what's the complication?"

Filamont smiled. "Really, it's simple because he's going to do a job for the nasty guys; they're keeping an eye on him, so the only chance we'll get to be able to take him out will be when he goes to the village to buy the opium.

"Now unfortunately, the village that he'll be going to is situated in Helmand province, that's your guy's area of responsibility. Again, no difficulty in that, but, and I've argued with the Hoover Building day after day on the point, if we go in and do this ourselves, your army types would take a great deal of exception to it and make a big noise. Also, if it got out that it was an official hit, then the whole of the exercise would be wasted.

"You see, we need the syndicate, the nasty guys, to believe it was a rival gang who carried it out, a gang that also want the opium this man was going there to get, so then they can take over the territory of the first lot who haven't got any opium, are you getting the idea?" Wilcox nodded. "Hopefully," Filamont continued, "if it goes well, we would start the gang war that only the government would win.

"So, and I'm getting to the point now, our problem, what we mustn't do is; one, we mustn't upset your side, or they will start a noise that will be heard in the States. Two, we mustn't let anyone think Uncle Sam was involved, or any other official unit of either ours or yours, or even the Afghans. Three, we don't want our contact within the syndicate to be in any way suspect. What we do want is a hit that could only have been carried out by a rival gang."

Wilcox was now able to think of the problems; Filamont arranged coffee whilst he did so.

Finally, he asked, "When would the hit need to take place?"

"That we don't know; our informant will know about two weeks before the man leaves the US."

"And how many people will be in the group, I assume he won't be going alone?"

"There will be two from the US, and they're going to meet up with some mercenaries who will be their guides and protection, so I would think there will be about six in all, maybe seven, but only this man" – he passed a picture across the desk – "is the target, although we wouldn't mind if this one" – another picture – "also stayed in Afghanistan. The mercs are of no interest."

"How can we be sure the one gang will think it's the other?"

"We can give you some clues to leave behind, maybe a gum wrapper or a water bottle, things that would be normal in Kansas but not elsewhere."

"How close can a shooter get to his objective?" Wilcox asked.

"I reckon he'll have to be across the river, which will make it a long shot, but it'll mean he should be safe from a follow-up attack by the mercenaries."

"Well, it seems we should be able to assist our cousins on a little matter like this, I mean what are families for? But something that might be useful, where about is this valley and the village that's going to sell the dope?"

"Yes," Filamont said, "I can't exactly tell you where it is, apart from, it's in Afghanistan, and it's north of Kabul."

"I hope you're kidding me?" Wilcox asked with alarm in his voice.

"Well, yes and no, out in those mountains, villages don't have names, as we know it, the only people who go there know where they're going before they set out. Us westerners have to rely on navigational information, so I can tell you the village is at about N36,01,48, E70,48,36, but apart from that, it's up to you; you see, the man who knew where it is, died.

"I just hope there are not too many villages at them co-ordinates," Wilcox said with a deep sigh. "Okay, I'll find it somehow, but there's one little point, who's picking up the tab for this? My boss was most insistent I ask."

Filamont said with a smile, "The US might be having to ask a favour, but I don't think it requires to be financially bailed out, at least not just yet, you just tell the minister to invoice us, and I'll see it gets paid."

Chapter 9

On his return to the office, John looked in on Jenny, a nod towards Sir James's office was enough to ask if the boss was busy, a replying nod was all that was required to say Sir James was alone and therefore available. With one deep breath, to steady himself, John pushed the door open and went in. Sir James looked up for a moment then looked down again saying:

"What did they have to say?"

John relayed the gist of the conversation he'd had with Filamont.

"So, who's paying?" Always straight to the point was Sir James.

"Oh, definitely them, sir, paying all we ask."

"Right, so you'd better be getting on with it then."

Briefing completed, instructions passed, time to leave, never any time wasted with Sir James.

Arriving at his desk, John started up his computer. Using Google Earth, he set about finding the spot on the earth where the Afghan village should be. Not being the best of map-readers, he was still able to find the location easily enough, but he could only hazard a guess as the distance from one side of the valley to the other, but providing he was someway right, even he could see it would be a very long shot to take out the drug buyers.

It looked like the shot would have to be taken from across the river as Filamont had suggested, and the distance across the river valley at that point was very wide. With the computer's ruler, he measured the distance from the map and got a figure of about a mile, and a bit. *A very long shot*, he thought, so he was going to have to find himself a very good marksman; he certainly couldn't make the shot himself, even on a good day he could miss a target on the fifty-yard range. So, his first requirement was to find someone who could make the shot.

Reviewing the contractors who had worked for the section before, there were one or two good shots, but they weren't up to this sort of job, even if they would be willing to go to Afghanistan, something he doubted.

Enquiring of the font of all knowledge, Jenny didn't help; she only knew the same two men John knew; besides, she pointed out how would you get them into Afghanistan without the army wanting to know why. Jennifer might not have known of a suitable sniper, but she had unknowingly given John the answer to the question.

"Where do you find people who can shoot well?" he asked; it was a rhetorical question. "Why in the army of course," he answered himself. Jenny looked on knowing she wasn't expected to take part in the conversation. "I wonder if the regiment who are currently in theatre have got someone who is an exceptional shot. Only one way to find out." Conversation over, he gave Jenny a pat on the cheek and returned to his desk.

Reaching for the phone and the 'special' phone book, he called the Section's contact man Jefferey Evens, who, he hoped, would be sitting at his desk in the HQ MOD in Bristol.

"Afternoon, Jeff, John Wilcox here," he announced in his jolliest tone of voice.

"Oh, no," was the pained reply, "what are you after now? Don't answer, whatever it is we've just run out." They were acquaintances of long standing although they had never met, but they talked whenever Wilcox needed military equipment or, as in this case, manpower.

"Now that's not nice," Wilcox responded, "anyone would think I was always asking for things, and it's been, let me see, nearly a month since I asked for anything at all."

"It was two weeks ago and the boat section hasn't got things back together yet."

"Was it only two weeks, are you sure? I suppose you are because you write things down, don't you? I never could do that, too much of a bother; anyway, enough history lessons. I need a marksman, one who's a really good shot, and I need him in Afghanistan, yesterday, can you help?" He'd finished on an up note trying to make the request sound routine but kept his fingers crossed.

"This is a joke, isn't it? If it is, it's not funny. If it's not, then my original answer stands. I've had enough jokers around here already today, and one more I do not want."

"Okay, I hear you, but no, this is not a joke," Wilcox replied. "I truly do need a marksman, and I need him in Afghanistan, and I do need him now. And, I don't want to make your life harder, but I also need to fly out there and talk to him about what I want him to do, which means I'll need an authority to present to which ever colonel is currently in charge, so can you help me, please?"

'The Section' through the various ministries did have the authority to ask for assistance from all other departments, and they were obliged to meet the requests even if it was difficult, but the Section had to use them carefully and not ruffle feathers, they could only apply through contacts like Jefferey or ministers.

"Right," said Jefferey with a big sigh, "okay, let me have it again then I'll see what I can do." Wilcox reiterated his needs and left Jefferey to find them for him while he sat back and thought about what else he might need. After five minutes, he couldn't think of anything he should be thinking about so stopped trying to think and picked up the paper he had intended to read when he had arrived this morning.

It was nearly two hours before Jefferey called back.

"Okay, I've got three marksmen in Afghanistan, and they're all very good. Before you ask, you can choose which one you want when you get there. I've provisionally booked you on the morning supply flight, the day after tomorrow. Your authority letter is with the minister's PPS, but the minister's in the house for the defence debate this afternoon, so it won't get signed till this evening, so once it is, the PPS will send it around." This last statement was really a euphemism, as neither Jeffery, nor the PPS knew just where the Section was housed, but they did have a post box in the MI5's building. "Now is that everything O' lord and master? Maybe I can now get back to the important things I was doing when you called."

"That will do very nicely thank you; I shall now leave you to your less important work and deign not to darken your door again, for now that is." A groan was heard from Jefferey before the phone reached its cradle.

Ω

The large, fat and ungainly Lockheed Hercules cargo aircraft landed at camp Bastion (was it camp or fort he never could remember), in the early morning. It had been an uneventful flight, although Wilcox, sitting in a para seat, did not find it the most comfortable, but at least the droning of the engines had eventually sent him to sleep so the time passed without it seeming too long.

The landing, when it came, did give him some small amount of apprehension; one moment they were flying along normally, then the aircraft made a sudden drop, that from inside felt like it was falling out of the sky, and it lifted Wilcox from his seat for a while. The loadmaster, with a smile on his face, retrospectively, explained this quick descent was in case any terrorist intended to use a missile to make the drop even quicker, very sensible, but a warning for the sake of his stomach would have been nice.

Stepping out into the bright sunshine caused him to pause for a moment or two unable to see anything after being in the dark interior of the aircraft for so long; he quickly reached out for a pair of sunglasses and returned his eyesight to a usable condition. A soldier was waiting for him close to the aircraft para door, having been sent from the orderly office, to escort him to the colonel's office.

Colonel Blackman, a tall, upright man with features as sharp as the creases in his combat fatigues, was standing at his office window, regarding the newly landed aircraft and more so the passenger who had just got off. Having had only one day's notice of his arrival and no information of who he was, or why he was here, he was a bit disconcerted, and annoyed. Being in charge of this post with all the responsibilities that went with it would have been only polite to have given him more notice. Normally, he would have had expected at least a week's notice if someone was to come in to theatre, but this time, nothing. What rank was the man? What was his purpose? What was his name even? How should he treat him? To say the least, Blackman was not in the best frame of mind.

There was also something about the man; did he know him? No, he was so familiar yet, no, he was definitely sure he had never met him, maybe he'd seen him at some function; you met all sorts of people at some of these parties, the more official the party, the stranger the guests.

It had been a bit of a shock when the MOD had told him this man, who they hadn't named, was coming out for a special operation, which he would, or would not, tell him about when he got there, very mysterious. He would be carrying a letter of authorisation with him as his identity.

They had also told him to facilitate the man with what he needed, whatever it might be, so, it wasn't a great leap of imagination to assume, this unknown man was a spook, a spy or some sort of intelligence thing, but he knew of no ongoing operation, and if there was, he would normally be put in the picture. But he was only a soldier one who was supposed to be running things out here, so why should they tell him anything.

Wilcox entered the colonel's office, introduced himself and they shook hands.

"Good morning, I'm Colonel Blackman," he said. "I hope you had a good flight."

"Call me John," Wilcox said using his most pleasant tone. "Yes, the flight was as good as a Hercules flight can be. Look, I'm sorry to be foist on you like this, but unfortunately, there's something I have to sort out, it's really rather important and has a strict time scale."

"No, that's fine," Blackman replied, his tone belying the statement. "We're here to serve." Strangely, Blackman was getting to like the man but was still reserving judgement, for the present. "Unfortunately, as we have no idea why you're here" – the emphasis on the statement was clear – "we haven't been able to arrange anything for you in advance."

"Yes" – Wilcox put a considerate look on his face – "I hope I won't be here for more than a couple of days, and I'll explain as much as I can, but first, you had better read this." He proffered the letter from the ministry. "I'm afraid it still won't explain anything, but at least you'll know I'm 'bona fide."

The letter began, "The person presenting this letter…" no name the colonel noted and read on. "Quite so," Blackman said after he had read, "perhaps you'd like some tea or coffee?"

"Tea would be fantastic; the stuff they're able to make on the aircraft is frightening." They sat and talked generally whilst they had tea, then Wilcox decided it was time to enlighten the colonel about his mission, or rather, the story he had concocted that he felt would get the best reaction.

"I assume we're safe to speak candidly in here," he asked, giving an inquiring look at the colonel who gave a nod of agreement, "well," Wilcox continued in a low voice, "and this is top secret. If it got out that we were working on information received, it would put our contacts in real danger, and it took a long time to get them in place, if you know what I mean." Blackman looked suitably impressed.

"For some years, we've been trying to catch an important terrorist; he himself isn't actually part of any particular group but more of a contractor type of position. Do you remember the case of Carlos the Jackal, the fellow who tried to shoot the French President DeGaulle back in the sixties?" Blackman agreed he did. "Well, this is the same sort of person; he works for any of the current rash of groups that are trying to hold the world to ransom. He's important enough for us and other security agencies" – the word 'agencies' led Blackman to believe the Americans were also involved, as Wilcox had intended – "to go to any lengths to remove him.

"So far, we've never had any luck; he always has back doors, people who will tip him off when we get near. Now, very recently, we've had a strong piece of reliable intelligence that the man will be in this country in the near future; he's normally well protected, but on this trip, he's working for himself and will be almost on his own. After all, if he brought an army with him, it would be a bit obvious.

"He's actually here to make an opium buy we're told, even terrorists need sources of money; it seems he's intending to supply some American gang. Why him? I don't know, as you might guess criminals aren't as tight an organisation as a terror cell, and the Americans have an informer on the inside. Now my task is to see that he does not leave here alive, he's just too dangerous, and who knows when we might get the chance again.

"Sorry to have been so long winded, but that's the basic situation, and normally, we would hand the problem over to yourselves, it being more your sort of work, but we also have an important consideration; it's a bit of disinformation really. We must make the killing and make it look like the action of another terrorist group or perhaps a criminal group. This would safeguard our sources, and there's a chance we could start an inter group dispute or even a war between them, so, most desperately, we need to ensure it doesn't look like an official hit, so we can't have your unit involved, in any visible way."

Blackman thought he understood the situation and was very pleased he didn't work for one of these cloak and dagger outfits, but he was still confused by one thing.

"I think I get what you mean, but I don't see what is it then that we can help you with? Are you looking only for somewhere to base yourself or is there something else?"

"Right, I'm sorry I haven't come to that as yet, this is where you can help us. I need a good marksman, a sniper, someone who's reliable at long distance shooting; it'll probably be over a mile, that's probably as close as he'll be able to get. I say probably because the man would have to decide for himself.

"Then I need transport, to the location and back for a recon so the man can get a look of the lay of land, perhaps he can see a better ambush site than I can using maps and Google Earth; it's got to be up to him where he'll take the shot from. Then the same trip again for the actual shooting. The trips also need to be sneaky both in and out; we can't have a big army helicopter waking every one up and giving the game away. He'll also have to be by himself, the way a contract killer would operate. I know it sounds complicated and melodramatic, but I'm hoping you can help."

Blackman had sat quiet through the rendition without questioning the story. "So what you're asking for from us is a marksman and discreet transport, nothing else?"

"Not unless you can think of something that might improve the chances," Wilcox answered. Blackman again went silent in thought, then accepting the story called in the adjutant.

"Henry, what marksmen have we got with us?" Major Henry Parton was the regimental adjutant, the colonel's number two, who was expected to know everything about the regiment and its doings, at all times, a post all officers had to go through if they wanted to eventually be a commander. He was very tall, maybe an inch or even two more than Wilcox who was not short, but whereas Wilcox was of average build, Parton was as thin as a rake.

"Well" – Parton gave the colonel's question some thought – "there's Corporal Dylan Williams, then Lance Corp John Devers, and Lance Corp Mike Erving, no, scrap Erving, he's gone sick, so it's just the two." Wilcox was amazed at Parton's ability to remember the names and abilities at a moment's notice.

"Who's the best of them?" Blackman asked.

"That's an easy one. Williams probably one of the best in the army."

"Would he be on duty at the moment?" Parton agreed he would. "Thanks, Henry." Parton left and Blackman turned to Wilcox again.

"So there's your first requirement; we've got a suitable man, a good one, but I don't know if he'd like to go on a shoot without back-up; he would normally have a troop in the background in case of trouble. Anyway, you can go and see him, find out if he suits your needs. I'll organise an ops team to see how we can get you in for a quiet shuffty, Private Jones." This last was to the colonel's orderly who quickly appeared. "Take this" – what to call him, he didn't want to give him a rank he might not be entitled to – "gentleman, to the armoury to see

Corporal Williams, wait till he's ready then bring him back here. I'll see you then" – this to Wilcox, again a slight hesitation – "John." It seemed a bit too informal on such a short acquaintance, but what else could he call him?

Chapter 10

Corporal Dylan Williams stood up from his desk as the orderly and Wilcox entered the armoury office; he couldn't have been said to have jumped up or that he was now standing to attention; he'd been in the army too long to do that for anyone, at least not for anyone ranking below the adjutant.

"Good morning, Corporal Williams," said Wilcox, taking the initiative, "Dylan, isn't it? May I call you that?" Suspicion crossed Dylan's mind at this opening, what have we got here? *Not an officer*, he thought, *not with an approach like that*. Dylan gave a slight nod, and Wilcox accepted this as agreement and continued.

"The colonel has allowed me to have a chat with you, could we go somewhere where we won't be overheard? Preferably in the open."

Now Dylan's surprise turned to suspicion, could he be in some sort of trouble, was this man from the SIB? (Special Investigations Branch of the Military Police) He couldn't think of anything that could bring them to him, or was this an evidence collection? Maybe someone else was in trouble?

He looked at the man, tall, erect, sure of himself, definitely every inch an officer, yet he was wearing cams but not showing name or rank badges, this was suspicious or at least unusual; he was accompanied by the orderly room lance corporal so it must be official, but civilians in the armoury? It wasn't allowed, but if the colonel had okayed it, then it wasn't Dylan's problem.

"Yes, sir," he said, working on the army adage, if it moves, salute it and call it sir, if it doesn't move, paint it not an officer, but the colonel knows him so be careful. "If you come this way, we can walk out to the wire." The wire being the fence that surrounded the camp, there's plenty of space there.

As they walked away from the buildings and tents, Wilcox regarded Williams; he already had the impression of a loner, not an outsider, but someone who was satisfied with himself, someone who could take or leave the world and all that's in it. Once they were a good way from the buildings and possible eavesdroppers, he began to outline what he was after.

"The adjutant tells me you're the best shot in the regiment, is that true?"

"Yes, sir," Dylan said shortly. Truth is truth and Dylan was not being boastful in saying so, and the one word was enough to answer the question so it was all he said. Wilcox accepted the reply. "You can drop the sir, corporal, I'm a civilian. I don't have any commission. What I have got is a shooting job that needs to be carried out; it's in theatre, but although cleared right up to MOD level and above, there are some complexities about it. Would you be interested?" Dylan was confused, to say the least, this man was asking him, not telling or ordering, but asking if he wanted to do what he was paid to do, is this official or not?

"I'm in the army; I'm not given to choosing what I do," Dylan stated. "I do what the colonel tells me."

"Yes, all right and proper," Wilcox agreed. "But the MOD has told" – he put an emphasis on the word for effect – "the colonel to help me and supply all I need, and the first thing I need him to provide is a capable marksman. He's okay with that and the adjutant says you are the best, so I've been given permission to ask you, so that's why I'm here. Unfortunately, I can't give you any real details until I know you're willing to do the job, as it's above the colonel even."

Dylan still looked wary but was impressed, this went all the way up to the MOD and even the colonel hadn't been told what it's about, but he said nothing.

After a short pause, Wilcox continued, "In itself, it's a straightforward shoot, but although it's been cleared right up at government level, we don't want the army to be accountably involved. As I say, there are some problems that would make it different and maybe difficult. It's a bit outside of normal, official army procedure, so you've got the right to say no, and I'll have to make do with someone second best, but I need to know now if you would be interested to take it on? I don't like to leave you in the dark, not knowing what you would be taking on by agreeing, but I can say it would be a very long shot, with interesting aspects, so would you be interested?"

This was getting weirder by the minute Dylan thought. *I'm a soldier I do what I'm told, now I'm being asked, I mean asked, if I wanted to do my job.*

"What are these problems," he asked finally.

"Okay," Wilcox said, "first and foremost, you will never be able to say anything about the 'OP' to anyone, not your mates or officers. You, me and the colonel are the only ones to know of it; it is classed as an official secret." Wilcox didn't mind stretching the truth or even lying. "If it meant you were being pressurised and had to make up a story, you've only to let me know and I'll back you up, could you live with that?"

"Yes, I can keep my mouth shut."

"Okay, so second, you would have to work totally alone, and in bandit country, if you got into trouble, you'd have to get yourself out, no back-up troop, no calling in air power, again, could you handle that?"

"That's how I'd prefer to work."

"Okay, lastly, the shot would be more than a mile and the target man sized, a fairly big man but not out of proportion, can you do it?"

This last point gave Dylan pause for some thought.

"How far over a mile would the shot be?" Mention of the shot immediately put Dylan into active role, his mind locked on to this crucial point.

"That I can't say, but the colonel is arranging for us to go to the location, and you can check it out for yourself. If you take the job, it's your call; you're the specialist; it's up to you to say what's needed."

"So, you want me to go out by myself into bandit country, shoot someone, get myself out, if I can, and then forget it ever happened, have I got that right?"

"Nicely put, in a nutshell, yes." It was Wilcox's turn to be short in reply.

Once again, Dylan was quiet as he thought out the possibilities. "And the colonel's okayed this?"

"Yes." Wilcox decided to elaborate, "The 'OP' is officially unofficial, and the colonel has been given very little choice."

Again, Dylan was quiet for a good five minutes, then he took a deep breath and said, "Okay, I'm prepared to do it, if it's possible and stick to the terms you laid out, but it's a long shot, and if I think it's too long for me, I'll say so and all bets are off, okay."

"Great." Wilcox released the breath he hadn't realised he'd been holding. "The colonel is arranging a trip now so keep yourself ready to go out for a look-see this afternoon."

They walked back to the armoury where Wilcox collected the orderly and then returned to the colonel's office.

Ω

"So, have you've got yourself a marksman?" Blackman asked.

With a smile, Wilcox replied, "Yes, I have, and he seems to be exactly what I require, and you'll be pleased to know he wouldn't agree to do it until I'd assured him you had given the okay." Blackman took this with a sense of pleasure. "Now, have you been able to work out how we're going to get there and let him have a look at the place?"

"So, you're going along as well?"

"Of course, sir, I need to know what the situation is, and if Williams has any problems or questions, then I'm the one to answer him."

"Well, okay, but I'm not sure about you going up there, being a civilian and all, but it's your call, let's see what the fly boys have worked out for you anyway." They both walked across to the 'OPs' tent.

"Have you organised anything for us yet, Jeff," Blackman asked the pilot who was bending over a map table.

"I think we have, sir," replied Captain Jeff Webb. "The place is easy enough to get to; it's the discretion consideration that makes it a bit tricky. Our best bet is to go wide and come in behind the ridge here" – he indicated the point on the map, across the river from the village – "there is very little, if any, human activity over that way. We'll be travelling over desert most of the way, and when we get close, the ground slopes quite steeply; it'll let us get in reasonably close while always staying below the mountain ridgeline. I think we'd be very unlucky to be seen; certainly, the village will never see us. However, the noise, as always, is the problem, we will make some, and this could echo off the mountains, letting everyone know we're there.

"One way out of this would be to be accompanied by an apache or lynx, which make a lot more noise than us, and can do a fly-by, taking a look at each village in the valley, as if they're looking for someone, and they can work their way up the valley until were ready to go, and then, we can call them in and reverse the procedure."

The captain looked up pleased with himself, which he had every right to be, as it was a good plan that Wilcox could happily go along with.

"Just a couple of questions," Wilcox asked, "how long would we have on the ground and how close to the ridge can you get us?"

"Good question, our Gazelle can shut down once we land so there is no fuel problem for us, the apache only has three hours max, so we would have to call it back in after an hour max, let's say forty-five minutes for safety. As for landing zone, I've spotted a place here" – again he indicated a point on the map– "it's about four hundred yards from the top of the ridge so not too far, and its level, almost, with the co-ords you've given us."

Wilcox was happy, the pilots were happy and so the colonel was also happy; the sooner this was done, the sooner the civvy would be gone, and he could get his post back to doing what they should be doing. It was arranged for take-off to be at three o'clock. Corporal Williams was told to report at two o'clock and to be suitably equipped. Wilcox went, with the others, for lunch in the officers' mess; it being taken for granted, he was entitled to that consideration.

Ω

To Wilcox, it seemed that Dylan was going over the top when he arrived at the 'OPs' tent; he was carrying his M24 sniper rifle and wearing a pistol in a shoulder holster, a similar one of which he passed to Wilcox.

Totally disregarding everyone else in the tent, Dylan stated, "I take it you know how to use that?" Dylan was now in his element, so the question held a presumption in the tone that stated who was in charge. Wilcox, who didn't answer, took the pistol out from the holster, released the magazine, operated the breach mechanism fired of the action and replaced the magazine. "I thought so," Dylan said, offhandedly.

"Why do we need all this fire power?" Wilcox asked.

"Because we're going into bandit country," Dylan replied in a peremptorily manner; he would have spoken to any new recruit in the same way if they had asked the same question.

Wilcox accepted the reproof but still asked, "Why the M24 then? We're not intending to kill anyone on this trip."

Dylan gave a shrug. "This is my everyday weapon. I take it to the range every day, and if I leave the fort, I take it with me." He gave a sidewise glance. "I've got five rounds in the magazine, so if I ever have the Taliban after me, then five of them will be dead before I have to reload or get my Glock out."

Wilcox wouldn't have questioned the statement. Dylan always sounded, when he was talking of shooting, that he was telling the absolute truth. As they reached the aircraft, Wilcox saw that the aircrew were also armed in a similar way but with the SA80 rifle rather than the M24.

The trip into the mountains was uneventful although convoluted, as the Lynx wound its way through the valleys, to avoid rising above the mountaintops. The landscape looked barren and uninteresting, nothing moved down there, no vehicles, no people, no animals. Wilcox couldn't even see any sign of wind either.

After fifteen minutes of flight, the aircraft was bussed by an apache, which circled them then angled off to one side taking a parallel path that would take it out and along the route of the river, while the Gazelle started a slow loop that would take it out into the desert, and then, bring it in behind the mountains from a completely different direction.

They landed well behind the ridgeline and the pilot cut the engine. Dylan was first out and scanned the surroundings; there was no sign of life; it had been a worry that there could be something like a goatherd, with a boy to look after them, but there was nothing and no one to be seen.

They synchronised their watches and position with the pilot, a precaution in case the aircraft had to leave for some reason, always a possibility, as the aircraft was more valuable than the two on the ground, and they all had to realise the pilot's first responsibility was to his aircraft. Dylan and Wilcox finally set off towards the ridgeline.

It was a short but steep climb, and as they approached the top of the ridge, Dylan waved Wilcox to get down and stay where he was, while he carried on to the very peak on his belly. At the summit, he raised himself enough to see over the ridge, then dropped down and moved to his left. Again, they took a look over the ridge and then moved again; in all, he tried ten different points before returning close to the original position he'd selected.

Keeping as flat as possible, Dylan now presented his weapon and sighted at the centre of the village. Taking and noting the reading from the range finder built-in to the Zeiss scope, he moved his aim and repeated the measurement. He did this four more times, focussing at different points in the village, then he laid down his rifle and took up a pair of binoculars. The next five minutes, he spent looking at the general situation across the river. Next, he crawled across to a large rock that stood above the ridgeline, stood up, and looked at the ridge around him. Ten minutes later, he returned to where Wilcox was seated, took out two bottles of water from his pack and handed one to Wilcox.

"It's a long shot," he said. "I measured at two thousand, four hundred and thirty yards."

"Can you do it?" Wilcox needed to know.

"Yes, I could hit a man-sized target at that range, but I could not be certain of a kill, at least not with this weapon." He indicated the M24. He sat thoughtfully. Wilcox took this in and thought of all the trouble to get to this point to be stopped by a few yards. He asked, "Is there another weapon that would make the kill certain?"

"Oh, yes," Dylan said with a smile in his voice. "This here" – he indicated the M24 – "is old, it's good, and for my usual work, it's fine. My usual shot length would be up to a thousand yards, but at distance, it tends to be a bit wayward; the army has now started replacing it with the 'LH115A3', now if I had one of those, that would be a different matter, then I could be sure, even of this shot."

"What's one of them?" Wilcox asked bewildered, his knowledge of rifles was limited and of sniper rifles totally non-existent.

"Probably the finest sniper rifle system in production today; it's made by the Accuracy International company in Cambridge; you can compare it to a Rolls Royce with a 32-inch barrel. I could choose which eye to hit at that range."

"Can you get one of those?"

"Not a chance, the army's bringing them in to service but regiment by regiment, and they haven't got around to us yet; we have to carry on using this" – he indicated his M24 – "it's good enough as I say for routine work, but not for what you want."

"What about getting closer?" Wilcox asked.

"Not a chance, we're as close as we can get on this side of the river, and over the other side, I would have to be out in the open."

"How about on the road before they get here?"

"No, again, I wouldn't be able to differentiate between passengers."

"So, what you're telling me is it's a half chance or a better rifle, no other option?"

"That's the size of it."

Ω

When they had returned to the fort, Wilcox went to see the colonel and asked about the superior weapon. The colonel called in his supply officer who agreed they should have the new rifle soon, but it was not yet their turn; the army has its procedures, and they will not be bypassed.

"Can't we borrow one from another regiment?" Wilcox suggested.

"Not a chance," the supply officer replied, "you see, they are issued as a personnel weapon. Once a man is classed as a sniper, he gets issued with it, and it remains with him till he leaves; the man sets it up for himself to how he wants it to be; he would never lend it, and no one would ask him to."

Wilcox could see he was getting nowhere; it seemed that if Dylan were to have the weapon he needed, he'd have to buy it. This unbidden thought started a memory running in Wilcox's head; he recalled Henry Filamont saying 'the US isn't short of a few dollars.' He smiled as he made up his mind.

"Would it be okay for me to go see Corporal Williams again?" he asked the colonel.

"Sure," the colonel said, "you know the way."

In the armoury, once again Wilcox told to Dylan, "Write me a list of exactly what you want to carry out the shot, don't cut corners, and I'll see you get it." Dylan hardly believed what Wilcox was saying.

"Including the rifle system?" he asked, with amazement in his voice.

"Especially the rifle system, plus the sights and ammunition and anything else you might need."

Dylan was thinking whilst he wrote his list. "The kill is the most important factor in this, am I right?" Wilcox agreed, not knowing what Dylan was thinking of. "Well, do you want me to use hunting ammunition?" Once again, Wilcox was at a loss.

"What's hunting ammunition?" he asked.

Dylan was a bit shy on the subject but went on, "Officially, the army is not allowed to use it. Geneva Convention and all that, but you say this is not really official, you see it changes size when it hits the target. I suppose it could be compared to the old 'Dum Dum' bullet the gangsters of old were so fond of, so if it hits someone, then it is almost certain to kill. Its only genuine use is to kill large game."

Wilcox knew what Dum Dums were and how effective they were at killing, and the thought of it not being allowed to be used by the army, would really help with the deception he wanted to create.

"Okay," he said, "that's a good idea; put them on the list as well." Taking the list from Dylan he asked, "You say this company is located in Cambridge?" Dylan confirmed it. "Okay, it looks as though I'm going to have to visit them."

Back in his room in the mess, Wilcox sent an e-mail to Jenny, back at the office, asking her to make an appointment with the Accuracy International company, for the following afternoon as late as she can, that was the one advantage of being six or seven hours ahead in time. By the time the C17 aircraft arrived at Brize Norton, there would still be time to get to Cambridge.

Chapter 11

Piet Botha was sitting in a hotel bar feeling dejected and depressed; his life was not the wild exciting thing it had been. What had happened to the idealistic youngster, he asked himself, full of patriotism, determined to defend his country, with his very life's blood if necessary. Now it was gone, the purpose, the comradeship, the feeling of belonging to something and somewhere, the knowledge of being right, all gone.

Born in Johannesburg in a segregated South Africa where everything was either black or white, both figuratively and actually, you were either on one side or the other, white and life had been straightforward. If you were white, you could get on and live a good life. If you were black, you were there to serve the whites and be thankful they were there to look after you. It was a simple concept that appealed to any child.

Born into an Afrikaans family that could trace their ancestry back to the original Dutch settlers, he had been taught this simple concept from the cradle, and he wholeheartedly accepted it, but before he had even reached his majority, it changed. The blacks got above themselves; they wanted to run things; they wanted equal rights, and they used terrorism to achieve it. It wasn't long before it became a civil war fought on colour lines.

As soon as he was old enough, Piet had joined the army; he saw it as his duty to hunt and kill those that wanted to take his country, a country that his people had brought out of savagery and ignorance. The blacks still didn't know how to be civilised but considered they could run the country; they wanted to displace the whites and take over what his forefathers had built.

Being in the army anti terrorists' detachment, he felt justified in killing these troublemaking blacks. Innocence, right and justice were of no concern to Piet; it was he who had the right to defend his country, so on the slightest pretext, he would kill, maybe the Kaffa wasn't a terrorist, but it would only be a matter of time before he became one, that was Piet's philosophy.

Eventually, Piet got noticed by his superiors, not, as he would have liked, as an ardent defender of his country, and its way of life, but as a renegade who was out of control, and they found his attitude could no longer be tolerated. He was considered to be too wild and uncontrolled, but they still needed him; his single mindedness though barbaric was effective. Piet was transferred up on to the northern border; up there, a lot of actual terrorists were still crossing into the south from Zimbabwe and Angola where they had support.

Eventually, the whites had to lose, both from numbers and international pressure; the apartheid regime could find no support in the rest of the world, whereas their black opponents were supported by the whole of the communist world; the whites had to give in sooner or later, but this was something Piet could not accept.

Along with a few like-minded comrades, he decided South Africa no longer wanted or had place for them, but now, they were battle-hardened soldiers and would find it hard to settle to a civilian life; they headed north. They were leaving behind the homeland that they had fought for, had been prepared to give their lives for but had now rejected them.

Taking the experience of their past, they headed into the war-torn lands, that constituted most of the rest of Africa, where their experience of fighting and killing were only too welcome, to be employed as mercenaries, working for anyone who would pay.

At the start, there were ten of them who hired out as a single commando, with Piet as their leader; overtime, some were killed and some others joined, always disillusioned South Africans. Life as a mercenary, Piet found very much to his liking; he felt it was what he was born for. Piet and his men were given the freedom to do pretty much as they wished, as long as they kept on the good side of the dictator of whichever country they were in. And when their paymaster was deposed, or killed, they would change sides, or move on; there was always another war or uprising waiting for them.

They lasted this way for maybe five years, but eventually, the wars petered out or at least the blacks were fighting amongst themselves and didn't want to pay for mercenaries. There were also the international attitudes that would no longer countenance their actions; there had been too many atrocities, and the changed situation now made them criminals; they became wanted, for trial rather than to fight.

It was time for them to move on, to get completely out of Africa and look elsewhere for their kind of work. Some of the commando returned to South Africa but had to change their identity first, if they didn't, they would be put on trial, and if they were lucky and didn't run into some of the people they used to fight, they might survive to do a long prison sentence.

Some moved on to countries where they would find work in the criminal underworld, being sheltered by the crime gangs and who didn't care about their war crimes, just as long as they could fight. The rest headed to Asia, where fighting was still a daily activity if on a smaller, more personnel scale.

Without minor wars to use their talents, the 'commando' as they still thought of themselves, reduced to just four and Piet. They had little trouble becoming bodyguards to the wealthy, self-important types, who did their killing on the stock markets and were just as ruthless as Piet and his men. After a few years, even this work began to dry up as governments improved their laws and conformed with the evermore dominating international laws and the better enforcement of them.

Now Piet, sitting in the bar, had almost given up, even he had been thinking of packing in and returning to South Africa, maybe buy a farm or a hunting camp or something like that, but the idea didn't appeal to him; he could see none of the enjoyment or excitement of his past life in that scenario.

It was while he was in this mood, the American, who called himself Bowman, approached him with an offer, one week's work as a bodyguarding team for two men. They needed to go up to northern Afghanistan, to buy a cargo then travel through Pakistan, unofficially, down to the coast to Gwadar, to meet a ship. The pay was fifty thousand dollars for the week, with Piet responsible to provide transport, two pick-ups and a Land Cruiser.

Piet wasn't impressed with the job; it was obviously an opium buy, why else would anyone go up north, travelling down through Pakistan wasn't the easiest thing either; they had a competent boarder force and were happy to shoot, but it was possible if you knew the way, and Piet knew the way. The money was reasonable, and the commando was running short of that, so they needed the work; he accepted the offer.

Chapter 12

Corporal Dylan Williams, British Army soldier, armourer and marksman, highly regarded in his speciality but not a man it was easy to get near to. He had friends but not close ones; he got on with those he worked with and those he supervised, although he was considered to be a hard taskmaster insisting on perfection in their work, or at least as close as they could get to it. All in all, no one disliked Dylan but when picking teams, he was not the first to be chosen, that is, unless it was a shooting competition, then he was the man they all wanted, likewise when out on patrol or defending a position, everyone felt safer with Dylan along.

Dylan's childhood had been nothing special, as far as others brought up in an English rural village. An only child, living in the countryside, he never had much in the way of playmates, and by the time he went to school, he was considered very much an outsider and not part of the class, not that this bothered him, he was big enough and tough enough to not have any trouble with the school bullies.

Dylan's mother, a regular Norfolk housewife, made sure he was fed, clothed, went to school, and did his homework, all of which he thought was a waste of time. His father, however, a gamekeeper on a local lord's estate, taught Dylan everything he knew about the natural world, how to stalk and hunt, how to shoot and when and why, in fact all the things Dylan thought great, and a proper way to spend his time, especially as he was good at it. By the time he started school at only five years old, he was already an accomplished woodsman and happy to be alone studying nature.

Every evening and weekend, when his homework and chores were done, Dylan would be out in the woods, and if his father's work permitted, they would be out together, with the guns, whatever the weather and any time of day or night.

Thanks to the owner of the estate his father worked for, who never minded them shooting his land, Dylan was able to practise whenever he was able. At first, with air rifle, Dylan learned to hit static targets like wood pigeon settled in trees or rabbit when they stopped bouncing about. When he was old enough to absorb the recoil, he moved on to moving targets like pheasant, or hare, with the shotgun.

His fourteenth birthday was probably the day he most remembered of all of his childhood, for that year his father bought him a .22, rifle. It was nothing special; the family didn't have a lot of income so his father had bought it second-hand in a boot sale, but to Dylan, it was as good as his father's Webley hunting rifle. It took only a few days before he could strip and clean it; he soon had learned its faults and had either repaired them or at least knew how to allow for them. By the time he was twelve years old, Dylan had been able to hit, and kill, anything that was in the sights of his shotgun, and by the time he left school, he could do the same with a rifle.

Educationally, Dylan, not the brightest or most dedicated pupil, left school with only maths and English for his academic qualifications, and those only because his mother would not let him out until his homework was done. The lack of certificates never bothered Dylan; what he considered important were the medals and cups he'd earned for shooting, both for club and county.

With his, self-limited, education, his options for employment were limited, and if he didn't want to follow his father and become a gamekeeper, which he didn't, the only job that he thought would suit him was the army. There he expected he would still be able to get plenty of shooting, so he applied, and finding they wanted him, he signed on for twelve years.

The year after he'd joined the army, his parents were killed in a car crash, and to his surprise, he found their death didn't cause him any grief. It wasn't a matter of having a dislike for them; he had enjoyed a normal family life, with no troubles or complaints with his parents, but now, they were dead, and life goes on, only not for them, but it still goes on. It was years later before he came to realise this was a part of him that was different; he was unable to understand the idea of grieving, in the same way that killing something, or even someone as he did in the course of his work, didn't cause him any sleepless nights.

In the army, he was trained to be a soldier and an armourer; this suited him, as did anything to do with weapons. The army, with all the tests and evaluations, could also see in Dylan's aptitude that he was most effective by himself, that in fact he was a loner, not an outsider. He could operate as a part of a team, as well as he could work alone, but he always kept his own council and never entered into anything whole-heartedly, unless that is it involved shooting.

He soon became the best shot in the regiment and consistently won shooting competitions, it meant he spent a lot of time by himself on the range; it was still a solo activity, but now, he was alone because no one could match him. He had no ties or responsibilities and was an extremely good shot, and the evaluation tests showed he preferred to work by himself; it wasn't long before the army found the right place for him as a marksman, 'a sniper'. The fit was perfect; it was as if he was made for it.

Ω

It was four days after the reconnoitre into the Afghan hills, when a small crate had been delivered to Dylan at the armoury; it took him by surprise, official deliveries were always addressed to the colonel and went to the stores before being sent on to the section. He never received personal mail, except for his magazine subscriptions, certainly not anything of this size, in fact not of any sort; it was definitely addressed to him, personally, so he opened it.

He stared dumbfounded at the metal gun case that the crate contained; he would have known what it was without any further information, but it did have a label, that clearly stated the sender was Accuracy International and addressee was Corporal D Williams. Dylan was not the sort to show emotions, but his heart had given a jump to actually have an AI LH115A3; he expected to get one sooner or later because of his position, but if this had been the issue, he would have had to be measured for it, and go up to the stores to sign and collect it when it came, not had it sent to him personally.

He finally found a small envelope stuck to the side of the gun case, opening it he found a note from the man he knew as John, the one who wanted him to kill two men sometime soon, not that it had any name on it, or needed one. It purely stated:

'This is what you wanted so get yourself ready; the target will be in position on the fourteenth so you've got just over two weeks, no more.'

So, he had one, an AI LH115A3, he expected to have to give it back at some time, no one gives away something that expensive, but at least he gets to play with it for a couple of weeks. This man John really did have a lot of pull, not only could he get the colonel to jump, he could get a private company to do the same, not only to get the weapon but to get it in less than four days, and not even second-hand; he must also have access to a lot of money as well. It was brand spanking new, even though he would have to give it back, he hadn't ever been so pleased to receive something, not since his father had bought him his .22.

Less than three weeks, that's two weeks more than I need, Dylan thought, but he got started anyway, like a child with a new toy, he couldn't leave it until tomorrow. What he was going to have to do in the next week or so was: to clean it, the weapon was brand new, but it still needed cleaning. The heavy grease on it was purely for storage protection, so it had to come off, this entailed stripping the rifle down to its component parts, and then, using a solvent to remove the heavy grease from each and every part.

Once it was clean of all traces of the protective grease, a minute inspection had to be carried out. Dylan would never have expected there to be the slightest flaw, not with a weapon from AI, still he couldn't be sure though, unless he had inspected it himself, which he set about doing. Finally, he lubricated all the parts with fine gun oil reassembling the weapon as he went. He now had to set the stock to his own arm measurements; this wasn't a hard task, as he knew his required settings by heart after the number of weapons he'd owned. After working the action and dry firing, he finally replaced the rifle, almost lovingly, into its transit case and locked it in, then deciding he could do no more for the present he headed for his bed.

Being in charge of the armoury, he was able to decide his actions for the day, so he had no trouble the next day booking himself time on the range, quite a normal thing for the armoury to do, as often weapons required testing, but this day he caused quite a shock when the range warden saw the weapon he was going to test. Questions were asked, but Dylan with his usual indifference ignored them and set about his work.

The Lupua hunting ammunition that had come in the box along with the rifle was technically illegal, certainly so for the military, so Dylan was having to use some of the armoury's equivalent standard 7.62mm ammunition. He would have to try the Lupua before he took 'the shot' in case there were any effective differences, but the substitutes would do for the initial setting up of the sighting and giving him the feel for the weapon.

Dylan started by firing the five rounds in the magazine in quick succession then changed the magazine and repeated. After the second five, he reloaded both of the magazines and fired them both again, but with a lot more care this time. After this initial warming-up of the rifle, he now placed a new target and spent the next three hours setting the sights by firing, taking note, adjusting the sights, setting screws, then firing again, and finally he was satisfied they were set as well as he could get them on this range, which was only five hundred yards. He now returned to the armoury and cleaned the weapon, once again with his eyes closed.

Having done all he could on the five hundred range, Dylan knew he would have to build his own three thousand yard range; after all, this was the distance he was going to have to shoot over when the time came. This new range would have to be outside the fort, so he would have to get permission from the adjutant. He set off to the orderly office, he knew the adjutant would say no, no one was allowed to play around outside the wire, but hopefully, mention of 'John' and the task he had to carry out, which he couldn't talk about, would make the adjutant relent.

The adjutant, who had been told by the colonel to assist Dylan in every way they could, surprised Dylan by agreeing without any argument, but he did make the limitation that he must take a protection detail and be back in camp well before dark.

First thing the next morning with two squaddies, who were detailed by the orderly room and Rick Jones, who was one of the lads from the armoury who he detailed himself, as a protection team, they set off to find a long level stretch of desert.

Dylan set his targets at two hundred-yard spacings from fifteen hundred yards out to three thousand, now, as there was no one taking close interest, except Rick Jones, specially selected as the man least likely to know the difference between a Lupua round and the rifle it was in, he could now use the Lupua ammunition.

Starting from the fifteen hundred target, he worked on placing five shots in each target, trying to achieve a two-inch group in each. If he failed, he would adjust the sights and try again, and with each success, he would move to the next target. The grouping was easy to achieve on the closer targets, but as he moved to the farther targets, he needed to fractionally adjust the sights, just a touch, but once, after four hours, when he had achieved his aim in the three thousand target, he was satisfied and called it a day. He now had the balance of the weapon and the sights were set as tight as possible, and although he intended to come out to 'his' range two or three times more, he would now admit to being ready in all respects.

Chapter 13

Tony James's house, like himself, was not excessively extravagant, six bedrooms and four receptions on a quarter acre site with patio and pool, and surrounded by a gated wall. Tony would often describe it as comfortable, but the locals, when comparing it to the local housing of farmsteads and block-built town houses, would call it a mansion. His mother had decided she preferred to live in the house in town, the one they had rented when they first arrived in Osage but now owned.

Tony could easily have afforded a larger house, his businesses, both legal and otherwise, were doing well, but making a show of his wealth would have made him more noticeable, and that's the last thing he wanted. What he didn't want was to be thought of as getting above himself, to be challenging the members of the syndicate in any way, and a more impressive house might make them think he was planning to move up.

Tony was having his usual post breakfast siesta by the pool, when the maid brought him the phone; she didn't say who it was, because she hadn't asked; she didn't want to know anything about his business. Everyone in town knew he was a crook, but the maid liked her job, and the pay was good, much better than anything she could get elsewhere, but it was safer to not know anything about her employer's business, then she couldn't be accused of talking about it. Tony liked her attitude, and she was good at her job, but it did annoy that she wouldn't even ask who was calling.

"Hello," Tony said to whoever was on the line.

"Tony, it's good to hear you." It was Phillip Marcosie; Tony sat up almost to attention, which was difficult in his lounger. "I've got some more information about the deal."

"That's good," Tony said, even though he had hoped the whole thing might have gone away, "have we got a date?"

"It's good to see you're still keen, I like that, and yes, we do have. You've got to be there on the fourteenth as early as you can. Sonny Minelli has arranged it all, so you'll be in country on the twelfth; we've got a team to support you on the trip. You'll meet up with the leader when you land and sort out how you're going to play it. Sonny's got it all, and he'll be over to tell you about it. So, you just relax, treat it like a holiday, and when you get back, we'll have a good long talk."

"Thanks," Tony said, "I'm sure everything will be fine."

"That's what we all hope, Tony." The connection was broken. Tony began to understand how a fish must feel when he's being reeled in.

Sonny called later in the day. Tony hadn't met him before but still took an instant dislike to him. Whereas Tony was quiet and dour, Sonny was full of life and exuberant. Tony's thoughts were always on business, but Sonny's thoughts were always flitting on to different subjects, but Sonny was a favourite of Marcosie's so Tony listened to what he had to say, trying, but failing, to look interested. Sonny gave a breakdown on the coming trip.

"It's all set," he told Tony, "we fly to Karachi, then to Kabul where we meet up with our bodyguard/guides; I go to the embassy to collect the money then we travel north; I'll leave you to negotiate with the tribesmen, then we load up and cut through the mountains into Pakistan and drive down to the coast." At this point, Sonny got out a map, but Tony waved it away.

"You keep the maps," Tony said. "You seem to like that sort of thing. I'll find out when we get there."

Sonny detected Tony wasn't being as friendly as he had expected, but although he could ignore it, he decided it was better to get this over; he passed over the itinerary he had prepared for Tony then left agreeing to meet him again at the airport.

Ω

The flight carrying Tony and Sonny landed at 3:00 in the afternoon at Kabul's Hamid Karzai Airport, as had been arranged. Piet Botha was there to meet them as they left the terminal. Piet indicated the Land Cruiser he had hired for the trip, and they got in having hardly said more than a few words of general greeting.

Tony got out at the Intercontinental Hotel, but Sonny asked Piet to take him to the American Embassy, which he was happy to do. Sonny seemed more approachable than Tony, so Piet explained his planning while on route.

"I've booked you in for two nights, but we'll be leaving late tomorrow; there are no roads, only tracks up there, and they will disappear from time to time, so it'll be a long trip, but you'll be okay in this." He indicated the Land Cruiser.

"It'll be a longer trip down to the port in Pakistan, and we'll have to slip across the border a bit carefully, because they've got an effective army, but I know a few places where we can cross with little trouble.

"It'll be about twelve hours up to the village and maybe twenty or thirty hours on the downward run, that's if the roads haven't been washed out. I will load supplies for three days and that should cover us, does that sound okay?" Sonny agreed it was.

When they arrived at the embassy, Sonny left Piet in the car and went in. At the reception desk, he asked for Keith Bowman. Keith came to the reception to escort Sonny to his office where Sonny took possession of a large briefcase. Through personnel connections of Marcosie, the case had been sent via the diplomatic channels, a not unusual procedure, at least not unusual enough to attract the attention of the consulate staff, unlike the interest that would have been taken if it had been brought through airport security.

Piet took Sonny back to the hotel agreeing on the way that he would be there at six o'clock the following evening then they went their own ways, Sonny in to the hotel, and Piet into a bar.

Chapter 14

It was purely by chance that, as Tony and Sonny were landing at Kabul so John Wilcox was landing at camp Bastion. He didn't really need to have flown out; he was sure that Dylan would have everything organised and be ready to fly up to the village, but although everyone at the camp had been only too happy to facilitate the operation while he had been there, with his ministerial letter, you never could tell what might happen when he wasn't. Now it was too late, to allow some minor hiccup to ruin the mission. His own experience told him that when junior ranks were telling senior ranks what to do, the good of the operation gets lost, in the hierarchical nose displacement that can be engendered. So, Wilcox, with his letter from the minister still in his pocket, thought a little moral support, for Dylan, would not come amiss.

This time it was late when Wilcox landed, so he left it to the following morning before going over to see Dylan; he had to admit he was feeling a touch tense about the operation, not that he doubted Dylan, he couldn't remember having seen anyone who had so much confidence in his abilities.

He was sure he'd done all he could to make the mission a success, but if it went wrong, he would have to face Sir James, not something to be considered lightly, and Sir James in turn would have to endure the 'can't you Brits do anything right' attitude of the Americans, and of course, the expenses he had already incurred would have to be paid by the section, necessitating a further interview with Sir James, not a pleasant thought.

Dylan, on the other hand, was fully relaxed pursuing his usual daily work routine. His Bergan backpack was standing by his desk; it was half full but still open awaiting the last of his equipment.

"Did you get all the items you asked for?" Wilcox asked.

"Yes, thanks," Dylan replied, "I've cleaned and prepped it and set up the sights. I've been able to get a small grouping at three thousand so there shouldn't be any problem." Dylan wouldn't normally be so talkative, but he sensed John was a bit uptight, so, as they were talking guns, he didn't mind; he even got the LH115 out of its case to show him.

"Very nice," Wilcox said, not knowing if it was nice or not, but it did look business-like.

"I've got one question though," Dylan said, and Wilcox felt a slight unease. "Why," Dylan asked, "was there an envelope in the box with a couple of pieces of litter?"

Wilcox smiled with relief. "That, my friend, is a bit more of the disinformation we want to spread. The gum wrapper could only come from Kansas as that's the only place it's sold, likewise, the cigarettes are a very popular brand there, so if you could sort of, leave them in the place you shoot from, but make it discreet sort of visible but hidden, know what I mean?"

"I'm with you, a good tidy up but miss a couple of things."

Seeing all was well with Dylan, Wilcox left him to his work and went to the ops to check up on the flights. The operation was planned exactly as they had agreed when he was last there; it would be almost a repeat of the previous time, but this time take off would be at 11:30 on the fourteenth and Dylan would be dropped off at one o'clock on the fifteenth.

The return was more fluid; the aircraft would try to pick him up as close to 6:00 in the evening of the fifteenth but that would depend on whether Dylan had called. He would have a radio with him, but he wouldn't switch it on unless the situation had changed and needed to be picked up, or if required help.

Satellite and overpass film had been taken over the past week, and there hadn't been any activity recorded on the side of the river that Dylan would be working from, so everything was looking good.

It seemed to Wilcox that he had nothing more to do so he spent the rest of the day in the officer's mess, talking if anyone was there and reading when there wasn't.

Ω

At six o'clock precisely, on the evening of the fourteenth, the convoy of two pick-ups and one Land Cruiser set off from the Intercontinental Hotel. Piet with Johan, Dutchy and Sam, three of the four men that were left of his commando, were in the pick-ups, and Deon, the last of Piet's team was driving the Land

86

Cruiser, with Tony and Sonny. Tony automatically sat in the back, while Sonny insisted he'd ride in the front, for a better view he said.

For Tony, it had been a very long day; a day with nothing to do, and this following a long day of flying, he was used to being busy, this sitting around did not sit well with him. Sonny on the other hand had no problems, apart from keeping the boss informed, he'd spent time walking around the town and socialising in the hotel bar. Before the trip had even begun, the two different attitudes could be clearly seen, and Piet only hoped it wouldn't change in to open hostility.

It was not long before they left the city and the metalled roads, from now on, they would be on rough tracks. Initially still close to the city, there were reasonable scrapes, but these soon faded out, and the road became rock-strewn potholed mud. It was fortunate there hadn't been any rain for some weeks, so at least the mud was hard, allowing them to keep up a steady pace of thirty to forty miles an hour, for most of the time, but often it became a matter of low gear and low speed as they negotiated the potholes and rock falls.

Tony kept quiet, sitting hunched up in the corner, looking as though he was sulking about something, while Sonny, living up to his name, was showing an interest in all there was to see, which was not much, mainly mountains, rocks and the rivers that crossed their path then disappeared. Eventually, they came to the one river that was coming from the way they were going, and from that point on, they always had it on their left.

Piet insisted on stopping every hour for ten minutes for refreshments and a leg stretch, then back in and away again.

Tony was not a patient person, and he also did not like discomfort, if he had been in the vehicle with his own people, he would have complained all the way, but he was not going to allow Sonny, or the driver, to think he couldn't take a bit of rough travel. Sonny on the other hand was quite happy, sometimes sleeping, sometimes talking to the driver, from the way he acted, you would have thought he was on the holiday trip Phillip Marcosie had mentioned, but that was Sonny; he always accepted what he couldn't change, rather than moan about it, and that was another thing that annoyed Tony.

Ω

At eleven o'clock, Wilcox again strode into the ops, there were only a few people in at that time; they looked surprised to see him, but they greeted him in a friendly manner. Looking around, he found Dylan, also an early arrival, sitting quietly, to one side his Bergan and encased rifle immediately to hand; he also wore two handguns in their shoulder holsters. As there was little happening in the tent that he could get involved in, he joined Dylan.

"I didn't expect to see you here yet?" Wilcox said.

"Regulations," Dylan informed him, "all passengers must be here two hours before take-off; it's to make sure everybody turns up and won't cause any hold-ups, or at least it gives time to find anyone who is missing, of course it was intended for troop movements on the 'Hercs' or C17s, but a rule is a rule," he said, philosophically. "I had nothing else to do anyway."

"I see your well-armed again, are those Glocks your personnel weapons as well as the rifle you usually use?" he asked, remembering the previous conversation they had had on the subject.

"No. they're from the armoury," Dylan told him. "Rankers wouldn't normally carry them, but as tonight I'll be by myself, I thought I'd best carry them, mind it would be nice to have my own, then I'd know its peculiarities, but we can't have everything we want. I've personally serviced and tested both of these on the range; they're firing pretty straight. I'm perfectly happy with them" – he gave an affectionate pat to the gun case – "and as for this, it's working perfectly."

By 11:30, the crew had arrived and checked in. Dylan now took the AI rifle out of its transit case, leaving the case for his return, then the group walked out to the aircraft. Wilcox went along, really just for something to do, but he gave one final reminder to Dylan.

"Remember the target first, then the other one, then anyone else who you take a dislike to." Dylan smiled; he was probably the least worried person there.

Once all were aboard, Wilcox stepped back clear of the rotors and then watched as the aircraft rose, and within a few seconds, it was lost to sight in the stygian darkness.

Ω

Dylan stood in the open, under the coal black, star-encrusted sky; he could hear the aircraft for maybe the next three to four minutes before it was gone.

Along with all other sound, he couldn't even hear any insects; he might have been deaf, for all the sound there was, but still, he allowed another ten minutes to pass to be sure his ears and eyes were fully accustomed to the conditions before he accepted he was alone.

Although there was a vast star field, it gave little light; it showed where the crest-lines of the various mountains were but leaving the ground totally invisible. Dylan could wait where he was for the moon to rise and give him all the light he could use, but that would not be for another two hours, and even if there was no one to see him, he felt exposed and vulnerable out here in the open. The first rule and action of a sniper is to get into cover and become invisible, until then he was in danger, especially now he had no back-up.

Shouldering his Bergan and stepping very carefully, he picked his way towards the ridge crest; it took him nearly half an hour to walk the distance that had taken less than five minutes when they had been here before, but he was in no hurry, finally, he arrived at the spot he had previously selected to make his hide.

Dylan laid out his mattress, took the AI from its case and placed it on the mattress standing on its bipod legs. He tested the position, moved a few stones and peered through the sights at the village, this was in as much darkness as he was, but the view through the sight intensifier made what light there was as good as day, so he had no trouble seeing the buildings clearly.

Satisfied his position was correct and his equipment ready, he took out his water and snack bars and sat against a rock eating what would be his only meal for the next few hours. It was only a very light snack he allowed himself, only two protein bars, but they would give him enough energy to last the day, if necessary, and a heavy meal, and then laying belly down on his mattress for some hours might give him indigestion, that would be disastrous.

Moonrise over the mountains came at the expected three o'clock, now he could see the whole of the valley, coloured in black, grey and silver and laid out before him. He took a quick general look around, saw nothing of interest, then got down onto his mattress; from now on, he would have to be very circumspect in his movements. If he moved about too much, he could show his silhouette above the ridge crest, the chances of there being anyone about who might see such an error was almost impossible, but there could be a village watchman, quite a lot of villages had them to guard against predators, either of the two or four-legged variety.

False dawn, a slight lightening of the sky, came a little after 3:30, but the sky soon returned to black. At the same time, the temperature dropped, to the dawn chill, dew creating level; it changed by only a degree or so, but it was enough to send a shiver through Dylan's body. A little after 4:30, the sky again started to lighten, but this time, it continued as the dawn stealthily arrived.

By five o'clock, the first of the villagers could be seen moving around the village; for them, it would be just another day the same as the one before and as the next one, probably would be. This day though would be very different, in so much that the American would be coming to buy the crop. Dylan however was determined he would die before he could do so.

When he and John had come here previously, John had asked if he had to take a dislike to the target before he shot.

"No," Dylan had replied. "If I allow feelings of any sort enter my thoughts, they would affect my aim, the target is just that a target, not a person; the villagers on the other hand were people who were going about their lives, and he wouldn't like it if he inadvertently killed one of them."

The villagers, farmers for the most part, were as hard as the land they lived in, both in their bodies and their attitudes. Life and death here were serious considerations and each man carried a large knife and a rifle, and he knew how to use both; they were prepared to kill, especially if they thought they were being slighted or robbed, and they did not like strangers, whom they would rather shoot than welcome. The aggression, that was a natural part of them, had managed to hold off the British Army for something like two hundred years, in the seventeenth and eighteenth centuries.

The Sun had just crested the mountain ridge behind Dylan when he heard the sound; it was very faint, but he was sure it was the sound of a vehicle, with the engine labouring, probably in low gear to overcome some blockage on the track. In a couple of minutes, he was sure it was not one but two vehicles, and finally, he could identify it were three vehicles labouring their way up the torturous track.

From his elevated position, it wasn't long before he could see the first vehicle, a pick-up truck, as it rounded a rocky outcrop, then came a Land Cruiser saloon, and finally another pick-up. The convoy was following the track that edged the river travelling slowly and carefully.

The villagers were now gathered in the centre of the village, awaiting the convoy. Dylan was settled in his hide, and the target was rounding the last bend. Now Dylan thought, as he took one final look at the general situation, all the pieces are in place. He put his head down and looking through the Schmidt & Bender telescopic sight, he aligned the hairs on the Land Cruiser, keeping it there as the vehicle came to a stop.

Ω

From the passenger seat of the lead pick-up, Piet Botha was studying the scene before him; the village looked safe; a dozen or so men, with rifles slung on their shoulders, were gathered in the open centre of the village. The river was wide, wide enough to give time to react if anyone tried to attack across it. The mountains themselves could have hidden thousands, but the villagers would have shown some anxiety if they knew there was a danger lurking there. Piet accepted it was safe to enter the village.

Ω

Dylan watched as the three vehicles approached the men of the village. Through the sniper scope, he could see faces through the vehicle's glass, two in the first and two in the last, but the Land Cruiser had tinted glass so he could only see the driver; the two Americans must be in the back, he surmised. As the convoy came to a stop, the men in the front and rear pick-ups rapidly jumped out and took up defence about the Land Cruiser, this manoeuvre showed good training; they knew what they were doing. A short, stockier built man moved over to talk to the waiting villagers, and after a short conversation, he returned to the vehicle and gestured to the occupants.

The first of the passengers to get out was a small man, definitely not the target, if Dylan had needed any more recognition, he had a briefcase chained to his wrist. *So he must be the moneyman*, Dylan thought, then from the other side of the vehicle, a large man climbed out.

Dylan's finger, now tight on the trigger had barely stopped moving when the large man's head exploded, the 7.62 LUPUA round had entered through the man's left ear. The impact caused it to deform, as it should have, so on the way out, it removed most of the right side of the man's head and all of the brain stem; the man was dead even though the muscles didn't know it.

Ω

Piet stood still for maybe a second or perhaps two, until Sonny's head also fell apart, finally his brain registered that they were under attack.

"Take cover," he shouted to his men, adding, "he's over there on the ridge somewhere." There had been no time yet to scour the ridge to find the sniper's position, but experience told him, the way the heads exploded, the shot had to have come from somewhere across the river.

Deon, who had been the driver of the Land Cruiser, was still getting out of the vehicle and so was distracted, all he heard from Piet was the sniper was on the ridge. Once he was out of the car, he spun around, aimed his 'Uzi' at the ridge crest and fired a full magazine; it had been a simple reaction, in other situations it would have been the correct action. In the jungles they had fought in, it had been expected; it was an attempt to make the sniper duck, loose aim, and stop firing, which he might have if the aim had been good and the bullets had had enough power to reach across the river.

Ω

Dylan was happy the shoot had been textbook, even though the range had been further than he had ever tried before. With an automatic reaction, once he fired the first round, he had pulled the bolt and put another round into the breach, hence he had been able to take the second shot before there had been any reaction to the first. Likewise when he saw one of the bodyguards firing at him, he was already loaded, and without any conscious thought, he shot the man; he hadn't intended to shoot any of the bodyguards; they were only doing a job, and he knew they had 'Uzis', which he also knew couldn't fire this far, but the subconscious is a reactive mechanism, so the man had died. Dylan had racked another round into the breach and waited to see what would happen next.

Chapter 15

Piet lifted his head and surveyed what he could see of the village; the men who had been milling around the centre had all disappeared probably as soon as the shooting started; they were almost certainly in their houses. Piet didn't see them go as his face was pressed into the dirt. Deon was lying by the side of the Land Cruiser with his head spread around him; the idiot had started firing, and that had earned him a bullet all to himself; he should have just dropped down behind the cover of the vehicle, which is where the rest of them were. He could also see the big American, as with Deon his head had blown apart.

Piet's thoughts were racing, trying to sum up what had happened, there had only been the three shots; shot one, the sniper had a target and he hit it, whoever the shooter was he had come to kill the two Americans, they were the target, that much was obvious, so shot two, the second American, job completed, so that far it had been 'considered fire'. The shooter was a professional, he had a job to do and he did it. Piet had a grudging respect for the man, in terms of one professional to another.

Deon was killed because of his own stupidity; the sniper couldn't have had any reason to kill Piet and his men, so now he thought he had the situation laid out, it was a hit on the gangsters, but who made them a target that's the question?

Those shots did not come from a Taliban fighter Piet was certain; they haven't got that sort of weapon or that sort of marksman, and it wouldn't be in the local's interest to kill the opium buyer, so the Taliban didn't do it. What about the 'Brits'? It is their area of responsibility, and they had as much of a drugs problem as the Yanks, and they wouldn't mind taking out a couple of Yankee gangsters if the Yanks asked them to, but no, they aren't allowed to use the hunting ammo. The three heads exploding like that, had to come from hunting ammo, what about the Yanks then? They wouldn't have any problem using banned ammo, and it was their crooks that were involved, but this would be well outside of their area, and if the Brits found out, there would be hell to pay, but when did they worry about a little thing like that, again no. Piet couldn't see it; if the yanks wanted to stop these guys, then they could do it in their own country, and no one would care one way or the other.

Was there another group wanting the opium? Now that idea had its merits, it could be, but the yanks hadn't been in country long enough for someone to set up a hit like this, so it had to have been set up by someone who knew they were coming, and then, it would have taken planning. It would have to have been arranged by someone on the inside.

The more he thought of it, the more Piet took to the idea. "Have we wound up in the middle of a gangland war?" he said to no one in particular. "If we have, then no one told us about it, so we weren't ready for any of this, how could we be ready? If we'd been told, we could have known what to expect. Ten years in war after war, Deon's been with me, and now, he's dead because we didn't know there was a war." Piet was angry, angrier than he could ever remembering being in his whole life. *They didn't warn me*, he thought, *they didn't even suggest they might have brought trouble with them.*

"It's only in case you run into Taliban or such like, and I suppose you can handle that," he had said. *Well, I'll show them I can handle it; I'm not going to lie down and accept it. I'm going to get the son of a bitch who shot Deon and stuff that gun up his arse and empty the mag.* So went his thoughts for five or ten minutes before he calmed enough to think of their current plight.

Piet knew he had to do something; they couldn't lie here all day. He took off his hat and held it up above the wing of the vehicle for a count of two, nothing happened; he gave it another couple of minutes, moving the exposed hat a little to one side to simulate someone moving, still no reaction, this should have got a reaction from the sniper, but it didn't. *Okay then, let's see if he's still there.* He sprinted to the front pick-up; again, there were no shots from across the river, quickly he did an up and down, still nothing, either they were not of any interest to the shooter, or he was playing it very cagey. At last, Piet knew there was no use in hiding here; sooner or later, he would have to take the chance, so now was as good a time as any. He stood up but still kept half of his body and his head covered by the car's pillar, nothing, he moved out still expecting to feel the sting of the bullet, but it didn't happen.

"Okay, you lot," he called, "it's over, get up and let's get this mess tidied up."

The villagers where still absent. If he could have found one of them, he might be able to find out if there was another buyer for their crop, but although Piet was sure they were watching, he wouldn't be able to find them, and besides, they knew how to use their rifles, so he didn't want to challenge them. The four of them set to cleaning up. They put the bodies in to one of the pick-ups. Piet found the key to the accountant's handcuff and took charge of the briefcase, then with one in each pick-up and two in the Land Cruiser, they left, to return the way they had come.

After some ten miles, they found a deep canyon; they drove the pick-up with the bodies in as far as they could get it, then Piet called a conference.

"It's not nice to leave Deon there like that," he said, "but if we go back with the bodies, we'll be lucky to get out of this country, ever. And I've been thinking Deon was not just shot but murdered because we were not part of this particular fight, whoever the shooter was, he shouldn't have killed Deon, so I'm going hunting. I really want to get this bastard and that's what I'm going to do, but you've got to decide for yourselves if you want to come with me, or go elsewhere, but keep in mind, you've not only to get away from here but you'll have to get out of the country before anyone finds out about what's happened. We've still got two vehicles so if any or all of you want to go, that's okay with me, and if you want to come with me, that's also okay, so what's it to be?"

They were quiet for a few seconds then Jonas spoke up, "I don't think you're being fair, Piet. Deon was our mate as well, and a part of the commando, and there's still enough of us to be a commando, so if you go then so do we." All three nodded agreement.

"Right then," Piet said, once again in command, "I think I saw a place to ford the river a little way back, we'll hide the pick-up along with the other one and take the Land Cruiser."

They forded the river and drove most of the way back to where Piet had considered the shots had come from but stopped the car some two miles short. They didn't expect to find the shooter still there, but he might be and so they walked the rest of the way in hunting mode, if he was there, they didn't want to warn him, and if he wasn't, it was still the place, so they could cut his spore and see which way he'd gone.

Chapter 16

Dylan wasn't expecting there to be anything happening in the village, or any other village, or in the whole valley for a while, although he would bet that word of the happenings would move faster than he could. He'd seen the bodyguards set out on their way back to the city probably to report the ambush, or maybe somewhere else, for someone was not going to be happy about the outcome of the trip and shooting the messenger was still a common practice.

The villagers, once they decided it was safe to venture out, still had their day's work to do, as well as find a new buyer for their crop. Dylan was sure they would not have to wait very long to do that, and life would go on as usual. Likewise, they wouldn't waste time looking for a solitary gunman, a fight between rival gangs was nothing to do with them; it was however something to do with the guards. He'd shot one of their numbers and cost them probably half their pay, now they might feel aggrieved, and come looking for him.

After he'd watched the three vehicles pull out, Dylan collected all his equipment, including the three spent cartridge cases. While he had been waiting for the situation across the river to resolve itself he'd lit three cigarettes; he didn't smoke them, he never had smoked and considered it stopped your nose from being able to smell the scents on the wind, and to alert the prey to your presence, but he left them to burn down over half way, occasionally flicking off the ash then stubbing them out. Having picked up all he'd brought with him, he buried the stubs but didn't bury them so well, that a good tracker couldn't find them. Likewise, the two gum wrappers he buried in the same way. Having brushed over the position but not well enough to disturb the cigarette ash, with some twigs, he moved off down the back slope of the mountain.

Although he wasn't expecting anyone to come looking for him, his professionalism told him that without a support team, he had to be doubly careful and to expect the unexpected, so having spotted a jumble of rocks a couple of miles downslope that looked a good place to await the six o'clock call time, he relocated. Staying as much as possible in dead ground and giving a very careful look around whenever he had to move in the open, Dylan covered the distance, to the rocks in half an hour; he was able to get himself comfortable and waited. When he made his radio call, he could direct the aircraft to his new position.

Ω

Johan was the first to discover where the sniper's hide had been, not a surprise as he'd been a game hunter all his life and was by far the best of the team at tracking; he called Piet over.

"Someone had lain in this place for some hours but had moved out maybe one or two hours ago," he told him. "The view from this position across the river is the perfect position for a sniper to cover the village; it's the very place I would have chosen." Nothing had been left in the hide to show the occupation, but he was able to see the ground was disturbed, and to his hunter's eye, that told him all; a few more seconds and he was able to point out the cigarette ash and butts, and then the gum wrappers.

Piet examined the evidence and rightly identified it as American.

"Not so good as he thinks he is, eh." Johan nodded his agreement then started looking at the ground down slope.

Piet called in the rest of team and described the options as to which way the sniper had gone, "There was only two, up river or down slope. If he'd gone downriver, they would have seen him on their way up." It took nearly half an hour before Johan finally found a trace, in a shallow gully on the down slope of the ridge. The mark was a slight impression of half a boot sole, but slight as it was it gave them a start point. With Johan in the lead and the other three spread out some distance behind him, they slowly followed Dylan's tracks, slight as they were.

Ω

Dylan, half sitting and half lying with his back against the rocks, fully relaxed and almost half asleep when he heard it, the sound of a small fall of gravel, at least, he thought he had heard it. He came out from his doze immediately fully awake, straining to hear any other sounds. A quiet crunch, because of his heightened state of alertness, this time he knew he'd heard it; it was the sound of

97

a boot on gravel, and it assured him he was not mistaken, there was someone near. Pulling the Glocks from their holsters, he turned on his front and very carefully lifted his head until he could see above the surrounding rocks, in the direction of the sounds, and as his eyes cleared the rocky obstruction, he found himself starring into the shocked eyes of one of the convoy's guard unit.

The shock was clear in the eyes of the man; he obviously had not expected to see Dylan, at least not yet; the shock delayed his reactions, by the merest part of a second, but it was enough to increase the time it would take to swing his Uzi into a position to shoot. Dylan, thanks to the misplaced boot that had caused the sound on the gravel, did not suffer the same shock delay; the Glock fired while the shock was still on the face of the hunter; it was an upward shot and took the man under the chin; he dropped like a sack, dead before he could fall. Dylan dropped back down as a fusillade of bullets sang around his rocky den, so the other three were here as well.

Ω

Piet, in the centre of the three followers and behind Johan, heard the shot and saw Johan drop; he fired his Uzi sending bullets and rock splinters all over the outcrop. Coincidentally, it was the same reaction that he had cursed Deon for making, but this time, it was close enough to be effective. Piet dropped to the ground and reloaded. Seeing the prostrate form of Johan, with a large hole in his head where the bullet had exited, there was no doubt he was dead.

Now Piet, Dutchy and Sam were in the open, with the sniper in cover, a bad situation for everyone, but at least they could keep the sniper down by alternately firing at the rocks. It had been a very unexpected attack, and Johan had had no chance, as would be the case for the rest of them if they were still where they were when the bullets ran out. Piet signalled to each of the other two to move around the location of the gunman, then silently indicated a count of three, and they both moved, with Piet firing short bursts at the rocks to pin the gunman down.

Ω

As soon as Dylan had shot Johan, he'd caught a glimpse of the others before he ducked down; he knew he was now in a bad position. There were three of

98

them left out there and were out in the open, but he was pinned down by the automatic fire they kept up; he couldn't aim at them without them seeing him.

Considering their options, he expected they would try to outflank him one on each side before he could organise a defence, so rather than defend, he had to move, rearwards. And keeping close to the rock, he raised his hand and fired three rounds from the Glock; this brought an immediate response from an Uzi, even while the bullets were incoming he holstered the Glocks, and taking up the AI, he moved. Keeping in a low crouch, he negotiated his way around the rocks behind him for maybe twenty paces, then threw himself down and took aim at the position he had just left.

Ω

At a run, Sam and Dutchy had moved, keeping low they ran in one from the right and one from the left; they both entered rocks with guns firing only to find they were alone.

Ω

Dylan had found an opening between some rocks that gave him a view into the formation he had just vacated; he had no cover behind so he could still be out flanked, but probably, the last member of the team didn't know that, as he hadn't given them time to reconnoitre the area; therefore, Dylan didn't consider it to be a problem, at present. He'd only had time to fall into the rocky cleft when the men jumped into his former rocky den, one from the left slightly ahead of the one from the right; both were firing bursts from the Uzis. .Without thought, Dylan fired the rifle, and the first man finished his jump dead, the other also fell but into cover.

Ω

Sam and Dutchy both heard the rifle and dropped to the ground, Sam for safety and Dutchy because he was dead. Piet called from his covering position.

"What's happening," a solo voice replied.

"Duchy's down," it was Sam's voice. "The bastard's moved out."

"What's your position then?" Piet demanded.

"I'm behind rocks, but I can't move out in any direction," was the slightly worried reply.

Ω

Dylan laid still and silent, one of two things would now happen, either the man in amongst the rocks would try to get out, probably firing his Uzi whilst doing so, or the last man would come around to get behind him. He waited, keeping the aim of the AI as before, ready for the slightest movement and listening for the slightest sound, that might tell him who was going to make the next move.

It was the trapped man who broke the impasse; he tried to jump up and out, but he was way too slow. Dylan had been shooting all his life; he could even take a snipe in full flight with a rifle; the bullet took the man as soon as his head broke cover.

Ω

"Are you okay, Sam?" Piet called out, but got no reply.

The lack of reply from Sam told Piet it was over; the commando was no more. Now he had to consider his own position; it was hopeless; he couldn't win against this man unless he could find a blind side; he didn't know this country or how the rocks were organised and couldn't see the man coming out, that wouldn't happen as he had the advantage that left Piet with only one choice. In a crouched run, Piet moved quickly up the slope, then along the ridge heading down river, his only way out was to get to the Land Cruiser.

Ω

Dylan heard the man move; he was ready to be attacked, but the sounds were moving away; he carefully raised himself and looked up the slope, the man was running. *No, you don't*, Dylan thought, *you started it; I'm going to finish it*. The fleeing man had made good time and was about two hundred yards away, but it wasn't enough. Dylan fired and the man went down.

Ω

The bullet hit Piet in the soft part of his thigh; he didn't cry out, and the luck, that had deserted him all day, now returned, and he fell into a gully. The gully wasn't deep but was deep enough to keep him below ground level and hidden from the sniper's view. He'd landed awkwardly, and he had a hole in his thigh that was bleeding badly, but he didn't move; fortunately, he'd retained the Uzi, quickly changed magazines and pointed up at the top of the gully, expecting the sniper to come looking.

Ω

Dylan watched the area where the last member of the guard team disappeared; he gave it an hour, and during that time, nothing stirred. He hadn't seen where the shot had hit, but with hunting ammunition, it didn't really matter. He could have gone over to the place where he'd seen the man fall, but he did have an Uzi with him when he went down. Dylan would be out in the open, so if he was still alive, he could be dangerous, best to leave it.

With the coming of dark, Dylan gave up his vigil; he packed up his kit and moved off toward the original landing place; he could have called the aircraft to him by radio but felt the need of a walk to relax him. He walked the mile plus to the landing place, and although he was now sure the other man was dead, he kept his surveillance to maximum right up until he was aboard the helicopter; he had nearly been caught and wasn't going to let it happen again.

Ω

Piet had managed to apply a field dressing to the wound in his leg, that had stopped it bleeding then he had lain back, resting but alert. It had become clear the sniper was not going to come after him. The Lupua round should have given a wound that would have made him bleed to death, but as it had hit in soft tissue, it had not deformed as it should but had passed clean through, he'd been very, very lucky.

Soon after dark, he heard the approach of a helicopter; he couldn't see it in the dark, but he could hear it land and take-off, not too far away. It made him think, was the shooter British Army after all? No, these days anyone could hire a chopper, he dismissed it; the army couldn't have fired those hunting rounds, as stupid as it seems, they were not allowed, and they never sent a man out alone.

Now that the sniper was gone, there was nothing to stop Piet from leaving except a leg that wouldn't take his weight. There was two miles between him and the car, but he had to do it; he had nothing he could make a crutch of so had to crawl dragging his leg behind. It was four hours before he finally reached the car; he was exhausted and soaked in sweat. He pulled himself into the back seat where the team had left their packs and drank two bottles of water straight off, then he allowed himself to fall asleep.

Ω

It was the following day when again, Wilcox and Dylan walked out into the desert for a debrief. Dylan described the events of the previous day, and the success of the mission. Wilcox asked only about the guard team, interested to know if Dylan was certain they were all dead.

"Three were defiantly dead," Dylan said, "the fourth should be dead. I certainly put a round into him; it was a low shot probably in the leg so if it didn't kill him, he would have bled to death. I watched for him but couldn't go look, if he was still alive, he still had an Uzi, so I stayed in cover."

"I don't think it would make any difference anyway," Wilcox suggested. "There's no way he could have made you as a British soldier, is there?" Dylan agreed there wasn't. "In that case, it would be helpful if he did survive and was able to tell them his story; they would have to believe it was a rival group who did it, so we win either way. That was a good piece of work, swift and sure, like an avenging Nemesis, exactly what we needed. Did you manage to spread the American trash before they came calling?"

"Yeah, as there was no wind, I even burnt a couple of the cigarettes so there'd be some ash. Who's this Nemesis you mentioned?"

"You're not a student of Greek history, are you?"

"Nemesis was the goddess of indignation against, and retribution for, evil deeds and undeserved good fortune. She was a personification of the resentment aroused in men by those who committed crimes with apparent impunity, or who had inordinate good fortune. Nemesis directed human affairs in such a way as to maintain equilibrium. Her name means she who distributes or deals out. Nemesis was regarded as an avenging or punishing divinity." After this explanation, Dylan still looked lost.

"You see," John continued, "the more important you are, the bigger the danger. These Americans thought they were important and couldn't be touched, but you, my Nemesis, proved them wrong."

"Right, that's it then. I'm on the afternoon flight. I doubt I'll be seeing you again. We don't often work with the army, but if you find yourself demobbed and looking for this type of work, give me a call. I can't guarantee anything, but you never know." He took a card out of his pocket. There was only the name John and a telephone number on the card, which left Dylan a bit perplexed. Wilcox explained, "We're a bit of a secretive organisation, but if you ring that number, someone will answer, just tell him you want to speak to John, leave a number, and I'll call you back. Right, well, like I say, I'm on this afternoon's flight, and you'll be back to doing what you do." They shook hands.

"One thing," Dylan asked, "where do I send the rifle?" Wilcox hadn't thought of this.

"When this regiment goes back to the UK, would you be able to get it back sort of unofficially?" Dylan confirmed he could.

"Well, then you keep it. I cannot use it, and the people who bought it wouldn't really care, but please let's keep it to ourselves; we wouldn't want to worry anyone." Dylan was only too please to help.

Chapter 17

When Piet awoke, he was confused and disorientated, but the pain in his leg soon brought him back to reality, he marvelled that it was full daylight, and he must have slept all night and into the day. A check of his watch showed him it was ten o'clock so he'd been out for about eight hours. He rifled in his pack for a fresh dressing and changed the original; he had to use a bottle of water to release the blood that had stuck the dressing to the wound and this caused the wound to start bleeding again but only slowly. He took some antibiotic pills and then drank two more bottles of water.

Whilst breakfasting on a protein bar and water he considered his position; he had failed to protect the clients, but that was their fault. They should have told him there might be trouble; he didn't expect they would see it that way though, and he had lost his team, that was Deon's fault, at least he started it all, if he'd just taken cover, none of the rest would have happened. The rest was down to the skill of the sniper, he had to admit it, but it didn't make him feel any better.

He had the money but not the opium, that was the wrong way around as far as those that were employing him would be concerned, all in all, they weren't going to be happy with the situation. It could be very dangerous for him to go back to Kabul; he was sure someone would try to try and put the blame on him and make like it was all his fault that he had failed to protect the clients.

Like he'd originally told the others in the commando, it would be better to run than to go back to Kabul. As for himself, he could take off, without going back to Kabul. He thought he'd got plenty of money now, but he did have a hole in his leg and that would have to be fixed, or he wouldn't get very far at all, neither in distance or in life, besides, they would not stop looking for him so for the rest of his life, he would be looking over his shoulder.

When the protein bars began to work and put some energy into his system, an idea, totally unbidden, appeared to him. Who was to say he had the money, he's the only one alive who knows where it is now, if he moved it elsewhere, he would again be the only one to know, but it would have to look as though someone else had taken it.

A plan took form in his head, getting firmer the more he thought of it, it would mean arranging some of the evidence to support the story he would tell, but then the facts and the evidence would be what he said they were; he was sure it was a sound idea. Although he had never opened the case, he was sure there would be enough in it to make it worth the effort, enough to support him for a long time.

After he'd finished eating, he did some exercise to try and make his legwork, it was going to have to if he was going to drive to Kabul. He tested his driving ability and found he could manage if he didn't use the clutch too much and set off back to where they had hidden the pick-ups to test it, even the few miles back told him it was going to be a painful trip down to Kabul.

Returning to the canyon, Piet sat down and thought about what he was going to say. The story he had thought out while driving would start with what had happened at the village, that was fact, the shooting was the shooting. Next, they had loaded the dead, there they were all three, on to the pick-up, and headed back. If anyone asked, the people in the village could tell what they'd seen so were his witnesses.

Now is where nothing but the evidence could support or contradict him. The next bit was again true but of course couldn't be proved, that because of Deon's death his team insisted on trying to track down the sniper, and they all got shot, including himself. They'd had to go out on to the mountain to check on the other three, and there was a hole in his leg. Then he would say he had come straight back to Kabul to get treatment, without stopping at the abandoned pick-ups, a good clean story with enough truth to make it believable.

So now, the first thing he had to do was arrange the evidence; he reattached the briefcase to the accountant by means of the handcuff and put the keys in his pocket. Selecting a large stone, he proceeded to smash open the case, once it was open, he took the money out, all dollars he was pleased to see, and put them into one of the backpacks.

The next part of the rearrangement he didn't like doing, but it had to be done, he stripped all that could be of any value from the bodies, wallets, watches, weapons and even boots, all this he put into another backpack and strapped it closed; he had no intention of taking any of the items for himself. Taking a slow long look around the site, to make sure he hadn't left any sign of his return, he took his leave.

Now what the evidence would say, to anyone who might and probably would come looking, was that someone had come along, seen the trucks and the bodies and ransacked them. He went over it twice more and was satisfied it would hold up, even if Mr bloody Bowman didn't like it. All that was left to be done was to hide the money, and he knew where he could do that. Now he was ready to go back and give them his story, the backpack, with the scavenged items, would be disposed of on the trip back. Finally, he set off for Kabul.

Chapter 18

As soon as he returned to the UK, Wilcox called Filamont and arranged a meeting for the following day.

"How did it go?" Filamont asked; he knew nothing of the detail as to how Wilcox was going to carry out the shooting; the fact that Wilcox had made the appointment said it was probably over, one way or the other. "Have I got a war to supervise or is my boss going to put me on the unemployment list?"

Wilcox smiled. "I don't know if you've got to supervise a war, but America has lost two of its drug dealers, and the world has lost one group of mercenaries." The satisfaction and relaxation that could be seen in every part of Filamont was palpable. "Even the trash has been spread, so if someone goes looking, they will be sure this was a wholly US affair. Oh, by the way, I've had to spend some of that money you said Uncle Sam had enough of; it had to be done, so I took you at your word and spent it. You'll see how much when you get the bill, but be prepared it is quite large."

This statement caused Filamont to pause a moment, should he get more detail or wait until the accounts and his boss called him in to explain.

"Too hell with it," he said. "They gave me a mission, and it's been successful. If it's expensive, it's down to them." His shear excitement was enough to let him forget any repercussions that might come later.

After Wilcox had left, Filamont called his office to spread the word; it was unlikely the message had already got there, and when he told them, there wasn't very much excitement about it; it was just another attempt to bring down another crime syndicate, but Filamont knew it would make a difference; he could feel it in his whole being. He hung up the secure line and used the regular phone to book a flight home; he couldn't get one in the next two days so it was three days before he left and was impatient for the whole time, and it was five days before he walked into his office.

Ω

It took Piet fourteen hours to reach Kabul, arriving in the outskirts at just before 3:00 in the morning. He made only one stop on the way and that was to deposit the money in an empty shop that he rented as a lock-up. He'd originally rented the shop to store the weapons the commando had needed when they had work to do, and there were a few items still there, proving no one had been in since he had last been there.

Having hidden the money, he once again, with some difficulty, got into the car. When he tried to use his injured leg, he nearly screamed with the pain and almost passed out. After giving himself a few minutes to recover, he tried again to get the vehicle in motion, but his leg would not work to operate the clutch. He was left with one option; revving the engine to maximum, he rammed the gear lever into second gear, the car lurched forward, and the engine nearly stalled but managed to keep going. In his totally exhausted state and keeping the car in second, Piet drove, crazily, through the empty streets to the Kabul City Hospital.

The nurses at the hospital were astounded when a dishevelled dirty and blood-covered man barged the door open and collapsed half in and half out of the entrance. Fortunately, Doctor Rasheid Al Maroun was already in the casualty department and was able to sum up the man's condition and initiate preparation for surgery.

It was 3:00 in the afternoon when Piet awoke; it took some time before he could remember the events of the previous day and night up until he pushed the door of the hospital, after that, nothing.

A nurse saw he was awake and alerted a doctor. Doctor Maroun came into the room, looked at the monitor, saw the saline drip was still running, then turned and spoke to Piet, who had observed all the happenings as if not part of the scene.

"How are you feeling?" the doctor asked. Piet made to reply but was unable to make his mouth operate so only a very quiet noise came out.

"Don't worry about that," the doctor said, "you're still under some strong painkillers and the residue of anaesthetic. My name is Doctor Rasheid Al Maroun; it was me who patched up your leg last night, enough to say we've sewn you up and filled you up with blood. So with plenty of rest, you'll be fine." This was the last Piet heard as he drifted back into sleep.

It was ten o'clock in the evening when Piet again awoke, this time he was more lucid and could remember the doctor's visit and what he had to say, although it meant little at the time. He found the bell push and summoned the duty nurse.

"Can I have a drink please?" His raging thirst was what must have woken him up; the nurse poured him a glass of water and helped him to hold it, as his hands had no strength to do it for himself; he drank two glasses then settled back into the pillows and once again slipped into sleep.

The sounds from the hallway outside his room awoke Piet, but this time, he felt refreshed and fully awake, the nurse looked in and bid him a good morning. He asked for coffee and something to eat but was told he would have to wait until the doctor had visited before he could eat, but he could have the coffee, this he happily accepted.

"I don't know how you managed to get a wound like that, and I know even less why you're still alive," the doctor told him. "When the bullet passed through your leg, it nicked the artery, usually that would have made you bleed out in less than an hour. I can only think your field dressing was pressing at exactly the right point and staunched the flow, but you still lost a lot of blood. When you collapsed in the emergency room, I thought you were finished, but I've managed to patch you up, and we've put the blood back in you, and from the look of you, I think we can now do without the saline. Food and rest is what you need now. So how did you come to get the wound?"

"I had a disagreement with a farmer up in the mountains; he thought I was someone else, I think."

"Yes," the doctor said thoughtfully, "the hill people can be very protective."

"Can you get a message to the American Embassy for me?" Piet asked.

"American Embassy?" Doctor Maroun said with surprise in his voice, confused by Piet's South African accent.

"Yes, it's a Mr Keith Bowman," Piet explained, "he's the man I'm working for; he'll be wondering where I've got to."

"I'm sure we can do that, but remember if you get visitors not to exert yourself, and don't get up out of that bed until I say so."

Ω

Within fifteen minutes of getting the call from the hospital, Keith Bowman was in the hospital; he listened to the nurse when she insisted he must not distress

109

the patient and could only stay for a few minutes. He agreed to obey by her rules and was let into Piet's room.

"What's happened, where is everybody?"

"And good morning to you," Piet replied, "if you sit down and shut up for a minute, I'll tell you what happened."

Bowman sat and Piet gave him his version of the events from leaving Kabul to arriving at the hospital. As he finished the story, Bowman could contain himself no longer; he jumped up and in a loud voice demanded more, and accusing Piet of stealing the buy money, his voice had raised to a level that brought the nurse running, bringing a security man with her.

"Stop this noise," she demanded, "this is a hospital, and this is a very ill patient who you are distressing, you will have to leave."

"I haven't finished talking to this man yet," Bowman stated.

"Oh, yes, you have," the nurse said and signalled the security man, that had now become two security men. Not wanting to attract more attention, Bowman left, giving a parting shot that he would be back tomorrow.

Chapter 19

When Phillip Marcosie arrived in his office, he found Martin Smith awaiting him. Marcosie gave him a sidewise glance before greeting him; it was very unusual for Martin to come here; he was standing in for Sonny, but he still wouldn't usually come to the office.

"Why are you here, is there some problem?" Marcosie asked.

"Yes, sir," Martin replied, "a serious problem. I've had an e-mail and phone call from Keith Bowman in Afghanistan." Marcosie thought on this, he couldn't for the moment place this Bowman.

"Who's this Bowman? Do I know him?"

"He's our man in the embassy in Kabul and has been for nearly ten years so that's probably why he's difficult to remember."

"Yes, I remember him now, so what's he got to say?"

"Sonny and Tony Spinelli have both been shot and killed."

Sonny, killed, the thought stunned Marcosie for a moment; he really liked Sonny, treated him as the son he had never had. "Who did it?"

"As of yet we don't know; one of the security team has managed to get back to Kabul and is in the hospital with a large hole in his leg," Martin continued to tell what Bowman had told them, of a sniper killing Sonny and Tony then the security team when they went to find him.

Marcosie had now put aside his feelings and was again the CEO of the syndicate.

"So, who's the sniper working for? And what about the money, where is it? What's this Bowman doing to find out what's going on?"

"Unfortunately, he's been thrown out of the hospital and can't get in to see this mercenary until tomorrow, err, like eight o'clock tonight our time, but he's putting together a team to go look at the place."

"Putting a team together, tell him to get his own ass up there and in a hurry. I want some details." Marcosie's anger was making Martin shake, this was why he hadn't wanted to bring the news; it had been known for the bringer of bad news to be shot, but if he hadn't, he would definitely have been shot.

"I'll get on to him straight away, sir." He looked to see if he was dismissed, but as Marcosie gave no indications either way, he quietly and quickly left.

Ω

Keith Bowman was in the hospital immediately after breakfast; he would have been earlier, but they wouldn't let him in. He was in a very agitated state, unable to sit down or to stop pacing the floor; he took out a map and asked.

"Where is this place you left the pick-ups?" Piet orientated himself to the map and let his finger trace a line up the dirt track the locals call a road.

"Here," Piet said, with a certainty in his voice. "Just on this bend, it's a deep crack in the mountain side; it's very deep so you'll have to go right in to see them, but you shouldn't have any trouble. I wouldn't think anyone's been in there for years."

"No, we won't have any trouble; you'll be with us."

"So, when are we going to go on this little trip?"

"Tomorrow, you, me and three others that owe me a favour."

"Oh, dear, I'm sorry, but you'll have to go without me. The doctor says I have to stay for another two days at least; it seems I did more damage on the drive back than the bullet did, so either delay or go yourself with your three friends to hold your hand," Piet said this with a tone that could just as well said, go shoot yourself.

Bowman had a problem; it was obvious to Piet that he had been told to go get the money soonest, but he wanted Piet with him in case there was a problem, like a missing briefcase.

"Okay, but don't think of running off anywhere before I get back, just in case things aren't as you say."

"At present, I can't run anywhere, as I'm sure you can see," Piet replied.

It was three days before Piet again had a visit from Bowman, he was not looking happy.

"The money is gone," he stated with a doubtful tone in his voice.

"Well, I haven't got it," Piet quickly replied.

"I didn't say you had. I did check the car and your apartment, we found your money, but it's not enough to make us think you took it from Sonny, so don't go off in a tantrum. I'm pretty sure you haven't taken it."

"So, wasn't it there in the pick-up?" Piet asked.

"No, we found the pick-ups, not a nice thing to see; the briefcase was still there and still attached to Sonny, but it had been smashed open and the money gone."

"Smashed?" Piet queried. "Why didn't they use the key, it must have been in Sonny's pocket?"

"Yes, it was. I suppose they, whoever they were, attacked the case before they emptied the pockets of the three men."

"You mean they took the money and still robbed the corpses, that's sick." Piet's act was very convincing. "So, what are you going to do now? Whatever it is don't include me."

"Why not, what are you going to do?" He was still suspicious of Piet, but all the evidence said it was someone else.

"Once I'm out of here, I'm going to be out of the country as fast as a flight will take me."

"Why what are you running from, Piet?" The suspicion was back in his voice and became more evident.

"Use some sense, man, if and when the pick-ups are found, there's going to be a lot of questions, enough questions to see I never leave this country. Remember, my name's on the rental for those pick-ups, so no, I'm not staying a moment longer than I have to, and the doctor says that will be two more days."

Bowman thought it was a good answer and probably sensible, and maybe he himself should consider doing the same; after all, they must have been seen talking together over the past few months, so any investigation could easily lead to him.

Ω

Philip Marcosie was not happy, and that was an understatement. With trembling hands, Martin Smith had given him the latest e-mail from Keith Bowman on the problem in Afghanistan. Marcosie had now not only lost the boy he thought of as his son and would have eventually handed the control of the business too but also one and a half million dollars. Tony James, the man they

113

had brought in to replace Tony Boscono, he didn't give a dam about, except to find out if he had anything to do with the shooting. The e-mail told the story very clearly, whoever Bowman had got to do the search was good; he'd even confirmed the mercenary's account and pretty much confirmed the hit must have been carried out on the orders of one of the other gangs in Philly, and that meant there must be someone on the inside who told them all about the buy.

"Martin," Marcosie called, "get back on to this Bowman. I want to know who is buying the opium now we're out of the market, and I want to know now. Denise" – Marcosie now turned to Dennis Fultard, one of his personnel guards – "get on the street. I want to know what's happening, find out who knows about the shooting, and who's looking to buy opium and who's crowding our outlets, and I want to know before tonight, so let's get to it."

The full activation of the Marcosie syndicate caused a serious ripple in the local underworld, and the inevitable was going to happen sooner or later and happen it did. Two o'clock in the afternoon, Dennis Fultard was in a bar; it was one of the places that an opposing but minor syndicate called the Grogan's, named after their previous boss, used as a meeting place.

Dennis was generally asking the questions that Mr Marcosie wanted the answer to, one of the younger members of the opposition who had heard something but not much was trying to build up the tension and cracking jokes about the Marcosie outfit being in trouble. An older gang member could see it would cause trouble if it wasn't stopped, so he intervened and told the youngster to shut his mouth. Dennis also said he should shut his mouth before he got taught a lesson. Dennis turned to the older to ask his questions, but the youngster feeling slighted, as only the young can, drew a gun and shot Dennis.

When the news of the incident reached Marcosie, he took it as a declaration of war, so now the syndicate was hunting.

Ω

Two days later, Piet left the hospital, he now had a lot to do, and he had to make sure no one saw him do it; he still had the Land Cruiser available, so wasn't stuck for transport, but he didn't dare use it. Bowman would have someone watching it; instead, he sneaked out the back of the hospital and walked to where he could get a taxi, which he took to his apartment, where he was able to pick up his own car.

He'd always kept quiet about the shop he rented and paid the landlord, who owned the whole parade, enough to see it didn't get broken into. When Piet needed to hide the money from the briefcase, the shop had been the natural place, so this was where he now headed.

The next problem was to get the money out of the country, without creating suspicion with either the authorities or Bowman. First stop, the post office, where he wired a large sum of the money to a post box in Italy. Next, it was the bank, where again he sent a large sum to a Swiss bank; finally, it was the Wells Fargo office, where he repeated the transaction to Italy.

Now apart from a few thousand dollars, his money was safely out of the country and waiting for him in Italy. He drove back to the hospital again, careful not to be seen re-entered in the back; he walked through and out the front to collect the Land Cruiser, while doing it he thought he saw someone watching him, he couldn't be sure but worked on the assumption there was.

At his apartment, the disorder showed that it had been searched, this did not bother Piet for this is the last time he would ever be in it; he packed his few things, the balance of the money he spread about his body, his own money he packed in the suitcase. He took the Land Cruiser and left it in the parking lot at the airport. The first plane out was going to Mumbai but not for another two hours so he found his way to the bar; it was busy in the bar, but he managed to find a table and settled down to wait.

While he was waiting, a young British soldier came to share his table. The lad was young and inexperienced and his idea of war was laughable, but he was keen and easy to talk to. Somehow, they got around to discussing guns, their merits and failings and Piet put him right about which was the best.

"It's not a matter of how good the gun is, it's about how good the man using it is," Piet informed him.

The squaddie agreed. "You could give me a LH, and I'd still be unable to hit a barn, but someone like Dylan could use an old Lee-Enfield and still take someone out at a mile."

Piet's sensors went on full alert. "Who's this Dylan you talk of?" he asked in an offhand manner.

"Oh, he's one of the regiment's snipers, probably the best in the whole army they say. I was watching him a few days ago and saw him get a two-inch group at three thousand yards, how's that for shooting?"

"Not with an old Lee-Enfield, I'll bet," Piet said showing indifferent interest.

"No, of course not, he was using one of the new AI's the LH115. A beautiful rifle it looked to me."

Just then, the public address called for the flight to Doha and London; the squaddie finished the last of his drink and jumped up. "Thanks for the chat," he said and was gone.

Piet was still puzzling on the information he had received, so there's someone called Dylan who has got an AI rifle and can shoot accurately at three thousand yards, maybe there's still a chance of a reckoning.

Ω

When Henry Filamont arrived back at his office, it was to find everything in turmoil. He started to look through his e-mails but had to stop when Mike Reynolds knocked on his door and walked right in.

"You wanted a war, didn't you?" Mike stated. "Well, now you've got one, as at the last reading; there are ten dead, an equal number in hospital, and thirty in custody, so what do you think now?"

"I think it went better than I could have hoped, who's been taken out?"

Mike slumped into a chair. "Obviously Marcosie is still operating, but most of the ones in custody are his men. It's the Grogan team that's taken the biggest hit, and now two of the others have decided it's a chance to break Marcosie's dominance, so they're on the Grogan's side. It's bloody hell out there, and we've even been able to identify six officers who are working for the gangs so it's gone federal and is now firmly back in your court."

Filamont couldn't have been happier if he'd won the national lottery; by having Tony Spinelli shot in the manner he did, he was finally going to make a major hole in the drugs trade in the state of Michigan. Silently, he said a thank you to the man who had pulled that trigger, whoever he was and where ever he was.

Part 2

Chapter 20

Jim Baker, an army corporal storeman, a man with a very happy-go-lucky attitude, a friend to all, always ready to see the bright side of anything, which was a surprise considering he was a Norfolk man born and bred, a county noted for its pragmatic attitude to the world in general, and day-to-day life in particular.

It had surprised his parents when Jim told them he was going to join the army. In the normal way of the people of the county, they had expected him to stay in the town, or at least the county, for all his life, the same as they had, and probably he would have if a recruiting sergeant hadn't explained the joys and excitement of a career in the army. Needless to say, the picture woven by the recruiter differed greatly from the reality. He did get some excitement, in terms of warfare in various parts of the world, but the joys of being an army storeman were few, especially when the regiment was in barracks in Suffolk.

At least he had joined an East Anglian regiment, so when in barracks, he could get home regularly, and he got a lot of pleasure from the social side of army life, always willing to join in with anything, and only too happy to organise an activity, whatever it may be. He always saw life as 'the glass being half full' and made the most of anything.

Jim was a friend to all, but his best and closest friend was Dylan Williams. No one could explain how the two had become friends; they were so different. Jim outgoing happy-go-lucky, Dylan the opposite, fairly dour, almost introverted, not a depressive but definitely a loner; he'd join in if pressed but preferred to do his own thing. If Jim had 'a glass being half full' outlook, then Dylan definitely saw things as 'the glass being half empty'. Regardless of their differing attitudes, they had a strong friendship of long standing, having first met when they joined the army on the same day and in the same entry.

This particular morning, Jim had been looking all over for Dylan, and finally finding him sitting at the bar in the corporal's club, staring into his empty beer glass. The beer glass had been emptied for some time, but Dylan wasn't noticing, lost totally in his thoughts he was oblivious to all around him.

"You look like you lost a shilling and found a sixpence," Jim said, "got problems?" Dylan acknowledged him and automatically asked the barman for two beers before deciding to explain his problem.

"Like you, my twelve's up soon, and I don't want to sign on, so I'm having to think of what to do now, how about you? Are you staying or going?"

"Oh, I'm going, most definitely," Jim responded. "I never should have joined in the first place, and apart from getting you to buy the beers, that's why I'm disturbing your meditation." Dylan cast a wary eye at his friend, inviting an explanation of the previous statement.

"I'm going to buy a shop," he stated, "a sporting goods shop." He now stood straight and looked very satisfied with himself. "It's up home in Norfolk, a small market town, but the shop's doing well, and with the ideas I've got, it's got a lot of potential."

"What do you know about shop keeping?" Dylan responded, with amazement in his voice. "You're a blanket stacker; you probably can keep a stock list, but what do you know about buying and selling?"

Jim refused to be affronted; he'd always wanted to run his own shop, ever since he was a boy, and he still dreamt of it, that was the other reason he had been willing to take up the recruiter's suggestion. He'd seen he would be earning enough to be able to save for the shop he dreamed of, something he would be unlikely to be able to do in Norfolk where well-paid jobs were hard to come by. If he'd stayed home, he would have wound up working in someone else's shop and hating every minute. Over the twelve years that he'd been in the army, he'd been able to save towards that end, and now, he was ready to fulfil his dream.

"I'll have you know I know a lot about shop keeping, unlike you I haven't wasted my time playing with guns. I've been studying. I've got qualifications in shop keeping, accounting, stock control, buying and selling, all that sort of thing."

"Well, I wish you well," Dylan responded, amused at Jim's pomposity. Dylan thought Jim was a great mate, but at times like this, he looked ridiculous. "So what has this got to do with my not signing on?"

"Well," Jim drew out the word, "this shop that's come up for sale is a snip. I'm surprised no one else is in the running for it, but although I can afford the shop and good will, I'm a bit shy where the stock is concerned, and I'm also short of some working capital, so I'm looking for a partner really." It was easy to see the look on Dylan's face that he had no interest in being a shopkeeper.

"I can't think why you should think of me for this; it's nice that you did think of me, but you know I'm an outdoor man. I couldn't be nice to people wanting to buy a new hat or coat. I'd wind up scaring away all your business. I really do thank you for thinking of me but no."

Jim wasn't one to give up that easy, he had known full well what his mate's answer would be, but he still had more shots in the locker.

"Look," he cajoled, "the reason that you came to mind as soon as I'd found the business was not only because I still need a bit of the money but that I will need someone to look after the guns."

"Guns, what guns?" Finally, Jim had mentioned something that got Dylan's interest. If Dylan was fast asleep, you would only have to mention guns and he'd be wide awake; guns and shooting had been everything in his life from a very early age.

"Well, it's a sporting goods shop." Jim made it sound like he was speaking to an idiot. "We've got to sell guns; you know, shotguns, target pistols, and even rifles, you know the sort of thing, and of course ammunition, and they'll be measuring and fitting the guns to the people who buy them, and filling cartridges of course. A lot of profit in putting together your own shotgun cartridges, all that sort of messing about, but of course, I would have to have someone who could get a licence to do that side of the business, just think it would be much like what you've been doing for the last twelve years, so what do you think?"

Dylan didn't know what to think; he had no plans of his own, but this had come along a bit sudden.

"I don't know," he said, "it would still mean dealing with people; you know I'm not too good at that." It was a true statement, but shooting was the only interest Dylan had, and well, he knew there weren't many jobs that only involved them. At least the job would be working with guns, and there might be an opportunity to get invited to some of the shoots they had in that part of the country.

Jim, being the good shopkeeper he wanted to be, could smell that he had a catch on the line, time to play him.

"You wouldn't be doing general shop work, that'll be for me and whatever assistants we employ. You'll only be doing what you do now, fixing guns and making sure the punters knows how to handle them, all that sort of stuff. If after a year or two we were still doing well, we could maybe build our own range, then you'd have your shooting as well." *Nearly there*, Jim thought. "I'll tell you what, come with me this Saturday. I'm going to see the bloke who's selling, and start the buying process; you could come and have a look at the set-up and have a chat to him about your bloody guns, what do you think?" Dylan couldn't really see a way out of it, so agreed to go along for a look.

As Jim had thought, the visit was enough to convince Dylan to invest, and as Dylan was not short of a few pounds, he bought fifty percent; they became equal partners.

Ω

Things turned out a lot better than Dylan had initially imagined. They had a readymade market among the local landowners, then there were the holidaymakers who often had come unprepared and needed their fishing kit and shooting needs supplied. The shop sold everything, from outdoor clothing to crossbows and wellington boots to fishing shelters.

The business was doing well when they had bought it and thanks to Jim, kept doing so. Contrary to Dylan's original scepticism, Jim was a natural, doing all the running of the shop, buying the goods in, keeping the books and such like. True to his word, Jim left Dylan out of the day-to-day running of the shop. Jim and Janet, Janet Summers the assistant Jim had taken on, looked after that part of the operation, as they'd originally agreed. Only on things that dealt with weapons and shooting did Dylan get involved; the fishing tackle and equipment was gradually moved across to become Dylan's responsibility as well, but it was done slowly so that he didn't notice or complain.

Janet had been a real find. A mature lady, she would never tell her age, who was married to Fred, a lorry driver who spent most of his time driving all around the continent. She was the mother of four boys, three of whom had flown the nest, leaving just Terry as the last one.

Janet like everyone had her good and bad points; on the good side, she knew just about everybody in the town and seemed to have been to school with most of them, at least the older ones. She was naturally talkative and knew all the local gossip. She was very good with people and could usually manage to send everyone who came in to the shop out with something they had had no intention of buying.

On the bad side, Janet was an organiser and matchmaker, and Dylan she considered to be unhappy in his bachelor state and would keep telling him to smarten up if he was to attract a woman. Dylan road with the blows when Janet started getting on to him and took the first opportunity to escape to the workshop.

As Jim had said originally, Dylan's work was more about weapon preparation and repair, just the sort of thing he'd spent a lot of time in the army doing, his only contact with the customers was finding out what someone wants, making it fit, showing him how to use it, or at least avoid accidents. He was often asked to repair weapons for the local gentry and farmers so it wasn't long before he got to know a lot of the locals, especially the police who were responsible for checking their gun licences, both the shops and Dylan's personal licence for his target rifles and pistols. They also had a licence to handle explosives, in terms of gunpowder, so that Dylan could make the shop's own shotgun cartridges.

Anytime he was lost for something to do, Dylan would disappear into the workshop, or as the work wasn't all-consuming, he would take the time off and go to one or the other of the local shooting clubs he had joined and practise the one thing he really loved, so it could be said that Dylan had made the right decision and was content almost. The only thing he really missed was sniping, target shooting was okay, but actually shooting someone who could shoot back was very different. Dylan would like to take a trip to Africa, to try some real big game hunting; it would be as near as he would be likely to get to the hunting he used to do.

After the first year, Dylan decided he would stay in Norfolk and settle down a bit, not that he had changed his mind about marriage and the like, his interests were all absorbing; he couldn't imagine any woman who would put up with his love for shooting.

He did however buy a small two-bedroom bungalow; this Janet thought of as nest building and renewed her attempts to interest him in all the local unattached girls in the town. He considered he only needed one bedroom but most bungalows seem to come with two. He converted the other bedroom into a workshop where he could indulge in his other interest of model making, a thing he'd done since boyhood, first with pre-cast plastic aircraft, then he moved on to wooden sailing warships; it wasn't an all-consuming hobby, but it did help to pass the time when he couldn't play with weapons.

His neighbours on the left were the Ables, Mr and Mrs; he never knew their forenames; in fact, he never saw much of them at all, they both worked in

Peterborough all week and had a sailing boat on the coast where they would go at the weekend, so if he ever saw them, it was only to say good morning.

In the bungalow on the right resided Mr Paul and Mrs Jean Jackman, they were very different to the Ables. They had moved to Norfolk from London when Paul had retired and didn't want the rat-race anymore and having had some holidays in Norfolk over the years, had decided that was the place for them. Having left their family and friends in London when they moved, they initially had trouble settling down, as Jean had explained to Dylan, when he moved in. Jean was a natural talker and gossip, who soon got to know nearly everyone on the estate. Dylan found he couldn't arrive home without a greeting from Jean; he didn't really mind, but sometimes this passing of information, gossip, could take maybe an hour, still he usually had the time.

So Dylan had settled in to the civilian world and was surprised to find he liked it; he was steadily building a social position, with many contacts who were fast becoming friends, that is within the limited amount of himself he was willing to expose, he could see himself staying, doing what he was doing for many years to come, if nothing changed, but how often did plans exist that don't change.

Chapter 21

When Piet Botha flew out from Kabul airport, it was only the start of a very long journey. The first stop was at Mumbai in India, and by the time he landed, his leg was again in a very painful condition requiring him to check in to a hospital. There it was found he had got an infection in the wound, this required another stay in hospital.

This time, he didn't find it a relaxing experience, because he'd flown on his own passport so could easily be traced, and he thought by now there was a good chance someone would be looking for him. He'd checked into the hospital on the second of his passports that was in the name of Peter Franks, so it would still take time for anyone to find him but not too much time. After three days, the doctor considered he was well enough to leave the hospital, and with great relief, he headed for the docks.

Because Piet was now using the Peter Franks identity, he couldn't leave India through normal channels, the Franks' passport hadn't got an arrival stamp in it, that would have showed he was in the country legally, and there would have been an official record. But Peter Franks didn't have the stamp, so if he tried to leave through normal channels, he would be stopped, and if he was stopped, even if he could talk his way out of the situation, a record of the incident would exist, even if he wasn't jailed.

Piet had spent a large part of his life skipping in and out of different countries, often without the correct documentation so knew how to do it. By going to the docks, it wouldn't be hard to find a ship with a captain or crewmember who, for a reasonable sum, would let him sail with them, no questions asked. This proved to be as easy to do as to say; a container ship was due to leave that evening, and the mate having been paid the required sum, squared it with the captain so that Peter Franks left India for points west, and Piet Botha was officially somewhere in India, and if he was being searched for, he would have vanished, at least for now.

He stayed on the container ship until it docked in the Yemen at the port of Aden, from where the ship would be going south. He had only to walk along the dock to find a local trading vessel that was heading to Port Said, again after payment of the required 'fare', the captain was willing to take him. From Port Said, he again changed to another small trader and was finally put ashore at a small fishing port on the mainland of Greece.

Now he was in Europe and the travelling to his final destination was easy, as most of the borders were open. Using bus and rail, he was able to get to Rome in Italy without ever having to show any of his passports.

Years before, when Piet had been avoiding an international warrant for his arrest, issued because of his mercenary activities in Africa, he had hidden, openly, in Rome and had made some good and useful contacts. He'd opened bank accounts in private banks and got to know people who could produce documents for him, things he now needed. He didn't need a new passport because he hadn't had to use the Franks' one, but he did need all the rest, driving license and birth certificate, he would need credit cards and so on, but for now, he only needed somewhere to stay and rest his leg.

He rented a small villa on the outskirts of the city; cash had negated his lack of documents. He did have documents, if he really had to produce them, but he'd just spent weeks having nothing recorded as to who he was or where he was, so he didn't want to prove who he was until he had got some new documents, which he wouldn't do until he had rested and convalesced his leg. The wound had not suffered any further infection during his travels, but he still had it checked out by a doctor as it was still hurting, and he couldn't walk far on it, but it turned out it only needed to be rested, something he was only too happy to do.

After being in Italy for a year, Piet felt rested enough to start putting his life in order. He'd changed his appearance simply by growing his hair; he'd previously kept his head bald, now after nearly seven months, he had a fine head of blond hair; he also grew a close-cropped beard and wore sunglasses at all times. His clothes were all fashionable in the Italian style even down to the shiny pointed shoes.

Now was the time to call on his contacts. First, he called on a forger he knew who lived in the Collatino quarter and arranged to have a set of Belgium documents produced, he chose Belgium because they spoke the Flemish, that was the origin of the Afrikaans of South Africa and sounded much the same. He kept the Franks name and even though the passport had that name on it, for his new identity, it still had to be changed.

It took a month for the papers to be produced and cost him a hundred thousand dollars, but they were very good. Next, he had to visit his bank, see that all was in order and deposit the money he had sent to his post office box, while there he changed his personnel details more as a precaution. Now there was only one thing to sort out, he had to get a gun; this would be no trouble, as he 'knew a man', his problem was what type he would be best buying. He would have liked to have the Colt 44 Magnum he had used for many years and was used too, but that might be a bit noticeable to carry around, in civilian clothes. In the end, he decided on the Sig Sauer P220, a nice small piece, easy to carry, but with a .45mm bullet, it would be very effective at close quarters, which is exactly what he wanted.

By the time he was fit and everything was settled, he'd been in Italy for nearly two years; he could now move freely around the world again, so he considered it was time to get on with the next part of his revenge.

He travelled to the UK this time openly by car and ferry, to make sure there were no checks that would reveal the pistol. He wasn't intending to stay in Britain for any length of time; the country was just too cold to remain in, and he was born and worked most of his life in a hot climate; he was only planning to stay until he had settled the one outstanding debt that still annoyed him. He was pretty certain the man he was looking for was called Dylan and was in the army, in a regiment that was stationed in East Anglia, at Colchester, so that's where he went.

Chapter 22

Dylan looked out of the shop window at the rain pouring off the roofs and overloaded gutters. "Norfolk sunshine," he said, "will it never end?" It had rained on and off for the past week. "And this is supposed to be one of the driest counties."

Dylan's comments on the weather, a thought spoken aloud and not directed at anyone, were however taken, by automatic assumption by Janet, to be directed to her.

"You're always moaning," she responded, "there's nothing wrong with a bit of rain now and again." The telling off was expected. "And what's the problem anyway you're inside, aren't you? Not like my poor Terry, he's out there in it, trying to make this a better place for us all." In fact, young Terry, Janet's youngest and only home remaining son, was actually in the pub, but that was something his mother didn't know.

"So, what's our Terry doing this week," Dylan asked, not really interested in the doings of young Terry, but it was as good a reason as any to put off the time when he would have to go out into the rain.

This particular day, he had to deliver a twelve bore back to farmer Sutton, over at Summerton farm, which was across the other side of the county and that would be a long trip for him in 'that disgusting car of yours' as Janet called it. The offending vehicle was in fact a 1960 short wheelbase Land Rover, and everything Dylan wanted in a car. He supposed it looked a bit disgusting, as he never washed it; he didn't really see the point, as it was guaranteed to get a fresh coating of mud every time he visited a farm, and that was at least once or even twice a week, but he did keep it serviced, and mechanically, it was in perfect condition.

"He's out there, in this weather, stopping the greedy farmers from ploughing up the footpaths and stopping people crossing their land, like what they're entitled to do; it's terrible the way they grab what's not theirs and then not allowing it to be used by anyone even though it's been allowed for hundreds and hundreds of years…" At this point, Dylan had switched off; he knew he shouldn't have started it, for now, it would go on for at least ten minutes or longer. Fortunately, a customer came in, and Janet stopped in mid flow to serve them; she was really a very good shop assistant, and Dylan was very good at spotting a golden opportunity, without a word he slipped out the door into the rain.

Young Terry Summers had left school and college, collecting six GCSEs and a diploma in environmental studies, plus a determination to put his qualifications to use, for the good of everyone, but it hadn't got him a job though. Currently, Terry and his group of friends were, as his mother thought, attempting to get public rights of way re-established, where land owners had absorbed them into their own property and opened again for public use.

The pathways, as Janet had pointed out, had been used by people for hundreds of years and had withstood attempts to stop them, both privately and government sponsored actions like, manor land rights and enclosure acts, but people fought back for the right to walk from place to place by the most direct route.

In the sixties and seventies however, as cars became more normal for moving people from place to place, the farmers had encroached on the largely unused paths bit by bit until they were unable to be recognised, then they would remove any markers and plough them into their other fields. At the time, no one noticed, but then came the late seventies and early eighties people once again found their legs and got back to walking for recreation and wanted to again use the paths.

The paths were clearly marked on ordinance maps, so people used them, which annoyed the farmers as a lot of the paths cut right across the fields and people were walking on the crops. Some of the farmers were happy to allow the right of way, and often would automatically maintain them, putting up new signs and fitting proper gates, but there were some who tried any and every way to stop the public from crossing what they now considered their land. They used obstructive methods, from putting obstacles like locked gates or mammoth-sized bales of straw to block the gateways, and so Terry and his friends would walk the footpaths exactly as they were marked on the maps, and damn these belligerent types of farmers.

Ω

The footpath the environmentalists had decided to walk on this particular day was across the land of Sir Peter Archer, locally known as Sir Bossy Balls, for the way he tried to run everything in the county.

Sir Peter was not a pleasant person, the small wood that bordered the field the footpath crossed, in the days before he had bought it, used to be a popular place for people to walk their dogs. He soon put a stop to that, by the simple but dangerous measure of putting barbed wire along the roadside of the wood and making sure to leave some offcuts in the long grass, which of course the dogs found, with their paws.

After a few dogs had had to be treated by the local vets for seriously injured paws, the dog owners soon got the message, but Sir Peter would still make a point of walking the wood, with his shotgun, each morning to make sure the no trespassing signs were obeyed.

The footpath that Terry and his friends had decided to walk had been incorporated into the farm some twenty to thirty or more years ago but was still listed as a public right of way. Since Sir Peter had bought the farm, he was the owner of the land either side of the path but considered the path was his land as well and had thought he had the right to defend it from trespassers.

Firstly, he tried blocking the entrance to the path, then if anyone got over that, he would threaten them with his shotgun, which he always had with him and was often seen to wave it about, with the breach closed, in a threatening way.

This morning to get on to the footpath, Terry and his group had had to climb a hurdle and skirt a manure pile. Then while they were walking across the field, keeping precisely to the ordnance survey maps route, Sir Peter had appeared from out of the woods.

"Get off my land," he demanded in a loud domineering tone of voice. The demand and the tone were like a red rag to Terry, who was not known for his patience or tact.

"We're not on your land," he replied, in as belligerent a voice as he could manage. "You might have ploughed up 'public' land and blocked the entrance, but that doesn't make it yours."

"You are trespassing," Sir Peter stated. "You climbed over the fence and are now on my land, and if you don't get off, I'll have the police on you," this threat he emphasised by waving the shotgun he was carrying.

"No, you won't," Terry sneered, "you only think you've got power, but you haven't, we have. And if you think the police will support you, go call them."

Now the two of them were only inches apart, and one of the swings of the shotgun hit Terry on the side of his face.

Terry was a big lad, six feet tall and fifteen stone; he was also not the type of person to accept being hit by anyone, as the local police could testify. On the few times he'd been arrested for brawling outside the pub, and as reply, for the side swipe of the gun, he landed two solid punches in Sir Peter's gut, and one under his chin, putting him flat out on the muddy field.

"If you ever touch me again, I'll put you in hospital for a month, and this is public land, and I'm going to walk it, today and tomorrow and any day I feel like." With that, he turned and with the rest of the group continued their way along the footpath, with the curses and threats of Sir Bossy Balls following them. This had been the first time anyone had got the better of Sir Peter since he'd left public school, to say he was not happy about it would be a great understatement.

"So, you're going to walk it tomorrow, are you?" he muttered. "We'll see about that." If there had been anyone to hear, they might have been worried by the vehemence in his voice, as he watched the group walk away.

The next day, Terry kept to his promise and went for a walk along the same footpath, alone this time, now that he actually wanted to go where the path went, but also so that Sir Peter would know what he thought of him and his threats. He kept his eyes open in case Sir Peter was about but failed to see him.

Sir Peter was inside the edge of the woods and not able to be seen from the footpath, but he could see, and he saw what he had come to see. Taking considered aim, he fired the shotgun, and as intended, Terry took the blast in the side of his head and shoulder. Sir Peter retired backwards through the woods, leaving Terry dead or dying in the field.

Ω

Dylan was in his workshop when Constable Bill Jennings came in.

"Hello, Bill, what're you doing in here?" Dylan greeted him, then noticed the look on his face. "What's the matter?"

"You'd better come through to the shop," Bill said. "I've brought some bad news for Janet, and she'll have to leave."

"What's happened?" Dylan asked as he got up.

"It's young Terry, he's been shot and killed."

"Terry killed? An accident or what?"

"We don't know yet, he was found over in 'Potters' field; he'd taken a blast from a shotgun."

"Who fired the shot?"

"We don't know; there was no one else about; we're still investigating, but we want Janet to do the identification, which won't be nice, his face took a lot of the shot."

"Does it have to be Janet; I know Terry pretty well; can I do the ID instead?"

"Thanks, I was hoping you'd say that. I know you, like me, have seen such things before. I didn't want to put Janet through that, and Fred's away." Fred being Janet's husband. "He's driving a load down to London today."

When they entered the shop, Janet was being consoled by policewoman Val Smith. Jim had also arrived and was calming Janet's fears about having to close the shop.

"It'll be best if Janet stays here for now, and you keep the shop open," Dylan advised. "She's got no one at home at present, and she'll be able to talk here. I'm going to the hospital to do the ID; I'll be back later." Jim thanked him, and Dylan and Bill set off together.

"You've got to have some idea who did the shooting," Dylan queried as they drove.

"Look," Bill replied, "and this is between us." Dylan agreed. "Yesterday, Terry had a run in with Sir Bossy Balls, in that same field. Bossy Balls hit Terry with his gun, and Terry hit him a couple of times and put him down, then as they left, he threatened Terry. Now that proves nothing, but we're investigating."

"That would sound more like it," Dylan surmised. "I can't think of anyone else who would have a problem with Terry, not unless they got into an argument in the pub; he's probably the most liked person in town."

"We're not saying it was a deliberate shooting, not yet anyway."

"Yeah, and who would run away from an accidental shooting?"

"That's as might be, but leave it to us to do the investigation, and don't make any observations till it's proved, okay?" Dylan agreed he'd keep his mouth shut, although Bill knew it wasn't necessary; it was always difficult to get even the time of day out of Dylan.

The identification of Terry's body was routine but unpleasant, half of his face was destroyed, but the other side was untouched. Later when he'd returned to the shop, he found Jim holding the fort by himself.

"I assume it was Terry?" Jim asked.

"Yes," Dylan assured him, "I'm glad I was able to do the ID. Janet would never have been able to look at that face, not till the mortician has done a lot of work, where is Janet anyway?"

"She's gone home with a neighbour; I think we're going to need another assistant for the next couple of weeks. Actually, I've been thinking of getting a second assistant for a while, this might be a good time."

"You'll have to make sure Janet okays it; I wouldn't like her to think we're getting rid of her."

"Yeah, I understand that. I'll even ask her if she knows anyone suitable to be a junior assistant."

Chapter 23

It didn't take long for the police to establish it was Sir Peter's gun that had shot Terry, and that Sir Peter was holding it at the time. Sir Peter who apart from being a cold blooded killer was also a coward, who had no intention answering for his actions, maintained he knew nothing about anyone getting shot but did admit he was in the woods at the time of the incident, with his gun. He'd gone out to shoot pigeons, but he'd missed all he saw and hadn't seen anyone else at all, and if it was his gun, then it must have been accidental when he was aiming at something else.

At the inquest, the coroner considered, because of the altercation between Sir Peter and Terry of the day before the shooting, plus the threats Sir Peter had been heard to call out after the incident, he did have a case to answer and so recorded a verdict of unlawful killing, and Sir Peter was bound over for trial.

The police prepared the charges they wished to bring against Sir Peter of wilful killing, and all seemed set for a straightforward trial. Now the situation changed, the crown prosecution refused to bring the charges the police asked for, they would not explain why they did not support the police, only stated they were going to bring a case of accidental killing, in other words, they were going to accept Sir Peter's version of what happened. The chief constable agreed with the CPS, even against the advice of his officers and ended the investigation.

"It makes you sick," Bill Jennings said to Dylan in the pub one evening, "the CPS is going along with Sir Bossy Balls and ignoring the facts; they reckon the argument on the previous day had no connection with the shooting." Taking a look over his shoulder to see no one was close by, and in almost a whisper he said, "We've found out the head of the CPS in Norfolk and Bossy balls are both in the masons, in the same lodge even. Now I'm not saying there is any extra consideration being given to Bossy Balls case, or that there's any collusion going on, but when you also take into account the chief constable is also in the masons, it makes you wonder why, why they're so ready to go along with the CPS version of it being an accident." Dylan had to agree with Bill's assessment, but as far as he could see, they would have to await the trial, to see what the judge and jury thought.

The trial when it was held was thought to be a travesty, by all those who knew about trials, it was such an open and shut case. The confrontation between Sir Peter and Terry, the threats that Sir Peter shouted, nobody had any doubt Sir Peter would be found guilty of something; he was a Sir so it wouldn't be anything serious, just a slap on the wrist, like maybe only being careless with his gun, but it wasn't to be.

The prosecution sent a junior barrister who looked young enough to have just passed out of law school, if not high school, to prosecute the case, while Sir Peter hired one of the best criminal lawyers in the country.

The judge was very quick, unusually quick, to direct the jury into disregarding any evidence, presented by witnesses, that was not proven beyond doubt, while allowing the defence to present volumes about how good Sir Peter was, in the things he did for the good of the county, and the country, this was proved by his being given a knighthood. Needless to say, the judge's summing-up was almost a direction to find Sir Peter innocent of all charges, which the jury had little choice but to do.

Now the talk of the town and the local papers was of a miscarriage of justice, but the CPS would not allow there to be anything wrong with the judgement and disallowed any appeal.

Ω

To Dylan, the worst outcome of the trial was to see Janet in the shop each day; she'd lost her sparkle, had no interest in the happenings in the town. She was improving though, when she had first returned she just sat in a corner lost in her own thoughts, at least now, she was doing her work even if it was in a half-hearted manner. Fortunately, the girl they had taken on, Judy Roberts, immediately after Terry's death was good at the work and surprisingly good at accepting Janet as the senior and deferring to her.

One evening, Bill Jennings and Dylan were sitting at the bar in the Kings Head as usual. Bill thinking his thoughts and drinking, whilst Dylan ate his dinner. As Dylan finished eating, Bill spoke for the first time in a long while.

"I think I'll retire," he said.

"What on earth for?" Dylan enquired. He didn't know how old Bill was, but he was sure he had to be less than fifty.

"Because there's no point anymore, when Peters and his mates can totally flout the law, it shows that justice is dead. The court has given them free rein, there's no justice when the case comes down to who your mates are, it's gone, and we're back in the days when the aristocracy can never be wrong. We've spent hundreds of years to get an honest police force and a legal system that was fair to all, now it's been proved to me that it's all a game and the poor are the losers; they're the ones who have to do as their told, really, I don't think I want to belong to this organisation anymore." He was of course referring to the police force. "You spend years and years learning to do the job, knowing what's what, then some pimply kid comes along and says it's all crap, and we don't know what we're doing, then your boss turns around and agrees with him. Policing is only to keep the low life in check; the money people can do what they like; the verdict on them is decided in their private clubs not the courtroom."

Dylan had never heard Bill talk like this; he'd always defended the legal system.

"Don't give in to them, Bill," Dylan advised, "we need you around here; you and your mates do a bloody good job. If you chuck it in, what's left for the rest of us, give it a chance. If you read your history right, you'll see that justice can and will come in its own time. We ordinary lowlifes have started already. I've already seen that Bossy has had to go much further afield to get anything he wants; no one around here will sell him anything. I've even had the pleasure of telling him I won't sell him any cartridges, because I wouldn't want to think they would cause someone's death; he didn't like that."

"That's great, but it might make people feel good for a day or two, but it doesn't make him pay, the same for all those that supported him, the judges and lawyers, chief of police and such. I've had enough of it." Dylan could see the corrosive effect the judgment was having on Bill, and if he felt that way, how did Janet and her family feel, and the thought of that made up his mind.

Dylan had been having the same sort of thoughts as Bill, about the state of the legal system and how it had treated Janet and family. Having now seen what it was doing to someone as stalwart as Bill Jennings, he finally decided it was time he took a hand.

"Look, I agree with you whole heartedly, but I've a feeling, a distinct feeling that Sir Peter" – Dylan could not think of using his nickname, and there was a good reason for that. If you start demeaning someone, then it gets into your head that they're worthless, and someone who's worthless, you won't think is worth any effort on your part, and in Dylan's previous employment, that attitude could make him be careless and miss the shot – "is going to pay and pay more than he ever thought he might, so don't give it up, not yet, because I think we're going to need you, maybe soon, maybe very soon. Two more pints here, Sid (this to the barman)." Bill was in too morose a mood to take in what Dylan had said, but by instinct accepted the beer.

When Dylan had returned from Afghanistan, he was in possession of a state of the art sniper rifle, an Accuracy International LH115A3. If anyone had asked, he would say it was in his possession, but he didn't own it, which was true; he'd been asked to look after it, but he knew no one would ever ask for it back because no one knew about it, well, no one except himself and a man whose name he didn't know.

When Dylan moved into his bungalow, he had to have a gun safe fitted; it was a legal requirement because he owned a shotgun, two target rifles and two target pistols and ammunition for all, but this he kept in a separate safe. He had the safe fitted into the side of the chimneybreast in the lounge, and a very good job the installers made of it. Once it was fitted, he got the police to verify the gun safe was very secure and suitable for the job, which it was, so they issued him a licence.

After the licence had been issued, Dylan took the safe out of its hole and proceeded to modify it. Firstly, he had to increase the depth of the hole it was fitted into, then he fitted another cabinet on the back of the safe. With sliders fitted to the modified safe, he could slide it out when he wished then push it back; he installed a lock mechanism that would have to be operated if the safe was to be slid out, and with no one the wiser as to the duel use of the safe, he was able to keep the, illegal, AI sniper rifle.

When Dylan got home after the conversation with Bill Jennings, he opened the secret gun safe and took out the AI; it was still in perfect condition, properly lubricated, wrapped in plastic, and nestled in its original formed foam. Dylan's mind had been made up as soon as he had seen the effect of the trial on Bill. Never a person to worry about the legality of his actions, he was never the less a moral man, and the way this trial had been twisted to make a guilty person innocent had touched that moral nerve. He spent the rest of the evening stripping and cleaning the rifle; he got the gun case out of the loft, and with its sights and silencer, he left it ready for use.

Chapter 24

The following day, Dylan went to work as usual, it was good to see Judy being shown by Janet how to set out the window display; he gave an inquiring look to Jim who silently acknowledged 'yes, there was more improvement'. Seeing all was as well as could be expected, he told Jim he'd not be in tomorrow and probably the day after as well. Jim agreed there was nothing for Dylan to do that couldn't wait, so that was no problem. Dylan spent the rest of the day in the workshop finishing off a few small items.

At two o'clock the next morning, Dylan set off for his reconnaissance; he drove to Potter's field. The field and surrounding area were very quiet; the harvest wasn't yet ready to be cut, so there would be no reason for the farmers to be working this particular area at any time soon. On the right hand side of the road was a large field, full of rapeseed by the look of things; he wouldn't have known that two years ago. Dylan didn't know if the field had a name, but it sloped away down to a small brook.

On the left hand side of the road was Potter's field, and this sloped gently up to the crest line of the hill; on the right hand side of the field was a wood, really it would be more correct to call it a copse, from the size of it, but locally, it was called a wood, so Dylan called it a wood. Finding a suitable parking place, just inside the wood, and off the road, Dylan changed into his cams and slipped on his backpack.

Things had changed since the shooting, for a start, there were no obstructions to stop access to the footpath, not even a gate, and a signpost had been erected pointing to the other end of the field, so it seemed Sir Peter had learned at least one lesson. In the slight pre-dawn light, Dylan walked along to about where Terry had been shot; there was nothing to see anymore, but he said a silent hallo and promised to sort out some justice; it wasn't any belief in the supernatural that made him say it, just a superstition about time and place, then he turned and set off into the wood.

Immediately upon entering the wood, he was engulfed in darkness, what light there had been outside the trees was now gone. The wood and the undergrowth were very dense, required careful concentration and footing to stay upright, nothing new to Dylan. It soon became obvious the wood was never forested, or cared for in anyway. Studying the undergrowth as best he could, he moved through the wood; there were signs that someone, probably Sir Peter, had walked through the area regularly, so he used these same 'paths'. It didn't take long for him to cross to where he could look across another field that started where the trees finished and finished alongside Sir Peter's farmhouse and out buildings.

With the use of his monocular, Dylan was able to see clearly the buildings, the gateways and doors, and being four feet back in the wood, and dressed in cams, he knew nobody would be able to see him.

Once the dawn had arrived and lightened the area enough, Dylan studied the house and outbuildings as well as the surrounding fields, there had been nothing much to see.

It was close to 6:30 when the first signs of activity could be seen; a dog appeared and spent some time sniffing around the yard. A little after seven o'clock, a woman crossed from the house to one of the other buildings; she was inside for a minute or two then returned to the house carrying something he couldn't identify.

Sir Peter appeared in the yard, about 8:30, as he came out, the dog ran across and Sir Peter petted him. While doing the petting he lazily surveyed the landscape. *Yes, Sir Peter*, Dylan thought, *keep a close watch; a lot of people don't like you*. Sir Peter now went into the same outbuilding that the woman had visited, but when he came out, Dylan could identify he was carrying his shotgun, then he called the dog to him, and they both headed for the gate that would open on to the field.

Time to go, Dylan thought, *but I'll be seeing you tomorrow, Sir Peter*.

Dylan was up very early again the next day, and when he came out of the house, he was already in his cams and more importantly carrying the gun case that contained the AI rifle. The previous day's reconnaissance had shown him a safe concealed place to leave the Land Rover and the best position to see Sir Peter as he came out of the gate and into the field.

By six o'clock, Dylan had repeated his journey and was in position with the rifle assembled and casually cradled in his arms. There was little wind and the cloud cover was delaying dawn, but Dylan found this peaceful scene relaxing and pleasant, most of his life had been spent in ways much the same as this; he always thought of the early morning as his time.

Movement by the farmhouse caused Dylan to forget his reminiscences and come to full alert; he swung the rifle to the aim and looking through the Schmidt & Bender telescopic sight, fixed his aim on the figure that had attracted him; it was Sir Peter heading for the outbuilding where he kept his shotgun; the dog was standing alert looking after him. Dogs could always be a problem to a sniper; they could see further, smell the faintest odours on the breeze, and even if their owner was dead, they might still try to defend him by attacking the assailant. *Best before the gate is opened*, Dylan thought.

In a re-enactment of the previous afternoon, Sir Peter called the dog to him and turned to the gate, but he never reached it, the 7.62mm Lupua round destroyed his head, and once the body realised that it was dead, it crumpled to the ground.

Dylan was still disassembling the rifle when the screaming started; a woman had come out of the house and found Sir Peter. Dylan was sorry she had had to see the mess he had made of Sir Peter, but then Janet might have had to look at Terry.

Dylan was about to leave when he remembered the shell casing. He had only fired the one shot and had not expected to fire another, but his training and inbuilt reactions made him operate the rifle's bolt and this had ejected the used casing, now it was nowhere to be seen. He searched among the bracken and other foliage for more than ten minutes with no luck, then he heard the sirens of a police car approaching and decided it didn't really matter if the police found it; they couldn't match it to a rifle that didn't exist; it was time for him to be elsewhere.

Chapter 25

Reginald Bates, known as call me Reg, or more often call me please, by most newsrooms in the country, liked to call himself a jobbing reporter. What made him think of himself this way was that no paper wanted to employ him, at least not on a regular basis. They were happy to print his by-line when he had something of interest or when they needed to fill a column or two, this meant Reg had to find his own stories, wherever they might be. Needless to say, most of his stories were of local topics, nothing to get a by-line in a national paper or, dream of dreams, an article on the television, but anything he could get, he made the most of and managed to keep the wolf from the door.

Reg had been researching an article on the rustling of sheep from local farms and had just spent a long, cold night, watching sheep. Of course, nothing happened; it never does when you watch, so he thought the night had been wasted, until in his rear view mirror, he spotted a police car. It was traveling fast, no sooner had he spotted it in his rear view mirror than it had passed him; it wasn't sounding its two tones but did have its blues flashing. Reg's antenna smelt a story, probably a road traffic accident, it usually was, but maybe it would be worth a column or two, his foot pressed the pedal, and he followed the police car.

The police turned into Potter's farm, as far as Reg knew, there was no one with the name Potter living there, but there was someone by the name of Sir Peter Archer, and that name sent Reg's sensors into overdrive. He followed the police car up to the gate of the farmhouse, no one had said he couldn't and could immediately see there was someone lying on the ground with a woman leaning over him crying fit to bust. As Reg got out of his car, he was already scribbling in his notebook, getting the scene recorded. Not being one to await an invitation, he joined the police looking at the body; again, nobody had said he couldn't.

"It's Sir Peter, isn't it?" It was a reasonable question as his facial features were unrecognisable.

"It certainly is, but you wouldn't know it," one of the police officers replied before he realised who he was talking to. "What are you doing here? This is a crime scene," he said as he stood up preparing to move Reg to outside of the gate.

"So, it's a killing?" asked Reg who was quick to pick up on the officer's words. "Not an accident?" The policeman by now realising he was talking to a reporter, became more careful of what he said.

"We're unable to say anything else at this time, so please move outside the gate," he emphasised this with a not too gentle push. Reg was happy enough now to obey; he had a story of national interest. Rushing over to his car, he quickly took his Kodak easyshare Z7590; it was a bit on the old side buy and had often served him well. He managed to get ten or more shots before the policeman once again became aware of him and blocked his view, but he had enough pictures of the dead knight, the weeping widow and even the ever-attentive dog.

Now for the part he would get the most pleasure from, he had to call it in to the news desks of all the national papers and start the bidding war. This was going to be the biggest payday he had ever had. So without delay, he must register the fact it was his story and get them to commit themselves, they would have to pay, he had the story and pictures, and if they wanted to have it, they would have to pay and print it under his by-line, and in return, he would have one thousand words before lunch, with pictures, and a double page spread by the day after. That done, he would be safe from losing the story to someone else who might arrive try to steal it.

Ω

When the story hit Dereham, there was a sense of total amazement and joy, someone had taught a lesson to Sir Peter and anyone else who might try the same; there was a sense of euphoria and suggestions that they should have a party. Dylan carried on as usual and was doing some repairs to a shotgun in his workshop when the police arrived, in the person of DCI Tom Cooper, along with his understudy Constable Mike Price.

"I'm Chief Inspector Cooper; are you the owner of this shop?" The question was addressed to Jim, who acknowledged he was. "I have a warrant to search these premises." Cooper proffered the paper.

"Why?" Jim quite reasonably asked.

"It's all written on the paper," Cooper said in a peremptorily fashion, "so if you don't mind, I'll bring in the search team."

Jim was always an easy-going friendly sort of person, but Cooper's attitude brought out the other side of him.

"No, you may not bring in the search team; you will wait until my solicitor has arrived and accepted the warrant."

"I was unaware your solicitor was on the way," Cooper queried.

"She's not," Jim told him, "but she will be as soon as I phone her."

"If that's the case, please do so; we don't have all day." Jim did, and it was only ten minutes before Marjory Willoby arrived, looking as if she'd run all the way from her office at the other end of town. Jim welcomed her with great enthusiasm, not only because of the matter in hand but because they had a thing going between them; of course, it was a secret, the sort of secret that everyone knew about, at least they did if they had a Janet on the payroll.

By this time, Dylan had heard the commotion in the shop and came out of the workshop to see what it was all about.

"What's going on?" he asked, without addressing anyone in particular.

"And who might you be?" Inspector Cooper asked.

"What's it to do with you?" was Dylan's dismissive reply; he decided immediately that he didn't like this person. Jim stepped in at this point; he didn't want Dylan to make the situation worse and explained what was going on then turned to Cooper.

"This is my partner," he explained.

Marjory who had been reading the warrant now spoke up, "This is fully correct; the officers have the right to search the premises in line with their enquires into an investigation." She now turned to Cooper. "Can you enlighten us as to what you seek? We might be able to help you."

"I require to search to see if a certain rifle that was used in a fatal shooting is on the premises and would now be obliged if we might get on with our work."

Now it was Dylan's turn. "What's the specification of the weapon you're looking for?"

This confused Cooper. "What do you mean?" he asked.

Dylan giving a sigh that suggested he was talking to a child asked, "What calibre, that is, what size bullet is it reamed for?" No reply, another sigh. "Is it a .22mm or a 9mm, is it a magnum, is it automatic, a single shot, what magazine does it take?" Cooper was lost; he had never had anything to do with firearms, nor any interest in them.

Finally, Constable Price spoke up, "We're told it takes a 7.62mm, magnum round."

"Finally, someone with some sense." He was of course trying to wind up Inspector Cooper, and he was succeeding. Time for Jim to again reel Dylan in, but he was too slow for now.

Janet, who along with Judy had been silent, spoke up, "Is this to do with that murdering bastard who killed my Terry, if so, it was a shotgun he used."

The situation was now turning into a farce, and although Jim initially had not liked Inspector Cooper, he decided enough was enough.

"Okay, let's get down to business, Dylan. Do we have a rifle like the one they're looking for?"

"No," Dylan replied, feeling disappointed he couldn't carry on making life difficult for Cooper.

"What do we have?"

"Only two .22mm and one 9mm."

"Right," this to Inspector Cooper, "do you want to see these?"

"Yes, I will require to see them and to take them to police headquarters to verify they are what we've been told they are. Now may we begin our search?"

"Yes, you may."

"Hold it," Dylan said again. Jim was going to stop him again, but Dylan held up his hand stopping him. He now asked Cooper, "Have you got a trained firearms investigator out there?"

Cooper looked perplexed. "Why?" he asked.

Again, he sighed. "Because they are going to be searching amongst firearms and explosives and only a licenced person may do that."

Constable Price had to interrupt again, "Can they search if they don't actually handle any of the weapons or explosives?"

"Yes," Dylan replied, with satisfaction, finally the search got underway and found nothing as expected by all, except Dylan who knew for certain they would find nothing.

Inspector Cooper now addressed Dylan directly, "I believe you own some firearms of your own, Mr Williams."

"That's correct, Inspector; are you going to tell me you've got a warrant to search my house?"

145

"I do not have a warrant, at present, but could you assure me that none of your firearms meet the description of the rifle we're looking for?"

"I do have one weapon that nearly meets the specification you are seeking, 7.62mm. Are you interested in seeing my weapons? They are all safety locked up in my house, as they should be."

"You say they nearly meet the specification, what do you mean by that?"

"I mean they do not take magnum rounds," Dylan told him, "and before you make a thing about it, the weapon is registered with the police, and they also have a sample bullet, which you should have been told before you came."

Cooper still had thoughts of going to look, but his eye caught that of Marjory, she looked like she would love him to suggest it. Knowing Dylan would love to make more of a fool of him, and he was sure there would be nothing to find with Williams challenging him to do a search and the solicitor would probably object, causing even more trouble.

Finally, the search team reported the rifle was not there, so Cooper had to collect all the team together and leave.

"What was all that all about?" Jim asked Dylan. "It's as if you were trying to make trouble; you don't know more about this than you're telling." Jim was the one person in the county who knew Dylan's background, and the one person he knew could have carried out the shooting, but he also knew that he would not find out from Dylan unless Dylan wanted to tell, but Dylan was saved from answering, when Janet, whose hearing had returned to maximum since Terry had been avenged, said:

"Don't you go accusing Dylan," she defended. "He's a good lad and wouldn't hurt a fly" – both Dylan and Jim had to smile at that – "and I don't think they should be wasting their time looking; it was probably an angel who came to see justice done, so there. But if them police want to hang the person who shot Bossy Balls, they won't get any help around here."

That evening, Dylan answered a knock at his door, to find Constable Price.

"I'm sorry to disturb you, Mr Williams, but I've been sent to ask if you would allow me to inspect your rifle."

"Why?" was Dylan's simple reply. He didn't have any animosity against Price and didn't object to the examination but would like to know why it was now necessary.

"It's only that I must cross check the serial number to check it is the weapon you say it is, nothing more." Dylan invited him in, and they went into the lounge where Dylan retrieved his keys from a dish and unlocked the gun cabinet.

"It's the 7.62mm you're interested in, correct?" Price confirmed it was, and Dylan took his Remington 700 from the cabinet and turned it so Price could see the serial number.

"Great," Price said, jotting the number down in his notebook. "That's a magnificent weapon; what do you use it for?"

Dylan couldn't detect any trap in the question, and as with everyone who has an all-consuming hobby didn't mind talking about his weapons.

"I use it more to keep my eye in these days," he told Price, "there are not many competitions for this calibre; it needs to long a range to be any sort of a contest."

"Well, that is impressive," Price said as he was putting his notebook away.

"One more thing," Dylan said as he put the rifle back in the cabinet, "we can't have you going off with only half the information." Taking his keys again, he moved to the other side of the chimneybreast and now opened a smaller cabinet, this was where he kept his ammunition; he took out a box of 7.62mm cartridges and passed it to Price.

"You'll see they are not magnum rounds; the rifle isn't set up for magnums." Price noted it down in his notebook, again apologised for calling and left, Dylan gave a slight smile.

Ω

Hot on the trail of the police, Reg Bates turned up in the shop, he introduced himself and explained that he had been the one to break the story and was now looking for the follow up story, and as Inspector Cooper had come calling, he wondered if there was anything they could help him with.

"Like what?" Jim asked a bit aggressively.

"Hold on," Reg said, "I'm not here to look for who shot Sir Peter, from what I've discovered, he should have been shot at least twice."

"Hear, hear," came the voice of Janet.

"I see the lady knew Sir Peter?"

Jim, back in his usual friendly manner explained, "This is the mother of the boy who was shot by Sir Peter."

"Ah," Reg exclaimed, "I'm sorry I didn't realise. I really should check my facts before asking questions."

"Oh, I don't mind; I'm fairly used to it now," Janet explained.

"Tell me, Mrs?"

"Summers," Janet supplied.

Jim said, "Perhaps you would like to go into the office if you're going to interview Janet."

"That's very thoughtful," Reg accepted. "If the lady wouldn't mind answering my questions, I assure you there's no way I intend to malign anybody; I purely want to be able to put the full and true story into the national press."

Reg was ecstatic; he not only did have the original story, he was also getting the before and after as well. The staff in the shop was able to give him so much of the background and when this was added to his own research, it might allow him to get a book out of it. After he'd conducted his interviews, Reg decided to thank them by passing on the information that the judge at Sir Peter's trial had retired; it was very sudden, and it was clear he was jumping before he was pushed, as well as being worried the 'paladin' who shot Sir Peter might want to repeat it on the rest of those involved. Likewise, the head of the local CPS had taken a transfer to somewhere else and no one was saying where that somewhere was, and the police chief was also hard to find, so that shot hit more than one person.

By the time he'd finished, it was closing time, and Reg invited them all to the pub for a thank you drink, but all had somewhere to be apart from Dylan who usually ate at the pub and was happy to take Reg up on his offer. They went to the King's head, and over a couple of pints, Reg explained how he'd happened on the shooting and what he'd been able to find out since, and that was, that Sir Peter was a very nasty piece of work, and if he hadn't moved out of London when he did, then someone down there would have shot him.

Dylan called for another two beers, but the voice of Bill Jennings told the barman these were on him.

"Bill, nice to see you," Dylan said, "this here's Reg Bates; he's a reporter doing a background story on the shooting of both Terry Summers and Sir Peter."

"Well, you're talking to the right man," Bill told Reg. "I got most depressed over that trial and was ready to quit the force, but Dylan told me to hang on, and it'll come right so I did and he was right. I don't know if he did me a good turn or a bad turn, but at least, he was right that Sir Peter would get his just desserts;

anyway, I'm talking to a couple of blokes so it nice to meet you, Reg, and I'll see you tomorrow, Dylan."

"That was very interesting," Reg said after Bill had left them.

"What was?" Dylan replied nonchalantly.

"That you've got second sight?"

"Ah, that's nonsense. I was just trying to cheer the bloke up and stop him chucking up his whole career; it was just the way the timing worked out." Reg, like Jim before him, treated this with a very large pinch of salt, but there would be no point in pursuing the point, for he could see Dylan was not going to say any more, but he'd bear it in mind.

Chapter 26

Piet Botha, now known as Peter Franks, having reached Suffolk in the UK, in his quest to track down the sniper named Dylan, would, each evening, visit the local pubs in Colchester and the other towns and villages around the area of the barracks. Whenever he saw a group of soldiers, which was reasonably often as they were easy to spot, even in civvies they were too smart to be anything else, he would engage them in small talk. To strike up conversations, he used his knowledge of Afghanistan; a place nearly all had been some many times, and also about weapons, as he had done with the soldier at Kabul airport, as soldier to soldier, carefully moving the conversation to find out any information about the sniper, but either the ones he talked to didn't catch on to what he wanted, or didn't know this Dylan.

One evening, he entered a pub, in a quiet village called Ardleigh; he bought a drink and surveyed the bar, almost with what might have been shock, he saw sitting in one corner, the very soldier he had talked to at Kabul; he had to think hard to remember his name. *Mick something*, he thought, *yeah, Mick, Mick, Jones, that's it, Mick Jones*. He was sitting at a table with a couple of his mates; Piet went across.

"Well, hi, man," Pete said, "remember me?"

The lad looked up and recognition dawned on his face.

"Of course, I do," he replied. "Fancy meeting you here, do you live around here then?"

"No," Piet said, "I'm only here looking up people I knew out there, having a sort of a holiday."

Mick introduced his friends and explained where he and Piet had met. Piet drew up a chair and joined in their discussion where he could, and as the regiment hadn't been back from yet another tour in Afghanistan so very long, he was able to integrate quite well.

With a little help from Piet, it wasn't long before the talk turned to weapons, something they all had an interest in. Pete was explaining the different merits between the Scorpion and the Uzi when Mick gave him the lead he needed, if he wasn't to create undue interest.

"Piet here knows just about everything about guns," Mick told his mates.

"Nice of you to say so," Piet said, "but I may know a lot, but that's not everything, for instance, that sniper gun you told me about, I still don't know anything about that."

"Oh, yeah," Mick told all at the table, "the AI AMW, you know, the rifle that Dylan had, not the issue M24 but that fancy one he kept locked up even in the armoury."

"Who's this Dylan then?" Piet asked. "I remember you said he was a great shot, is he here still?"

"No," Mick said, "he'd finished his twelve and left."

"He joined up with Jim Baker, I think," added one of the others.

"That's right," the third soldier said, "they've opened a shop up in Norfolk somewhere, don't ask me where. I doubt Dylan ever told me, a close one he was, lucky if he said a word all day."

Piet let it lie at that and let the conversation move on into other areas; after an hour or so more and a couple of rounds, he made his excuses and left, happy in the knowledge of the who and approximately where to look.

Chapter 27

Jennifer Dolton was, as usual, removing her coat when, again as usual, Sir James spoke on the intercom.

"Wilcox to my office, when he manages to arrive that is."

John Wilcox happened to arrive exactly as the instruction was being passed; it was unusual, but the train had been on time this morning, so to Sir James's surprise, not that he allowed it to show, Wilcox entered the office almost as soon as he'd finished the request.

Passing a file across his desk he asked, "Have you got anyone who can sort out these two?"

These two, Sir James was talking about were the O'Brians, a pair of criminals, brothers, whose activities had finally come to the attention of 'The Section'. There had been meeting after meeting, at the highest levels, trying to work out how to handle the pair, but no section could come up with a solution that would remain within the law, but now, they had become too much of a problem, and it could not be left any longer. The imbalance they were causing in the criminal underworld was very unhealthy. The decision had, in the end, to be taken by the prime minister's office who requested 'The Section' to solve the problem.

Wilcox leafed through the file and thought for a moment.

"I've been expecting these two to become our responsibility. I've even done a little investigation; they're a bit difficult to get close to. But I think I might have just the man; he's worked for us before but under very different circumstances, and surprisingly, he has just re-appeared on our RADAR; he doesn't know anything about us yet, but he could be just the man if he'll take the job."

"Well, go and find out if he'll take the job, and don't stand here wasting time." Wilcox left.

Ω

For nearly a month after the death of Sir Peter and the visit from the police, nothing much happened in Dylan's life; he went back to his normal routine, at least as normal as they could with Janet still having bouts of grieving for Terry. He couldn't understand her grief; Terry had been killed and so had his killer, end of story. He couldn't understand it, but he realised she had need of the display of grief, so he just ignored it and kept out of her way when she was down.

One evening, while Dylan was putting some finishing touches to a model he'd been making for the last year, a pastime he enjoyed, it gave him something to do with his hands when he had no weapons to work on, the doorbell rang. It being fairly late in the evening he couldn't think who it could be. He had made some friends and acquaintances, having now lived here for a couple of years, but they were not the sort who would call on the off-chance, late in the evening, so he checked his camera monitors too see who it was.

The visitor was standing at an awkward angle to the camera so Dylan couldn't see his face; he couldn't see anything that caused him concern, although wary, he had no reason to think it suspicious, but it was unusual enough to make him show caution as he opened the door. He certainly knew the person outside the door but stood dumbstruck for more than a few moments upon seeing him.

"John," was all he could think to say.

It was for sure John Wilcox, didn't need to be told his name, but it's all that Dylan could think of; he was so astounded; they'd only met twice before, and that was, what seemed to be a long time ago, in Afghanistan. After the job he'd done for John, they'd debriefed, then John had got on an aircraft and that was it, Dylan had never expected to hear from John again. Now to see him standing outside his front door, this was totally confusing.

Dylan didn't know exactly who John was, or who he worked for; he was something to do with security and could make the police, the army and quite a few other departments jump to do his bidding, that was about all he knew about him, what could he want with him now?

Shooting Sir Peter, could he be part of that investigation? No, he couldn't tie him in to that; okay in the past, he'd done an unofficial shooting, but that was only doing what the army paid him to do, maybe a little different, but basically the same, it didn't relate into civilian life, or did it? He'd used the same rifle on both shootings, there had to be some connection there; John wouldn't visit just for old times' sake, of that Dylan was sure.

"You've got a blind spot in your camera setup," John said, "so you opened the door to someone you didn't know, that's bad practice. I expect you are wondering why I'm here, aren't you going to invite me in?" Finally, Dylan got over his paralysis and invited him in.

"You thought you'd seen the back of me, eh?" he said; he wasn't wrong but why now?

Dylan made way, and John walked in. Dylan showed the way to the lounge and invited John to sit. A thought struck Dylan.

"Are you working with the police now?" he asked, thinking he'd been too confident, about having left no tracks after the shooting.

"No," John said thoughtfully, "but you could say the police are working for me, at least I can ask them to do something, and they will, straight away, just like the army did before." He gave an uncustomary smile. "Don't worry; I'm not interested in your local troubles."

So, Dylan thought, *he does know about the shooting of Sir Peter, how?* He remained silent. John again flashed the twisted smile.

"Although your way of solving them I am interested in. You've no reason to worry about your recent reversion to type; the police are still totally in the dark, and they're happy to forget about the whole thing and would be pleased if everyone else would do the same. Of course, you want to know how I know all about it." *How right he is*, Dylan thought.

"You, my friend, were messy; you left a cartridge case on the ground under the tree, where the police search team were able to find it, and although I agree the police are a bit poor at finding a killer, they are very good at finding evidence and identifying where it came from."

"Winchester LUPRU 7.62mm, not common ammunition in this country, we don't have too many big animals to shoot. Now as you would know, or maybe you don't know, the manufacturer, Winchester Arms, in this case, keeps very good records. Every batch they make is properly listed as to the who, where, when, and such like, and the batch that the bullet that killed Sir Peter came from was sold to my department, indirectly at your instigation, and it seems this was a very good choice, they seem to have worked well twice." He lifted a questioning eyebrow, as if asking if maybe some more had been used. Dylan remained silent. "If you remember, I didn't even know what they were until you told me.

"We, my department that is, only ever brought one batch, of five hundred, for the job you carried out in Afghanistan, and I've every reason to believe there were some to spare, not really great detective work, but very messy on your part. I would expect better if you are going to work for me."

He was right again; it was a very messy procedure. Of course, his previous shooting had been in the military, so no one worries about clearing up cartridge cases, something to remember in future, Dylan silently agreed, something he needed to remember. Now what John had been saying brought his thoughts to a standstill.

"What's this about working for you?" he asked, genuinely mystified. "And, just for the record, I think I know what you do, but who are you, and who do you represent?" John had never given his surname while he was in Afghanistan, not even to the colonel.

"Good questions," he said, "but I can't tell you that; in fact, I can't tell you anything about the organisation I'm asking you to work for, that is work for as a contractor, not as an employee; we would call you only as and when we need your particular skills."

Dylan thought for a minute before answering, "Let me get this straight. The only real skill I've got is shooting, so I assume, you want me to go around shooting people, and to do it at the request of someone I don't know, for some organisation I've never heard of but who control the police, and so by implication are a sort of official department and can make the shooting of someone easy to dismiss? I think I'm going to need a bit more information than I have so far."

"That's a pretty good summation of the situation. There would, of course, be good remuneration, very good remuneration if it helps, but I can assure you it will always be in the national interest, unofficially, government sponsored, so what do you say? Are you interested?"

"Yes," Dylan eventually said, "you prove to me it's really official, national security type work and I'm in."

"Good, I thought you'd join; it's work you were made for." His smile was back. "Okay, so now for my bona fide. If you look online, you can find the phone number of MI5 in London. I could give it to you, but then, you couldn't be sure I wasn't trying to fool you. If you give them a call and ask for 'Mr Williamson in the lodger unit', you'll be transferred to another line, in a different building, a long way from MI5, and Mr Williamson will answer; he's actually expecting a call from you, so just tell him who you are and what you want, which is, am I genuine. I could give you the number now but that would prove nothing, so when you're ready."

Dylan found the number and made the calls; it all checked out. John was recognised and did belong to a government department; they could not tell him which department, but they could say it was part of the home office.

Dylan thought for a while if the proposition was true; it would be much like being in the army again, but with the flexibility of being able to say no, it sounded like it would suit very well. It would give him back that missing part of his mental balance and would certainly be more interesting than working in the shop, work he enjoyed, but where his true vocation could not be exercised, he had already thought of re-enlisting in the army for that very reason.

"Right," he said, "you've got me; you are what you say you are, as for your name? I doubt it is what you say it is, but does it matter? No, I don't think so, and you work for the government, so now tell me about the work. Who will give me orders? What's the pay and how do I contact you?"

"There, I thought you would agree; the work is in your blood, and you're probably already thinking of ways you could change this domestic life you're leading."

This man is reading my mind now, Dylan thought.

"Now let's get the ground rules sorted first. One, you will never be able to directly contact me. I'll occasionally contact you when I want to get more information or to explain something in greater depth." He took a small mobile phone from his briefcase. "Any contact you need to make will be with this phone; it's totally untraceable, and the only number you will ever need is pre-loaded. Someone will always be monitoring the number but will not answer you, so, when it's picked up at the other end, give your code name, say why you are calling and hang up. You'll be contacted, if necessary."

"What code name?" Dylan asked.

"Oh, yes, we've still got to give you one, have we not? Let's see." He thought for a moment. "I've got it, Nemesis, yes, that will do nicely. You remember who she was?" Dylan said that he did. "So when asked, just say Nemesis, whoever answers will know who you are and pass on to me what you have to say, so you could say I'm your controller, but it's possible even likely another member of the unit will need your services, but the person who answers the phone will know if that's the case."

"We will always help where we can, but bear in mind that if you make a mess-up, like with cartridge cases" – he gave a stern look – "we will not know you, but if circumstances cause a problem with the police or the like, we will help where possible. But don't take it as a licence to do as you like; we do have a lot of pull, with the police and such like. You'll be sanctioned by us, but that doesn't make you free to go hiring yourself out."

Dylan was beginning to wonder if he had made the right decision. John took a large envelope from his briefcase.

"This," John said, "is how you will receive your orders, probably by courier. If I need to explain some point, then I'll deliver it personally." He passed the envelope across. "In there is everything we know about the target, everything you should need to complete the task, open it, have a look."

The envelope contained a summary of the target, which was in fact two targets, two brothers named Sean and Rory O'Brian, who they were, where they lived, who their confederates were, where they could be found, at any time of day or year, and finally, a statement of why they were a prosecutable problem.

The men in this folder were criminals, not a bank robber type of criminal, but a controller of lesser crooks. They were men with connections, who could cause problems as high up as parliament. Dylan was impressed, not that there were criminals who could get help from parliament but with the detail in the folder, and it was all very detailed but left one or two questions unanswered.

"Why can't the police or special branch sort them out?"

"Yes, why not?" John replied. "You must remember they have connections. If the police try to create a case against them, they would be blocked, subtly, but blocked none the less, not in any way that could be used against the blocker, evidence would disappear, witnesses would change their mind, that's if they didn't also disappear; it has already happened, many times.

"So, what needs to happen is for their demise, and like with the last job you did for us, it needs to look like a criminal act, one crook shooting another, a burglary gone wrong, something like that. We have actually thought of a burglary, but it wasn't feasible; they live on the top of a tower block, and it's well guarded, that is where I think you, with your special talents, would come in.

"You'll get a lot of latitude in this job, to start with, you don't have to accept the task we give you, if you don't like something about it, use the phone and say you won't take it and give a brief summary of why. Likewise, if you are going to take the job on, just say that, and once you've accepted, the first half of your fee will be paid. You can carry the task out however and whenever you choose, but usually, we're in a bit of a hurry.

"In the file, you won't find any suggestions, only information. If you really need more, you can use the phone, but you'll have to work out the how for yourself. If you get any serious interference, again use the phone and we'll see what can be done, but it must not, repeat, must not be able, in any way, to be blamed on the government, or the security forces, understood?"

Dylan assured him that it was.

"Is this the first case you want me to solve?" he asked, indicating the file he'd been reading.

"Yes," John confirmed, "we would like it finished as soon as you can, but don't take any undue risks, keep it tight, and tidy if you need any special equipment, or help, use the phone, but not too often. Now I need you to sign these forms." He handed over a bunch of papers.

"I'm still cleared with the official secrets," Dylan pointed out. John's smile reappeared.

"If you started talking about the Section, or your contracts, it's not prison you'll be resting in, believe me." Dylan believed him; after all, that was what he was being employed for. He studied the papers; they were to open a bank account in the Isle of Man.

"I do have a bank account, you know."

Again, the smile.

"Not a bank that would accept large deposits without telling the taxman, and police." John stood, as the forms were handed back, he put them in his briefcase and turned to leave but stopped and asked, "When we discussed what weapons you took when on assignment, you said you always took a pistol, in case there was any close quarters action required?"

"Yes," Dylan agreed. John again opened his briefcase and handed Dylan a small package.

"I assume you don't have a pistol at present?"

"No, they're difficult to get hold of in this country."

"Well, then, that" – he indicated the package – "might come in useful, good night."

Dylan opened the package to find a new Glock 17, with a laser sight, silencer, and a spare magazine.

Part 3

Chapter 28

After John had gone, Dylan spent full five minutes looking at both the pistol and the file. He still could hardly believe it; he'd signed up to be a contract killer, albeit it was for National Security, he could say it was no different to what he did in the army, only a different department, for as before someone said kill and he killed. The only real difference was that now it would be a British citizen or someone who was living as a British citizen, but why should this bother him? He'd just acted as judge, jury and executioner where Sir Peter had been concerned, at least working for John's department or was it a section or even an organisation John had used all three, not that it mattered, he only had to be the executioner.

One part of what John had to say did bother Dylan, that was that he had been untidy, and if John had wanted to make life difficult for him, he could have, with the one little cartridge casing. He also didn't like the clause that he couldn't shoot anyone other than the people nominated; he was pretty sure if a situation, like the Terry killing and trial of Sir Peter, should come up again, he might want to do the same as he did this time.

Looking at the bulky folder on the table, he was tempted to start reading but decided he needed time if he was going to give it full justice; after all, two people's lives depended on his opinion. He could wait a few days before he decided to take it or not, at least he had that option.

Dylan slept well that night but still awoke feeling tired. He knew the reason, because this only happened when he had something on his mind, and the subconscious had been working it out. Over breakfast, the thing he had been worrying about now came to his conscious mind; it was the restriction on freedom of action with regard to an independent job. In the army, he had only killed the enemy, but now, he was a civilian and had the right to do as he pleased, not that he imagined he would be going around shooting people on a regular basis.

If he wished to shoot someone, not given to him by John, then he was going to have to have another illegal rifle, one that couldn't be traced even if he left a cartridge case behind. So, that was his first task, to get a rifle, preferably a 9mm because that ammunition was more freely available in this country, and he could get the bullets almost anywhere; it would need to be accurate, up to, say five hundred metres.

Armed with the current editions of the gun magazines he subscribed to, Dylan went to work.

When he arrived at the shop, all but Judy were in. After the usual greetings, Dylan nodded to Jim indicating they should go to the workshop. They could have gone to the office, but they knew only too well that Janet's hearing was back to normal and would probably detect everything they had to say.

"What's the problem?" asked Jim, in a worried tone.

"Nothing to cause any trouble but maybe a slight difficulty," Dylan said. Jim waited for an explanation. "Last night, I had a visitor. I can't tell you who, the fact is I don't know his name, but I do know who he works for, and this is top secret, no joking, he works for the government, but you'd never find the name of his department. Just take it I know he is what he says he is." Jim kept quiet and let Dylan get the story out.

"Now," Dylan continued, "they want me to do some work for them, not on a continuous basis but from time to time, and this means there would be times when I couldn't come in to work for maybe a few days—" Holding his hand up, Jim interrupted the flow of Dylan's words.

"Would this be the sort of work you did in the army?"

"I knew you'd catch on." Jim knew Dylan's previous work. "But the problem for us is my absences; you could say I'm working for the army as an occasional weapons trainer, or something like that, but the main problem would be the time I couldn't put in in the workshop."

"It's a pity you didn't tell me this last week; I had Rick Davies on the phone, you remember him?" Dylan agreed he did. "Well, he was looking for a job, and if I remember right, he was a pretty good armourer."

"He should be," Dylan said, "I trained him, have you still got a number for him?" Jim searched his mobile and found the number. "Well, call him and see if he's still available, if so get him up here."

Rick Davies was still looking for work, as he had been for three months now; it seems there wasn't much work for armourers in civvy street. Like Dylan and

Jim, Rick had finished his twelve years engagement and hoped he could get a more interesting job outside the army; he was wrong, at least until he received the call from Jim.

"Are you still on the unemployed list?" Jim asked.

"You'd better believe it," Rick replied. "Why? Have you found a job for me?"

"Maybe if you can get yourself up here to have a chat with Dylan." Jim told him.

"If you're on the level, then I can be with you this afternoon."

"Okay, will see you then." Jim hung up. "He'll be here this afternoon," he told Dylan.

True to his word, Rick arrived just after one. After the introductions to the ladies in the shop, the one of which, namely Judy, showed a little more than normal interest in Rick, Dylan took him through to the workshop and explained the setup and what would be expected. Rick took it all in and didn't see any reason why he wouldn't be able to manage. Dylan was happy with Rick's attitude and told Jim so, the terms of employment and salary were sorted out, and Jim asked when he could start.

"Would tomorrow be too soon?" he asked. "I would like to start straight away as I've been cooling my heels for some time now, and there's nothing to keep me down in Colchester." Jim and Dylan agreed he was welcome the sooner the better.

"Are you going to stay living in Colchester or moving up here?" Jim asked.

"I'd like to move up if you know of any rooms I could rent?"

"I've got a spare room," Janet cut in; she hadn't missed the look Judy had when she first met Rick and was already into matchmaking mode. But it was true she did have a spare room now that she didn't have Terry, and it would be good for her as well to have a man about the house when Fred, her husband, was off on the road.

"If you've got time this evening, you can come around and see it," she pressed. Rick agreed to do that but that he wanted to go get his things first, so it was agreed and Rick left.

There was still some time till closing so Dylan slipped into the workshop where he could look through his magazines. What he was searching for was someone wanting to sell a rifle of the sort he required; he didn't want to go to the dealers because they would want to see his licence and would record the sale and that was the last thing he wanted.

It was in the personal ads, of the fourth magazine he searched that he found what he was looking for, a private sale of a Markel Helix RX 9mm; it was listed as being in 'useable' condition, which could be read as poor, but he thought it was worth a try and got out his phone.

The person with the rifle was wanting fifteen hundred pounds for the weapon, which sounded a bit high for a 'useable' rifle, but Dylan agreed to have a look at it. They agreed to meet at the owner's house in Birmingham the next day, so Dylan told Jim he'd be out all day but to let Rick find his own feet for the day, and he'd be back on Wednesday.

Dylan's trip went well; he would have called the rifle in poor condition, but nothing he couldn't sort out, so they settled on a price of one thousand pounds, which Dylan had on him. The seller was more than pleased to get that much and didn't make a fuss about checking Dylan's licence, which was good by Dylan.

On Wednesday, Dylan took the rifle with him to work. Rick seemed to be settling in; he had accepted a room at Janet's house and was happy to be getting on with servicing a twelve bore. He saw Dylan's new rifle.

"What on earth are you doing with that?" he asked. "It looks like it needs to be scrapped."

"Listen here," Dylan responded, "this here is a good bit of machinery or at least it will be when I've finished with it, but you've never seen it because it doesn't exist, understand?"

Rick understood; he along with Jim knew Dylan's past, but still, he thought it was going to take a lot of work to get it into good condition, as Janet had apprised him of the shootings in the area. Rick wasn't the best at maths but 2+2 to him made 4, so he decided not to ask bloody silly questions, as Jim had put it.

Weapons manufactures and sales had by law to record all weapons sales but didn't have to do so for parts, so before even taking the Markel rifle apart, he ordered a new barrel from a manufacturer to the same specification, only longer. He had no knowledge of if the man he had bought it off had ever registered it or carried out a sample shot, so by changing the barrel, the rifling marks would be different and so the rifle would have disappeared. He then set about stripping the weapon down to its component parts. It was going to take at least a week to return it to its original condition, and it would take that long for the new barrel to arrive, but he didn't have a job for the rifle yet so he had the time.

That evening, Dylan started to read the file John had left; it was very bulky, and Dylan intended to read it carefully so expected to take a few evenings over it, but a start had to be made and this was it.

Chapter 29

Patrick and Rory O'Brian, not Irish, as the name suggests, but American, the third generation to be so. Their grandparents had come from Ireland in the 1920s, and taking up residence in New York, they had set out to build themselves a new life in 'the land of opportunity'.

Born of hard-working parents, who were greatly respected in the New York, Irish community, the brothers, from an early age, had been trouble, seeing their parents going out to work day after day, coming home worn out but well satisfied with their way of life. The brothers however had decided that it was not the lifestyle that would satisfy them. As usual, they together decided they did not intend to spend their lives scraping a living, working for someone else who took the profit of their labours, neither did they ever intend to spend the time and effort necessary to create their own business; they quite rightly considered that would still be hard work, and therefore not for them.

Even from an early age, they realised they could use the not small intellect, which they both had, rather than their muscles, which they also had, but from inheritance rather than by effort to make their fortunes, and the way to do that was in the criminal world. Rather than work, they would take whatever they could, whenever they could.

In their early years, they pilfered what they could and sold it where they could. By their late teens, they stole cars, burglarised warehouses, or private houses; they never specialised. If they could steal something that a fence would buy, then they stole it. They were both tall in height and burly in build and found their size was also good for low-level intimidation and protectionism, but here they had to be careful. Where they operated, there were already larger gangs who, with bigger and harder men, would react very unfriendly if the brothers stepped on their territory, doing so would probably end their careers and probably their lives, but they realised this and were very careful most of the time and carried weapons all of the time.

By the time they had reached twenty, they had made enough money to finance the next move on the path to success. Having watched the fences making more than them, out of the crimes they committed, they could see they were taking the risk and the fence was taking the profit; they decided that was the wrong way around so set about changing things.

As usual, the brothers didn't have any interest in putting in the effort to develop this new business. Herman Smith had been their fence for some years, so they considered it reasonable, that as they had indirectly paid for the business they should take over. Herman, of course, wasn't really given any alternative; the brothers paid him something for the business, and they let him continue to front the business for them, but as an employee, taking ten percent of the profit as wages. There was no negotiation about the takeover, only the suggestion that it would be much healthier for Herman if he sold out to them and then came to work for them. Herman had always avoided paying for protection now he regretted having done so.

Without realising it, the O'Brians had become businessmen, and they saw, that if instead of doing the dangerous work of stealing for themselves, they could use the myriad of lesser crooks, of which New York abounded, to supply their facilities, and with Herman to front the business, they would make more money but with no risk. Of course, fencing was also a crime but only if caught with the proceeds of a crime, so that was still Herman's responsibility.

They soon learnt, from Herman, where the most money could be made, when the merchandise was moved on, thinking if they were going to still be in danger from the law, then they wanted to make it worthwhile, to this end, the brothers would keep hold of the high-value items, gold, silver, jewellery and such like, leaving Herman to handle the rest.

As they built up a larger and larger collection of these items, they realised they didn't know what to do with them. Not knowing the first thing about handling this type of merchandise, and with Herman only too pleased to point out that they couldn't sell them, any jeweller would recognise them and report it to the police. Herman explained that he had always in the past moved that type of item on to other better connected fences.

Now the brothers could do the same as Herman had done, but that would mean someone else knowing their business and having to take a smaller return on the goods. Their problem was solved by chance when one of their 'suppliers' idly mentioned that a jeweller he used to deal with was about to get out of jail, it seems he had been caught modifying the jewellery for resale. The brothers were not slow to realise they would need a jeweller if they were going to make the most out of what they had.

Jerrold Hempton, a young man who was reported to be a very good jeweller, if a dishonest one, would not be welcomed back into the legitimate business of jewellery. He had been trained and employed by a reputable jewellery chain but had been caught 'working on the night shift' and had been imprisoned for three years; he had now done his time and was due to be released, coincidently just when the brothers had moved into the line of fencing jewellery.

The day Hempton came out, the brothers met him and made him an offer; they would set him up with a jewellery shop, and he would modify the jewellery they brought him. It was a perfect arrangement; the stolen gems would change size and shape; the settings would be melted down and made into new then sold in a legitimate shop. His return on his work would be ten percent of the profits, but he would have to be very careful, to keep a clear and honest accounting; it was a win-win setup; the thief who brought the item to the O'Brians got paid, Hempton got paid, and the O'Brians got the rest. The original item would have disappeared and be untraceable, so everyone was safe. Hempton knew he would never be able to find honest employment, but honesty was not what the O'Brian brothers dealt in; he accepted the offer immediately.

By the time they were twenty-five, the brothers had become very successful, and wealthy, but like many who are doing well, they began to think they could do anything they like and no one could touch them. Of course, they were wrong.

Ω

The poet Jonathan Swift once wrote:
Big Fleas have smaller fleas
upon their backs to bite them,
And smaller fleas have lesser fleas
and so, ad infinitum.

The brothers had never been big fleas while they lived in America, but by the same token, they were not the lesser fleas, but they occasionally forgot their place in the general scheme of things, and eventually, the day came that they 'did bite' the wrong person, and their luck ran out.

On the day in question, one of the sneak thieves who supplied them came with the news that another fence had set up and was insisting they take their pickings to him, and he had some bullyboys who were there to impress upon him the importance of doing so.

The O'Brians had good reasoning abilities, but when they thought they were being leaned on, they tended to get a bit rash, so it was this day, they didn't bother to find out who was backing this new fence; they could see it was some sort of a takeover and reacted in their usual way. Making a personal visit to this new fence, they wished to correct his ideas. In the course of discussions, O'Brian-type discussions, two of the bullyboys protecting the fence got shot and killed; the fence was also shot but only wounded. When the brothers had calmed down, they quizzed the fence and found out from them he was protected by the local syndicate; they were in trouble.

It didn't take long for them to realise their mistake; they agreed they were in trouble, serious trouble; it looked as if they'd finally made the big mistake they had always tried to avoid. What to do, there could be no question of saying sorry and making up; they'd killed two syndicate soldiers, that wouldn't be forgiven, and they didn't have sufficient firepower. There was never more than the two of them to protect their businesses, so they again shot the fence, killing him this time, at least he wouldn't be able to tell, that would buy them some time.

A night of talking and arguing about their options left them with the only possibility, and that was to run, to run as far and as fast as they could. Fortunately, they had always thought someday they would have to leave but thought it would be the law who would be after them. They already had obtained false papers and passports, that had been common sense considering the line of business they were in and could leave almost immediately.

In the morning, Patrick went online and booked tickets to Miami, then with another ticket agent from Miami to Spain and finally from Spain to the UK. Rory in the meantime had gone to see Hempton; he explained the situation and that it wouldn't be safe for him when the syndicate made the connection between them. So, the suggestion was that Hempton should liquidate the business, then make his way to Europe. Herman would once again be the owner of the fencing business, but he could tell who the backers were, so for safety' sake they killed him. By the evening, the O'Brian brothers were on their way; hopefully, they would be clear before the hue and cry started.

By the time Hempton had arrived in the UK, the brothers had already found a shop and workshop, taken delivery of some of the items from the New York shop that had been smuggled over, and so Hempton was able to get back in business almost straight away. The brothers had also been lucky in finding a thief by way of being accosted in a pub and offered, what had to be stolen, watches; they'd bought all he had and told him they would buy anything else that he came across, and to spread the word.

Their entry into the British underworld didn't go unnoticed by the local members, and this brought about a visit from some representatives of the same. After the visit and the disappearance of the three members of the deputation, the O'Brians were left to run their business how they wished.

As their legal, jewellery shop, and illegal fencing businesses prospered so they were welcomed into the social side of the community. They were invited to join, the round table and rotary, and eventually joined the Masons. This last elevated them into the upper level of society, where they made the contacts that would increase the value of their businesses and their importance. They became known in legal and government circles, with many people willing to assist them, in any way they could.

Now they were accepted as members of higher society; they considered they should have all the trappings of that status so had decided they should have a country place, just like the Brits, somewhere they could invite their 'important' friends and acquaintances to. They considered Scotland, with its shooting and fishing, a good attraction for the important people, but that was considered too far; they would want to be able to get back to London in a hurry if needed. East Anglia looked good but was too crowded; in the end, they decided on Wales.

The O'Brian illegal businesses thrived, mainly because their opposition knew of them and steered clear of them, and those that didn't steer clear, moved away, at least that's what was all that anyone would say if someone asked where they were. It was this dominance of the criminal world of London that brought the O'Brians to the attention of the police.

The Metropolitan police had a large file about them held as an 'eyes only' file, but in all the file, everything was speculation; there was nothing that could be held against them. When someone decided to review the file and start an investigation, they would come up light of evidence and heavy of lawyers, and if an investigator suggested he might be on to something, it would be decided, by 'someone up there' to move him onto other work, that more suited his talents. So, in fact, the brothers, through their contacts, had become untouchable.

Ω

In the morning, Dylan followed his usual routine, but although there wasn't much workshop work to do, and what there was Rick could handle, so he continued working on the new rifle, he wanted it to be perfect by the time he finished, even going to the trouble of re-varnishing the stock which he had re-set to his own requirement. At the end of the day, the three males of the shop workforce visited the pub, and the ladies went home. Rick had been told when dinner would be ready and to make sure he was there.

"I see you're getting to know Janet," Jim joked. "I suppose we should have told you but that would have spoiled our fun." Rick took it all in good part. When Jim and Rick left. Dylan had his dinner then went home to re-read the file.

Chapter 30

The following morning, Dylan made the first call on the phone John had given to him; the voice that answered spoke in a monotone, with no sign of any accent; there was nothing that could give any idea of where he might be. He told the voice he was Nemesis and that he would be accepting the task that John had given him. Dylan stopped talking, and then after five seconds, the call was ended by the other party. "As John said, no conversations," he said to the silent phone.

After the call, he went into work to find his new barrel for the Markel rifle had arrived, now he could spend the day finishing the re-build. Rick had finished the shotgun he had repaired and asked about testing it.

"That's what we'll be doing tomorrow," Dylan told him. "We'll go over to the army camp in Swanton Morley and use their range."

As soon as Dylan had arrived in Dereham, he had looked for somewhere to shoot; the previous owner had had to travel to Cambridge, to find a range that would suit all the requirement of the shop. Dylan, however, being ex-army went to the close-by camp and asked for an interview with the adjutant, asking to join their shooting club. When he recited his previous experience, they welcomed him, with open arms.

Once he was a member of the club, he asked if it would be okay to use the range when he had weapons to test after repair, this needed the Cornel's permission so the request was put in, and he okayed it. Dylan hoped the shop would be able to make its own range one day, but that would have to wait until they had made a lot more money.

Thursday was spent at the army camp with Rick testing the shotgun and Dylan testing and setting the Markel. When they returned to the shop, Dylan informed Jim he would be away for the next few days, probably all next week as well, but with Rick now happy with the work involved, Jim had no objections. Janet, however, did her best to find out where he was going, but try as she might she failed.

That evening, Dylan felt he had absorbed all that was relevant from the O'Brian file for him to start his own research. Taking out his laptop, not something that happened very often, he set about finding just where the O'Brians might be found. They owned three nightclubs, located in Bayswater, Paddington and Shepherds Bush, five jewellery shops, generally spread across London, and a penthouse in the Riverside apartment tower block in Pimlico.

The brothers might be expected to visit any or all of these on a day-to-day basis, but he could disregard the shops; they would be far too public to have any chance of making a shot.

The night clubs offered a better chance, depending on the layout and level of occupation of the streets they were in, all three were situated in the west end; one in Spring Street in the Paddington area, one in Ossington Street in Bayswater and the third in Dewhurst Street in Shepherds Bush.

Finally, and the most likely, would be the penthouse apartment where they lived, again, this would mean he would have to find another building that was at least as high as theirs or even higher if possible. Using the internet, he saw buildings on the south side of the river that looked promising.

Dylan was up early enough on Friday to catch the 7:30 commuter train from Norwich to London's Liverpool Street station, where he arrived at 9:30. Then he had to face the stifling heat and crowds on the underground, not a new experience to him but not one he had carried out very often, and being an outdoor type person, not one he wanted to repeat very soon.

He'd decided to start his recon, by taking a look at the nightclubs, and from Liverpool Street, he was able to take the Central line, all the way to Shepherds Bush without changing.

The building was an old Victorian townhouse; it consisted of four or five storeys in height and the front door opened directly on to the street, with no more than couple of wide steps. The street was lined on both sides with similar houses.

Looking at the street from a sniper's point of view, Dylan could see nothing but problems. The choice of a shooting position would have to be from one of the houses opposite, or at least reasonably close to the club, but they were all residential and all looked occupied. Even if he found a vacant one, or one that had been converted onto a business, the distance from the club's door, to where a vehicle would stop, was about ten feet, so when the target came out he would only be in sight for a maximum of two seconds. If the target was going in, the time might be longer as Dylan could anticipate his getting out of the car, but it still wouldn't be much time, unless he decided to stand and have a chat with the doorman. Dylan didn't consider this a reasonable possibility, and even if it was, it would only get him one of the two targets he was looking for, this he had to consider was a no go.

Returning to the underground station, he took the train back as far as Notting Hill Gate where he changed on to the circle line to Bayswater, then walked to Ossington Street. The second of the clubs. Dylan was starting to get the opinion that the same architect must have had a very busy time at the end of the nineteenth century, for the buildings in Bayswater look no different than those in Shepherds Bush; they also offered no better chances, and there was just no good position from which to take a shot. The same, once again, could be said when he moved on to Paddington. It was clear now that he only had one option left if he didn't want to have to follow the two brothers around, day after day, for who knew how long, just looking for an opportunity to get a walk by shot at the two of them.

Once again, he returned to the underground, now taking the Bakerloo line to Oxford Circus then changing on to the Victoria line and travelling the four stops to Vauxhall. A short walk from the station and he was looking at the famous River Thames.

For all its history, and all the poetry and prose written about it, the swollen turbid mass of water, that was the great river, was a disappointment when first encountered. No more was it a free-flowing dangerous artery of the seething city of London, with its waters contained within the concrete and stone walls, and its vastness crossed by many bridges, it looked almost placid, at least this was Dylan's opinion as he looked over the parapet of the Vauxhall Bridge. To be fair, it was probably at high tide so would be resting until the tide turned.

From the centre of the bridge, he was able to take a good look at the Riverview Apartments. Leaning back against the parapet, drinking the coffee he'd picked up at a coffee shop outside the station, he studied the apartment block.

Situated on a corner where the Vauxhall Bridge Road crossed the Millbank just as it started over the Vauxhall Bridge, the apartment block was impressive, sixteen storeys high and rounded on all sides, looking like three tubes stuck together. All the apartments had balconies apart from the top two that had terraces, which is only reasonable considering the extra price the owners would charge for being at the top, weather balcony or terrace they would have exciting views over the Thames and south London.

With the MI5 building directly across the river, the O'Brian brothers must have thought it a tremendous laugh, that from the luxury of their terrace, they could look at the top British criminal detection organisation positioned directly opposite, the very place that housed the people who would most like to get rid of them.

Having had a wasted morning looking at the nightclubs, Dylan now, having looked around and along the banks on both sides of the river, could at last see, this was the place, and the only place that had the potential to offer the opportunity he needed. On the south bank, there was plenty of building work in progress, and most of it looked like it was going to be in the region of thirty or forty storeys high, so provided he could get into the building sites they would make it an easy shot, providing of course the O'Brians used the terrace, he was sure they would sooner or later, even if only for a smoke.

Dylan moved from the bridge to the Millbank, here he leaned against the railings outside of an impressive house made of Portland stone that shone stark white in the afternoon sunlight. It was positioned right across the Millbank from the apartment block, a useful position where, for the next half hour, he could see all the comings and goings through the main entrance.

In the vestibule of the apartments was a reception desk with a receptionist who controlled the opening of the main doors, that would definitely stop any idea of getting into the building unseen, unless there was an underground garage, something to think about if he wanted to make a close quarters attack, but this was unlikely. If they had positive security in reception, then it was pretty sure they would have the same in whatever parking arrangement there was. His information folder told him the researcher had thought the same, but he liked to check things himself when he could.

He moved back, once again, on to the Vauxhall Bridge where he could take another look at the apartments from the riverside of the building. As with the front, there was an entrance, but inside it was the same vestibule, again with receptionist-controlled entry.

John in his notes had anticipated the only way to attack would have to be from a long shot. Dylan was now coming to accept this to be correct; it should be no problem to get the necessary height for a shot. Looking downriver, he could see at least six or seven likely buildings, and it would not necessarily need to be an overly long shot if he could use them.

Some of the buildings were residential and some commercial, both offering security problems, in that they would have active security; nobody took a chance in this end of London. If you could afford the apartment, then you could afford the security. But that still left four that had not yet finished being built, and although they would also have guards roaming the sites, they would be more interested in stopping thieves, who would be looking to steal the equipment, not to use the building itself. Once inside the building, he would probably have the whole thing to himself.

Although he knew he couldn't work inside the apartment building, he still crossed the road and rang for entry. The girl at the reception desk looked at him through the glass assessing if he had a right to enter. Finally, she decided he was not a resident and pressed the intercom button.

"Can I help you?" she asked, never taking her eyes off of him.

"Yes," Dylan replied, "I'd like to know about the apartments if any are available, would you be able to help me with that?" In response, the girl pressed the button to unlock the door. Dylan entered and approached the reception desk.

"What would you be looking for in particular?" she asked.

"Something towards the top and on the riverside."

"We do have some vacancies," she said, passing him a fancy brochure, "but they are on the lower floors, I'm afraid, and generally not so popular as the higher levels, though they are the same size and layout as the other higher floors."

"That's a pity," Dylan replied in a sombre tone, "but just how high are the highest vacancies?"

"We've two on the fifth floor," the girl informed him, "and there's still a really good view from there. Would you like someone to show you?"

"No, thanks, I had been hoping you might have something about the tenth or above, but if you haven't, then you haven't, but thanks for your help." Dylan made his way out still holding his brochure.

Ω

Standing once again, in the middle of the bridge, he again surveyed the riverbanks on the south side of the river, but this time concentrating on the Eastward downriver direction. He ignored the building directly opposite the apartments on the opposite bank; he didn't think the security at MI5 would be that lax, as to let him use their roof. There were some very tall buildings within easy shot of the Riverview Apartments, but again, they looked like they were fully occupied so would probably have some good security, or at least the chance of meeting a resident, but their roofs could be used if he could get access, but he would only try that if it became really necessary.

There was one building that did catch his attention; it was still being built, a very good possibility depending once again on access. The building currently stood sixteen storeys high, but the staircase and elevator shaft had already been constructed and was at least ten or more storeys above that. If he could get in, he would have plenty of levels to choose from, to get the right downward angle onto the O'Brian's terrace; it would also mean the range would probably be no more than six or seven hundred yards.

Dylan left his place on the bridge and walked on to the south bank; he had to go around the MI5 building then cut back between the next two before he was able to walk along the riverbank. He followed the bank until he reached what would, he now found out, become the Dumont building, so the hoarding informed him.

Sitting on the embankment wall, he took his time to look at all there was to see, with an eye to the position he would need for the shots. This would be the first time he had shot in a built-up area, previously his work had been in the open country, so now he not only had to consider where to take the shot from but who could see the position from another building. Some of the buildings close-by were taller than the one he was considering, but mostly, they were unoccupied.

Despite the problems he would have with the shot, one thing he was certain of was that the shot would have to be at night after the surrounding buildings and building sites had quietened down and the workers gone home. He would need darkness to get through the ground level of the building; it would be the area that most of the security guards would concentrate on. So, he would have to take up position after dark and be gone before dawn, that meant he had a window of maybe six or seven hours.

He was obviously going to have to spend some nights watching, just to get an idea of the O'Brian brothers' movements. As for today, he would be happy if he could test a way onto the site and up to the higher levels. The site fronted onto the road and had a high fence made of plywood boarding up to a height of perhaps ten feet; the only break on the fence was an entry gate, but this was controlled by a gatekeeper.

Dylan slowly strolled along the embankment until the hoardings finished, and he could see the fencing along the side of the site was normal chain link all the way to the rear of the site. Taking a good look at the fencing, he could see it wasn't in the best of repair; the potential was clear to see.

Dylan had seen all he could for now, he decided to move away return when the workers knocked off and the site got dark.

Ω

He walked along the embankment till he reached the Lambeth Bridge, here he crossed back to the north bank. He walked back to the Vauxhall Bridge Road and turned left towards Victoria continuing to walk until he found a café where he could get a full meal.

Over his meal, he glanced through the literature the girl at the reception desk had given him; he still had it, although he couldn't say why he had kept it, for there was nothing in it that gave any more insight to what he had expected the apartments to be like.

When alone and with time on your hands, you are likely to read anything that is available, so it was with Dylan all he had was the brochure so he idly read it not with any interest, but surprisingly, it did become useful. Towards the back of the booklet, he spotted an item; it told him that all the glass in the riverside apartment building was extra toughened, so as to make it impossible to fall through.

This was important information; he was well aware of the problem that toughened glass could cause, with a bullet coming in at an angle, it could skid slightly instead of making a clean entrance and become deflected. Also, the extra pressure needed for it to penetrate the glass would make it distort thus changing its aerodynamic characteristic. The hunting ammunition relied on this deformation but only after hitting the target. Really, to be sure of the shots, he needed the O'Brians to be on their terrace, so he was hoping they were the sort of people who liked giving parties, or at least smoked outside the apartment.

At six o'clock, he was back on the south bank close to the building site; the workforce was beginning to leave, checking out at the main gate. By 6:30, they had gone, and the gate had been locked. In the evening twilight, the security lights started to glow gradually increasing in intensity as the sky darkened.

Dylan now, from his position across the road, saw four security guards come out of the gatehouse and split up into pairs and begin to walk their patrols. The amount Dylan could see was limited because of the hoardings and his need to stay out of sight of the gatehouse. He moved a little way along the road to the next site; this building was not lit up, but although the building was not completely finished, there was no equipment around the outside of the building, and there was a light on inside though so they did have security.

Intense lighting has two effects; firstly, it illuminates the area it's directed at, but secondly, it makes the darkness not in those areas more intense. Dylan could see a path passed the second building right up to the fence of the Dupont building site. The site-surrounding fence at this point was not totally joined and a gap that had probably been used as a back gate at one time or another was wide enough for Dylan to enter unseen from either building. From this point on, everything became illuminated, but once again, the two effects of lighting came into effect, it could clearly show Dylan to the guards if he moved in any further, but at the same time, it showed the guards to Dylan. So by watching them and timing their patrol and using the dead ground supplied by the equipment in the yard, Dylan was able to work out a way across the yard and into the building.

He stayed for long enough to twice time the patrol length of the guard's routine. The one pair walked the outside of the site while the second went into the building. After thirty minutes, the pair who had gone inside came out and returned to the gatehouse. The outside pair took another fifteen minutes to complete their patrol. Thirty minutes later, the four reappeared but this time changed which patrol they took. So, Dylan thought the patrols took an hour with a thirty-minute break between; the guards inside only took forty-five minutes so couldn't have gone very high up the building.

"Mission accomplished," he said to himself, "time to go home."

Chapter 31

The poet Rudyard Kipling wrote:

"I knew six little china men, they taught me all I knew. Their names are What, and Why, and When, and Where, and How, and Who."

Piet Botha, who didn't know any of Kipling's poems, or even that he had existed but as far as his quest went, he was working his way through Kipling's six requirements for knowledge. So far, Piet had established: the who, Dylan Williams, the why, was what drove him so he knew that well enough, the what, was simple, to shoot and kill him, the same as Williams had done to Deon, Johan, Dutchy, and Sam, when they all met in the mountains of northern Afghanistan. The how would be by surprise and the small Sig Sauer P938 he had brought with him from Italy, leaving only the where and the when to be established, they were what he was working on at that time.

Fortunately, for his first day in Norfolk, it had been dry. The rain of the past couple of weeks had passed, so Piet, who had spent most of the day walking around Dereham, had remained dry. Coming to a new town or city, he always liked firstly, to get a feel of the place and then to locate his objective; in this case, the objective was the sporting goods shop half owned by the Dylan Williams; he thought this would be the most likely place to find him. Dereham isn't a big town, so finding the shop wasn't difficult; there was only the one. There was a small café along the road so he settled in to observe the shop.

The comings and goings to the shop did not reveal anything of interest, not that he could have recognised Williams, even if he bumped into him. When they had last met, Piet had been running for his life, not waiting to get an introduction.

He asked the woman running the café if she knew a Dylan Williams, and she was only too pleased to tell everything she knew, and that was that the sporting goods shop was owned by Dylan, along with his partner Jim Baker, who was a member of the chamber of commerce and the round table and numerous other things. All this information about a Jim Baker he didn't want to know, but until he found an opening, to get the talk back to Williams, he had to listen. Eventually, she did finish regaling him with the merits of Jim Baker and returned to the subject of Williams.

She gave a very good description of Williams, which Piet knew, from his observations, meant that he was not in work today, at least he hadn't been seen going in or out of the shop. He asked if she knew where Williams lived, but on this point, she wasn't sure; she thought it was somewhere out by the Tesco's; it was down that way, but she wasn't sure exactly where.

It had taken nearly an hour to get all he could from the café owner. Piet wasn't unhappy when he managed to finish the, largely one-sided, conversation and got out of the place.

"They'll know in the shop," she suggested, but Piet didn't think that would be a good idea, but he went that way when he left the café to make it look as though he was going to ask. Once out of sight, he instead followed the advice given, as to the area of town the lady thought Dylan might live.

The area only had one housing estate, and a few other houses spread along the road, but Piet, not being a natural sleuth, couldn't think how to identify which house belonged to Williams. He accosted a number of people, but they didn't know; he could just wait and hope to see him arrive, but that would not only be a bit hit and miss, anyone seeing him might think he was a burglar looking the area over or something like that. Either way, hanging around would cause suspicion so he decided to go and find a hotel for the night, and in the morning, he could probably find a postman, the one person who would know where everyone lived.

Ω

It was late when Dylan returned from the big city, but first, he had to decide on his plans for tomorrow; he was torn between going back to London and getting on with the job or taking up the invitation he had received to take part in a shooting competition from a gun club on the coast, up in Lincolnshire. He felt he really should get on with the job, but John had said he could take what time he needed too. He finally decided on the competition; it would be a nice relaxation, and he could also test the resurrected Markel rifle, for the first time in competition over a thousand yards, and a few practice rounds with the AI at that range would be useful.

Although he'd been late to bed, he was up and about by 6:00 the next morning, and after a quick shower and an even quicker cup of tea, he was off to spend the day doing the only thing he really enjoyed.

Ω

Piet arrived back at the housing estate at a little after 8:00, the next morning; he hadn't expected the postman to be any earlier than that. He picked up a coffee from the close-by McDonald's, found a seat near a bus stop and waited. The postman arrived in his van at a quarter to nine, drove a little way along the road into the housing estate then parked; he was getting his mailbag out of the van when Piet asked him where a Dylan Williams lived.

"It's just up there," the man said, "number five, the one with the cream paint on the side." Piet thanked the man; now he was committed, if he didn't go to the house, it would seem suspicious; it didn't really matter he intended to shoot the moment the door opened; he didn't have anything to say to the man and would be away before the locals had any idea of what had happened.

He slowly walked to the bungalow the postman had indicated; he saw no one else around, obviously it was a dormitory estate, and the workers and school children who lived there had already left for work, leaving housewives and pensioners, who wouldn't start their day until later.

The postman had started his deliveries in the other direction and now was out of sight, leaving the street empty. Piet opened the gate and went up to the door; he thought Williams would probably be able to see him arrive if he was looking out of the window but considered this wouldn't really matter, because Williams had never seen him up close. He rang the doorbell and at the same time removed the Sig Sauer from his belt; it was his intention to shoot whoever opened the door; he'd learned the day before that Williams was not married, so it should be him who answered.

Nobody answered, Piet rang again with the same result, then he heard a female voice behind him.

"He's not in," the voice said in a friendly tone; he quickly re-pocketed the pistol and turned to the woman who was looking over the fence. "He went out early this morning, much the same as yesterday."

"Have you any idea when he might return?" Piet asked.

"No, sorry," she replied, "it's his work, you see, he often has to go a long way to deliver guns and things. I wonder that old Land Rover of his keeps going the state it's in. You're not from around here, are you?"

"No, I'm just a visitor."

"I thought so, it's your accent, you see. Australian, isn't it?"

"No, it's South African; they do sound a bit alike though." That was a mistake, Piet thought. Never give away information that might be used to identify you later, but it was that habit the British had of always calling him Australian, and like most of his countrymen, he detested it.

"Well, I'll try again tomorrow," he said.

"That's a good idea," the woman said as she also turned to return to her house.

Well, at least I know he's got a Land Rover, so until I see it in his drive, I've no need to knock at the door, he thought.

Ω

It was gone midnight before Dylan's Land Rover pulled into his drive; it had been a long day, although he wanted to go straight to bed, his discipline would not let him. The next day he would establish himself in London and hopefully make his first attempt to carry out his mission. His recognisance had shown him the where he needed to be to take the shot, and that told him what equipment he would need. He didn't want to leave it to the morning to get things ready, for then it would be a rush, and he was sure to forget something.

Diligently, he set about getting his equipment ready for the following day when he would start the observation and hopefully the shots.

The German style grey camouflage coverall and mask he had decided would be the best match if he was going to be resting against new concrete. Food wouldn't be necessary, for he would have to leave his hide each day well before daylight and the arrival of the builders, so he would have all day to eat, but he packed some bottled water and a flask for coffee; in London, there was always a café close by, where he could get a flask filled.

He placed all his equipment in a pull-along case, including the Glock and holster. The rifle he left in its own case; there was nothing to identify the contents of the case, although a person who knew weapons might recognise it for what it was, but to anyone else it was only a silver-coloured, metal case with locks and a handle. Having prepared everything he thought he would need, he finally allowed himself to go to bed.

Chapter 32

After arriving in London, Dylan spent the morning finding a suitable hotel, he needed one that could accept what would be a nocturnal working pattern, this turned out to be a lot easier than he expected, not being a regular visitor to the big city he hadn't realised the life of a big city operated on a 24/7 system. The hotel he found was a little off of the Vauxhall Bridge Road and that was well within walking distance of the building site that he intended to establish his hide.

He settled himself into the room, putting the small amount of clothing he had brought along into the draws, then reviewed his equipment. Taking the small backpack from the pull-along case, he placed the items he would need this evening, water, Glock, cams, monocular, and protein bars in. It was at this point that he saw he had made one important mistake, in that the colour of his gun case was a nice bright aluminium, which in the night time lighting of the building site would shine out like a beacon, this was something he must fix, now.

Leaving the hotel, he found a hardware shop, in a small parade of shops a little way along from the hotel and was able to buy two tins of acrylic spray paint in a dark blue colour. Returning to the hotel and considering he didn't have a balcony attached to his room, he thought he might have to go outside to find somewhere to spray the case, but in doing so, he would be bound to cause interest. He climbed the stairs to investigate the roof, being pleased to find an easy access and room to do his spraying.

The best thing about using an acrylic paint was that it dried very quickly, and within an hour, he had been able to give the gun case two coats of paint and take it back to his room, fully dry and nicely toned down, to the extent that it would be as invisible as himself, this evening, although it still smelt of acetate, so he left the room's window wide open. Having completed these preparations for the evening, he settled back on his bed and fell instantly asleep, something he had always been able to do under almost any circumstances, day or night.

Dylan awoke at 4:00 in the afternoon, took a shower, dressed and collecting up his equipment left the hotel. He found a restaurant not far away and had a meal, before heading along the road, and over the Vauxhall Bridge, and coming to the building site as the last of the workers left. A quick scan of the situation told him everything was looking the same as on his previous visit.

The evening was drawing on and the light steadily reducing; he considered he might be memorable, carrying his pack and case, so decided not to loiter near the site. Carrying on down along the south bank of the river, he reached the Lambeth Bridge, crossed it and walked back towards the Vauxhall Bridge along the Millbank, stopping to sit for a while outside the Tate Britain art gallery.

Ω

By the time he had returned to the building site, it was full dark, at least as dark as it ever got, with all the lights of London glowing bright, but the streetlights and the security lights only increased the darkness in the covered and sheltered places. Slipping into the adjacent, nearly completed site, Dylan concealed himself in a dark corner and put on his cams. Leaving his pack in the dark corner and only taking the gun case with him, he carefully moved to the gap in the security fence he'd found the last time, now he waited.

It was a little after 8:00 when the security patrols came out of the gatehouse and began their slow way around the site. Two of the guards separated from the other two and went into the building, while the remaining two strolled around the perimeter as before.

The guard's patrols once again took a little less than an hour, and they were back in the gatehouse by 9:15. Dylan now moved, slipping between the machinery and building materials until he finally was able to enter the building. Stopping a little inside the building, he now waited, everything was quiet, he'd caused no alarm, and the guards were all in the gatehouse.

A quick look around to establish the position of the stairs, he walked over to them and began to climb. Fortunately, a short while after, they took over the shop; Dylan had noticed how Jim's waistline was spreading, it made him think, the same could happen to him, what with standing around the workshop or sitting in the car.

PT and gym work were something he'd always hated when he was in the army, but he had to admit it did do what it was supposed to, and that was to keep the soldiers fit. So, Jim's waistline had inadvertently been the cause of Dylan joining the gym in the local leisure centre. He didn't want to overdo it though, just twice a week he felt was more than enough, now as he plodded his way up the staircase, he was glad he did. Arriving at the nineteenth floor, he took a few moments to steady himself; he might be reasonably fit but nineteen floors equalled a lot of stairs.

Taking the monocular from his pocket, he took his first good look at the O'Brian penthouse. To an outsider, there was nothing to see, to the sniper, there was a whole book full of information; he could see the range and declination of the target; he could see there were no lights visible, so he could surmise there was no one there, so this told him the brothers must still be out. *Well*, he thought, *they did have clubs that they would have to keep an eye on*.

In truth, Dylan had not expected to see anyone this early in the evening, one or two o'clock would be a more natural time for them to get home, and it was only Monday, not a night for having people around for a party, although they might have a meeting or such like and so he would and be ready if or when they came out onto the terrace.

Dylan made his preparations; he assembled the AI rifle, checked the sights and measured the range; he allowed himself a coffee from the flask he had filled at the hotel and ate a protein bar, being careful to put the wrapper in his holdall.

What a good boy am I, Mister John, he thought.

While still smiling at his own witticism he sighted through the Schmidt & Bender sight. Everything was almost the same as when he had looked through his monocular, apart that he could see a light, not in the main room but shining through the doorway into the room. Not knowing the reason for the light to come on, he kept the sight on the doorway, watching for anything. After something like ten minutes, the lounge lights came on and a maid came in; she was carrying a covered tray. *Putting out some supper for the bosses*, Dylan thought, as he watched the maid put the tray on a coffee table then leave the room turning the lights off after herself. "Not expecting the brothers home just yet," Dylan mumbled to himself.

In the end, his estimation was right; it was a quarter after one when the lights came on in the penthouse, and he was able to see the brothers. They made themselves a drink, took the cover off of the tray and helped themselves to whatever was on it. They stood talking in the centre of the lounge, not sitting down so looking like they would not be staying up much longer, this proved to be the case. A little before 2:00, they left the room switching off the lights including the one that must have been in the hallway and left the penthouse in total darkness. Dylan watched until 4:00, then descending far enough down the building to be able to watch the guards; he was able to leave the site unobserved at 6:00 and return to the hotel.

Ω

On the Tuesday, Dylan again entered the building site in his usual manner and made his way to the now familiar nineteenth floor. As on the day before, the lights were out in the penthouse across the river, but the nature of his work meant that he had the patience to wait without suffering boredom.

A little after midnight, Dylan heard voices. They were coming up the staircase, as yet he could not define what was being said, but they were definitely getting closer; it had to be the security guards coming up to inspect the upper floors, not a thing they had done before. He now had to quickly decide whether to remain where he was or to go down on to one of the completed floors. If he stayed, he would be trapped, as the only way out was down; however, if the purpose of the climb was for the guards to check the complete floors and he went down on to what was currently the roof, he could be caught out in the open; he decided to stay where he was. Dylan could now hear the voices clearly.

"I hate it when we get new men on the team," said one voice. "That's the only time we have to come all the way up here, and there's not much point in doing it anyway." The man was obviously unhappy about coming up to the top of the site, but from what he was saying, it seemed to be company policy for all new men to see the whole site.

"Do we have to go up the staircase to the very top?" a second voice asked.

"If you want to go up there, you're on your own," the first voice answered. The voices had suddenly lost their echo and diminished, telling Dylan that the pair had gone out on to the top floor.

"No," the second voice again, "I don't want to go up there, this is more than high enough for me, maybe I'd go up if the lift had been installed."

The men had now stopped moving but continued to chat about the view and the job and life in general for a good half hour, then started on their way down. Dylan relaxed and went back to watching the penthouse.

As on Tuesday morning, the brothers returned home after one, had a nightcap and snack then went to bed, and again, Dylan stayed until 4:00 then returned to his hotel.

Ω

On the Wednesday evening, he was back in place by ten o'clock; he'd readied himself but saw this was going to be another repeat of the previous nights, but then he heard a noise, a scraping sound, that was followed by a knock, something hard gently hitting against the concrete wall; someone was coming up the staircase.

His first thought was it was another inspection by the guards, but he soon disavowed this idea. The guards had been noisy and talking, and he'd heard them from a long way down, so not a guard, to light a tread, this was someone in soft shoes or boots, like his own.

Dylan estimated the noises were about two floors down but definitely moving up. There was no time to collect his things, so he moved three steps up the next staircase and took out the Glock, muffling the sound with his coat he cocked the pistol and stood ready to meet the intruder.

There came another knock then a quiet curse, then a figure rounded the bend in the staircase, as the figure came into sight, Dylan could see it stop and look at his rifle that was still standing on the landing.

"Stay perfectly still," Dylan said, the figure took a pace back and gave a short scream that was quickly stifled, then stood totally still, that is apart from the trembling. The muffled scream had told Dylan he was dealing with a woman.

"Who are you?" she asked while Dylan was still coming to terms with the gender of the intruder.

"I'm the person who is likely to shoot you if you don't do as I say, and I say put the weapon down against the wall, where you are, then move into the far corner and sit on the floor, with your hands under you." She complied, and Dylan came down the three steps to stand before her but at sufficient distant away in case she knew martial arts.

Then speaking slowly and quietly he said, "I won't ask who you are, it doesn't matter, but I am asking why you are here and with a weapon?" She was quiet for some time; Dylan let her be, giving her time to think of her predicament. Finally, she took a breath in a way that said she'd decided.

"I'm here to kill Rory O'Brian," she said, with a belligerent tone in her voice.

"Why?" Dylan asked. Again, there was a pause.

"Because he killed my partner," she replied now with a softening in her voice.

"I'm going to put my pistol away, please let's have no heroics; it could be out quicker than you could get up." He carefully made the Glock safe and put it away. Now, while still watching her he picked up her rifle. He took out the magazine and inspected the ammunition then assessed the rifle. A Ruger .22 target rifle with a phoenix sight.

"Have you ever fired a rifle?" he asked.

"Yes, I have," she replied in an affronted tone. "I'm a member of a club, and there I'm considered to be very proficient I'll have you know." She was becoming emboldened as her fear was wearing off.

"Well," Dylan said in an instructional fashion, "you came to kill Rory O'Brian, with a .22 target rifle; it's as well I was here to stop you. You might be a good club shooter, but I'll bet you've never fired over three hundred yards?" The unasked question remained unanswered. "I thought so, the shot you were thinking of taking is over eight hundred yards with a ten knot cross wind. If you fired this rifle, you wouldn't have hit the building let alone the man, and you would have ruined my chance to do the job."

"You're here to kill Rory O'Brian?" she asked, amazement in her voice.

"Yes," he replied.

"But you said it can't be done from here?"

"No, I didn't. I said, you couldn't do it with this" – he indicated the rifle – "from here." This made her think for a bit.

"Why do you want to kill him?"

"Because someone asked me to do so, and I don't like what I know about him."

"But why would someone ask you to kill someone?" This was not the way he should be acting, telling her his business, but he couldn't seem to stop himself.

"Because I'm very good at it," he continued, "and have spent most of my adult life killing people." Dylan didn't know why he was telling things he had never told any other person. What he did know, by instinct, was that this woman was no killer, just angry and distressed. If she was able to kill O'Brian, she probably wouldn't be able to live with herself, and in fact, he liked her; he didn't know how that could be on such a short acquaintance.

"Look," he said, "this is not the place to discuss this. I can see there is not going to be a chance of a shot tonight so let's go somewhere we can talk it out," she agreed and got up. "Just one thing please, promise me you won't try to do this again, you couldn't kill anyone, but if you leave it to me, then you'll know they will have got their just desserts sooner or later." she agreed. He picked up the AI rifle and started to disassemble it.

"Is that the rifle needed to do this shooting?" she asked.

"There's plenty that can do long shots, but this is probably the best there is." It was very poor light in the stairwell, but she could see the length of the weapon and compared it to her own poor example.

They worked their way down the stairs, as they approached the third floor, they heard the guards moving about below them; they stayed quiet, and it was only a short time before the guards left. Dylan moved over to the edge of the floor where he could observe the compound; it wasn't long before he saw the guards moving towards the gatehouse, and as they entered, Dylan signalled to move. They left the site with no problems the way Dylan had come in. He took the time to change out of his cams then they moved out and headed up the Vauxhall Bridge Road aiming for the McDonald's at Victoria. The walk was at a slow but steady pace and in silence all the way, each tied up in their own thoughts on the happenings of the night.

When they arrived, the restaurant was nearly deserted with only one or two customers. They each ordered coffee and burger with fries then moved to the corner farthest from the counter. Finally, Dylan broke the silence.

"What's your name?" he asked.

"Jackie, Jackie Reynolds, what's yours?"

"I'll tell you, but please let's avoid the associations. It's Dylan, Dylan Williams." She managed to supress a smirk.

"That's nice, err, colourful. How did you get named Dylan?"

"I don't know I was a bit young at the time, but I think Mum was into poetry and Dad into protest music, well, that's all there is to it," he said dismissing the subject as he usually did. "Now tell me about your partner, what was his name?"

"Archie," she said in a quiet, subdued voice, "in full it was Archibald, but like you he didn't really like it; it took me a long time to find that out, so everyone knew him as Archie." She went quiet, reviewing her memories.

Dylan gave her time, then asked, "How did he come to get on the wrong side of the O'Brians?"

"He had a burger van; he'd bought it when he came out of the army."

"What regiment?" Dylan couldn't help asking.

"The Paras. Why? Were you in the army too?"

"That's the only place you can learn the type of work I'm good at, but you were saying?"

"Well, Archie had a good pitch, close to the Chelsea football ground, and he made very good money there; anyway, one day they came up to the van and said he would have to sell the pitch to them and move on. Nobody told Archie what to do, so he told them to bugger off while they still could, one thing led to another and that animal Rory took out a gun and shot him in the face, then they got in their car and drove off." Jackie was silently crying during her recitation, but once she'd finished, she blew her nose and brightened.

"So, you decided you would kill Rory in return," Dylan suggested.

"It's all I could think of. Two witnesses told me what had happened but refused to tell the police. The O'Brians of course had alibis that proved they couldn't have been there and lawyers to back them up, the lying shits." She obviously felt better for having told her story, for she was now sitting more erect.

Dylan went to the counter and got more coffees, when he returned, she'd made up her face and was more aware of her surroundings.

"How did you get in to shooting?" Dylan asked, more for something to say, he wasn't the most eloquent conversationalist; in fact, he rarely put more than ten words together at one go.

"That was Archie," she told him, "he was a good shot, competed for his regiment at times. He was always going on about how good it was and that I should take it up, so I agreed and joined the same club as Archie." She gave a longing look at the rifle-carrying bag. "That was one of Archie's old rifles that he gave me to get started, and I wasn't half bad; he had to help me a lot at the start, but once I got going, I got much better, and a few weeks ago, I came sixth in the club annual competition," she said this with great pride. "Archie was so proud of me. But that's enough about me; tell me about how you got to doing what you do."

Dylan gave a short summation of his life; he told of his time in the army and of the shop; he even admitted to shooting Sir Peter, but John and the section he left out just giving John's name as the friend who wanted the O'Brians killed.

"Do you do the round of the shooting competitions?" he asked.

"No," she replied, "I don't think I'm that good."

"You only get better when you try," Dylan admonished her, "put yourself in for a few, you'll soon get your face known; it's only really a very big gun club."

"Well," she prevaricated, "maybe, at least I'll think about it." Dylan gave her the names of some of the magazines that would let her know when and where to find out about upcoming competitions and left it at that.

When dawn came, it took them both by surprise. They'd been sitting in the McDonald's for five hours. If asked, Dylan would be unable to say what they had talked about for all that time.

"Well," Jackie said, "I'd better be getting home."

"Yes," Dylan agreed, "it is pretty late or should I say early. Maybe I'll see you at some of the competitions one day, or if you're up Norfolk, call in, maybe I can give you some lessons." Jackie said she would but both of them knew it wasn't a strong possibility. When Dylan returned to his hotel, he didn't feel tired at all, but as soon as his head hit the pillow, he was asleep.

Chapter 33

The next night was a replay of the previous nights, except Jackie wasn't there. The maid had put out their tray at 11:00, and it was half past one when the lights came on, as before the brothers made themselves a drink and stood talking in the centre of the lounge, Dylan was so tempted to take a shot there and then but restrained himself. He was sure the terrace doors of the penthouse, which were made of toughened, if not armoured, glass, and although the bullet would go through either with no trouble, the resistance of the glass would cause the LUPRU round to distort as it was supposed to, and once this happened, the round could and probably would lose its accuracy. In fact, it could go anywhere; it might hit the target, but the odds were against it, no, he would have to wait until an opportunity occurred when either the doors were open or the brothers were outside.

It was only a matter of fifteen minutes later when the brothers emptied their glasses and headed to the lounge door, switching out the lights on their way. *Bedtime*, Dylan thought. He waited another two hours, but there was no change so he packed his equipment and left the way he had come.

On Saturday, Dylan was again in position by ten o'clock, but when he looked through his monocular, he saw everything was different. There were lights and people on the terrace of the penthouse. *A party*, he thought as he prepared himself, *tonight should be the night*. At least, it looked as though it should be. Putting away the monocular, he prepared the rifle and took up his stance, now as he viewed through the scope, he was able to see clearly the individuals.

There were maybe twenty people over there, and they were milling about, drinking, talking and some even dancing; he could see Rory O'Brian who was towards the front of the terrace, but initially, he was unable to pick out Patrick, then he saw him coming out of the door on to the terrace. *Decision time*, Dylan thought, *which one first?* Patrick was close to the door talking with a small group.

Rory was close to the front of the terrace with a woman; he would have to cross the whole of the terrace to get to safety.

Dylan sighted on Patrick and fired; he saw it was a good shot and chambered another round and moved the sight to pick out Rory, but he was gone; he must have thrown himself down, and into a group of people making a shot impossible; it would mean he had the fastest reactions Dylan had ever seen.

It was a few seconds before someone started screaming, and everyone looked to see what the problem was, then there was a stunned frozen tableau until they came out of their shocked stillness and stampeded for the door, and somewhere in the chaos was Rory O'Brian.

It took only a few seconds more before everyone had gone, and the only person left on the terrace was Patrick, and he was lying in a pool of blood with a large part of his head elsewhere.

Dylan settled back to see what would happen next. Rory was not going to present himself as another target, so there was no good reason to stay, but he had nothing else to do, and it would be a very long time before anyone would work out where the shot had come from. Using his monocular, he had another look at the penthouse terrace.

The first police to arrive at the scene were two constables who immediately called for back-up, then sometime later came two detectives, who looked at Patrick's remains. The next person to arrive gave Dylan a shock; it was the man John. It only took a few seconds for Dylan to realise the man John would want to know how the shot went and had probably been listening to the police radio. Whilst Dylan was watching John wandered over the terrace then looked directly at Dylan's position as if he could see him, then without taking his eyes off of Dylan, he stooped mimicking picking something up; the message was clear, a reminder to Dylan don't leave anything behind.

Dylan had already picked up the cartridge case but was amused that John thought to remind him. He packed his equipment and made his way down the staircase, with the suppressor fitted on the rifle, it was certain anyone more than twenty feet away would not have been able to hear any sound, so, as expected, when he got to the bottom of the stairs, everything was as it had been the last few nights.

Dylan decided not to cross the river by Vauxhall Bridge, as the sirens, on the police cars over by the Riverview Apartments, told him there might be checks, or at least delays, so he used the Lambeth Bridge and the back roads to the hotel.

On his way, he took out his special phone, and when answered said, "Patrick down and out; I'm hunting the other one." Then he hung up.

Ten o'clock in the morning found Dylan booking out of the hotel. The receptionist told him there had been a shooting down the road during the night; they didn't have any details, but the radio thought it might have been a gangland related incident. Dylan showed due surprise then left to go home.

Chapter 34

Rory O'Brian had not been the leader in the partnership with his brother. Although quite bright, he was always a follower. Patrick was the brains and Rory his Lieutenant. Patrick would say do this and Rory would do it. If there was a plan to be made, then Patrick would make it, and Rory would agree. If the matter in hand required action, especially violence, then it became Rory's province, and he would be sure to carry out quickly and cleanly, while Patrick would step away. But now, Patrick was dead, and Rory had to deal with the police, left to himself, Rory would never have thought to call the police; they were the opposition and were too be avoided.

When the police had arrived, Rory was shaken. He'd not called them, in fact, all he had done since the shooting was to sit in the kitchen with his head in his hands, not doing or even thinking of anything, so one of their guests must have called, or maybe the maid, but she was sitting on the other side of the table and crying still. Whoever had called them knowingly or not may have landed the entire O'Brian empire in serious trouble, not that Rory was thinking clearly enough to register the problem; it was noticeable that all twenty-five guests had now gone leaving only the housekeeper/maid and Rory to face the situation.

The police arrived in the guise of two constables, who had been diverted from their nightly patrol. Their job was to confirm the authenticity of the call that had claimed a shooting had taken place. It took the pair very little time to establish that there was a dead body on the terrace, and it was missing half of its head. They called it in and requested CID backup, and then, they started asking questions, perfectly normal questions, but questions from the police were just the thing to bring Rory out of his grieving state, even though his mental torpor, they had activated an automatic response. In his head, he could almost hear Patrick calling to him; it was one of the lessons Patrick had always told him. "If someone was asking questions, call the solicitor, and don't say anything until he arrives."

Rory now carried out Patrick's order and called the solicitor. Of course, the two policemen present should not have allowed the call to be made until the CID got there, but they were still quite inexperienced and only knew anyone was entitled to a call, which they were but only after the investigator said so.

Phillip Braithwaite had been the O'Brian's solicitor for some years; in fact, since shortly after they had arrived from the States, he was good at his job and especially good at handling the nefarious activities of the brothers O'Brian, not an easy task, but when it came to criminality, he was very good. He'd learned the hard way having had once to defend himself from charges. This history had appealed to the brothers; they always liked to deal with their own sort. From then on, he had acted for them on many occasions, in the role of company legal advisor and personnel solicitor. Now the situation was entirely different from the problems he'd had to look after before; he now had to help the police solve the murder of Patrick whilst making sure Rory's and the company's position was protected. If the police were allowed to proceed unchecked, they would soon uncover the true operations of the company O'Brian.

Fortunately, Phillip had not been in bed, having only shortly before arrived home from an after-show dinner. When he arrived at the penthouse, he could see the state of Rory and realised that he wouldn't be in any condition to answer police interrogations. So far, Rory had kept silent, thank god, and for some reason, the CID hadn't yet arrived; this allowed Phillip time to head them off, but this could only be a temporary situation, sooner or later they would arrive and start the investigation properly. It was certain Rory could not handle the police questioning and would be sure to say something; he would lose his temper with them and without thinking, let slip something that the police could get their teeth into.

Phillip somehow had to stop the questioning; the only answer that was sure to work was to get Rory away before the CID arrived, then he could make them stick to the known facts of the case and not go delving into the dark areas. Phillip made a call.

"John," he said, speaking quietly into the phone, "I'm sorry to wake you this early. Have you heard of the situation at the Riverview penthouse?"

John Carter had the position of number three in the O'Brian companies; he'd earned the position by teaching the brothers how the London underworld worked and how to collect information and use it, as well as how the police could be manipulated, but now, he was going to be tested.

"What situation?" he asked in an annoyed and sleepy tone. "I've heard nothing; I rarely do when I'm asleep."

"I'm here at the penthouse now," Phillip told him. "Patrick's been shot and killed."

"When?" John asked, suddenly fully awake and with astonishment loud in his voice.

"About eleven o'clock last night. Look, we've got a problem; I'm here ready to fend off the police, but so is Rory, and he's not in any condition to know what he's saying. We've got to get him away from here, before he drops everyone in the shit. Can you get him away?"

John was now fully awake and already getting dressed; he didn't hold his position in the organisation just because he knew the O'Brians but because he was a good, clear thinking planner, and now was the time to prove it.

"Right," he said, "keep him quiet for as long as you can; try to get the police to let him go or sneak him out, either way, get him out. I'll send two of the lads around, and we'll bring him over here for now. Once we know the situation, we'll have time to think, then I'll get him away somewhere."

John called Tommy and Michael Callaghan, a pair of brothers, both were ex-boxers and street fighters, but they had managed not to get their brains damaged. The two of them had worked for the O'Brians since John had once needed some muscle to fend off another gang that was trying to cut themselves in on the brother's patch. By intimidating their people, the Callaghans solved the problem, their way, and it became known far and wide who they were giving protection to. The pair was not the sharpest in the knife draw, but they were both big, tough and willing to do anything Patrick asked. John got them out of bed and instructed them to go get Rory and bring him over to his place.

Phillip had managed to convince the two constables that Rory was in no condition to answer questions; he was in deep shock and required attention from a doctor. The two constables didn't like making the decision; this was the CID's problem, and they should have been here long ago, but without them, the pair suggested as a compromise they called out the police doctor, but with an implied threat of legal action if they did not let Rory go and get attention from his own doctor. The two could see no option; after all, it was medical and might become legal, so they agreed, although very reluctantly, and Phillip was able to get the maid to take Rory to the building entrance where they waited to be taken away by the Callaghans.

Chapter 35

It was gone 4:00 on Sunday afternoon when Dylan arrived home; he was not feeling too bright and didn't like to have left the job half done, although the night's work had been as good as he could have managed, and John would be happy the shot could be blamed on some unknown gang who wanted the O'Brians gone. He was amused at the thought that if Jackie had been a good shot, then the idea might have been true.

He parked the Land Rover and was removing his equipment when the voice of Mrs Jackman called him from over the fence.

Not now, he thought, *I don't want to get involved in her gossip now.*

"You've had a visitor while you've been away," Mrs Jackman told him, with a note of intrigue in her voice. "A South African man he was. I thought he was Australian, and I don't think he liked it, so he quite quickly put me right, in a bit of a sharp tone of voice I thought, but he only called the one time, but I think I've seen him around the town from time to time, looking a bit lost, if you know what I mean."

Dylan was a bit taken aback at this news; he'd expected to hear the usual tittle-tattle that was her specialty. Mrs Jackman had to tell everyone anything she knew or thought she knew, but a South African, that was a bit out of the usual.

"What did he look like?" Dylan asked.

"Well," she wasn't hesitating; she would never do that, someone might jump in before she could start again if she did that, she was just collecting her thoughts, for Mrs Jackman was known to see and remember everything, "he wasn't very tall, a little less than you. He had very big shoulders though and slightly bandy legs; I suppose that's from living in a hot country and not getting proper food." Mrs Jackman always assumed other parts of the world were backward. "His face was solid like it had been made from stone, you know, all sharp edges, oh, and wiry hair. He said he knew you from Afghanistan, so it was probably from when you were a soldier. He said that he'd call back another time but hasn't." You could be sure if he had called then Mrs Jackman would know. "But like I say, I think I've seen him since maybe in Tesco's." Dylan quickly took advantage of her pause for a thought to jump in.

"Oh, yes," he told her, "I think I know who you're talking about; it was just someone I met in a bar, somewhere like that, just in passing, you know. Well, if he's going to call again, then I'll know if it's the same man, but thanks very much for letting me know, now I must get unpacked." With that, Dylan lifted his things out of the Land Rover and went in the house; he always had to cut Mrs Jackman off short, or else he'd be there all night, but it didn't seem to worry her; she was probably used to it.

The description Mrs Jackman gave could only be one man, the mercenary that was security on the convoy he'd wiped out, up in the mountains. He thought he'd killed him, obviously he hadn't, and now he had followed him here, and there could only be one reason. Dylan was going to have to be careful and watchful.

When he had cleaned the AI rifle, he put it in the gun cabinet and at the same time took out his Walther GSP expert target pistol. The pistol fired a .32 bullet, which in the normal run of things wouldn't be thought of as a killing weapon, but like all weapons, it would kill if it hit a vital point on a body, and Dylan was good enough to hit exactly where he was aiming, making the pistol as dangerous as a 9mm. The reason he chose the Walther was that it was a licenced weapon, and he was sure he could talk his way out of trouble if he had to kill the man. Using the Walther, he could claim he knew the man was armed so using the Walther was really just self-defence if and when he had to explain to the police. It was sure the man would be armed, or else there would be no point in him coming to find him, and thinking of that he wondered how had he found him?

Ω

Piet Botha had been checking Dylan's bungalow for over a week without seeing any sign of him; he again checked out the house on Sunday morning and again drew a blank. The situation was starting to annoy him, but it just fuelled his anger so he was prepared to continue watching and waiting.

On Sunday evening, Piet had decided to have one last look at Williams' house so he parked up and again went into McDonald's, a place that was starting to feel like home from the amount of time he was spending in there, when from the window, he saw a decrepit Land Rover turn into the road where Williams lived. Piet could see clearly the vehicle turn into the drive and the man get out.

He watched as Williams was accosted by the woman next door, maybe she was telling him about Piet. He decided he would wait for dark to call on Williams, his approach would be easier then and best to get it done as quickly as possible, both because he had had enough of this town, and from what he'd seen, Williams might be gone again tomorrow. Piet did not want to wait another week.

Piet went off to book out of his hotel, have a drink and a meal; he planned to call on Williams about nine o'clock, not too late to surprise but late enough for it to be dark with very few people about.

It was a little before 9:00 when Piet checked the road and houses as he walked up towards Williams' house. All was quiet, with not a soul to be seen, most of the houses had the curtains drawn and the lights on, in others could be seen the flickering of the television. Piet walked up to the door without hesitation and took the SIG out his belt just before reaching out to ring the bell.

"Put the gun down by your feet now, or you won't see the rest of this night," the voice came out of the darkness, over by the Land Rover. The shock paralysed him, and the tone of the voice seriously suggested he do as he'd been told.

Ω

Dylan always had weapons and ammunition in his house, all properly licenced, well, at least most were, because of this, the police had done a thorough examination of the property before issuing the licence. The gun safe was a good one and acceptable for licensing purposes. During the inspection, the police had suggested a real-time, recorded surveillance system should be fitted, a very useful thing if you needed to make an insurance claim. So Dylan always keen on safety where firearms were concerned had had this done, but in his usual way, the system he had fitted was well over the top for a domestic house, with discreet cameras and sensors. On his one visit, John had pointed out that one camera was badly positioned and had left a blind spot. Dylan repositioned it the same night, so from the time Piet came along the road to the time he was standing in the doorway, Dylan had seen him, and Mrs Jackman's description could not have fitted anyone else.

After the talk with Mrs Jackman the previous night, he had kept the Walther pistol close by. When he had seen Piet on the security monitor coming up the road, he picked up the pistol, and in a few seconds, he'd slipped out the backdoor, around the back of the garage and got behind the Land Rover by the time Piet reached to ring the bell.

Ω

Piet froze in the doorway; he did think of trying a snapshot but a dead team and a bullet in his leg told him he'd be a fool to try it. He decided to try bluff.

"You can't shoot me, man," he said. "How would you explain having a gun; it's not allowed in this country." Having said this, he began to believe his own theory; he braced himself ready for the sudden move.

"Don't do it." Dylan had read Piet's intentions. "This weapon I'm holding is a Walther target pistol; it's licenced and loaded with .32 ammunition. At this range, I could put a bullet through your eye, and it would be justified because of the footage of you preparing to use a pistol, so, if you don't put it down, you'll die."

Piet didn't doubt Williams could and would do as he said.

"Okay," he said, "I'm putting it down, don't shoot."

Dylan maintained his aim upon Piet, watching very carefully as the SIG was very slowly put onto the doorstep at Piet's feet, and he took a step back.

"Now very, very, slowly turn around, I thought so," Dylan said, after Piet had complied, "I wasn't sure if I'd killed you the last time we met, maybe I should have followed up."

"You'd have been looking at the wrong end of an Uzi if you had," Piet replied.

"Yes, I suppose I would have, but I don't get why you're following this up, you and the other men were soldiers, you knew the risks, why haven't you got over it? As we all usually do."

"Listen, man," Piet said with fury in his voice, "you had no right to shoot Deon; he was only driving the car; the two crooks, who cares, but it wasn't necessary to shoot Deon, if you hadn't done that, we wouldn't have come after you. I don't know why you had to kill the crooks, and I don't care; the crooks and you had your parts to play, something my team was not a part of, but you made us a part of it. You shouldn't have done that."

"Don't put the blame on me; you're the one responsible; you should have trained your men better? If he hadn't started shooting wildly, he could still be

205

here. Anyone who shoots at a well-placed sniper is going to die, which is exactly what happened, and you all should have known this; you should have trained him not to start shooting at a well-positioned sniper."

"You don't get it, do you, man?" Piet was emphatic. "We weren't security guards, we were soldiers; we were only looking for a stake so we could get out of that stinking place; we were trained soldiers and bloody good ones. When you're fighting in the bush, if someone shoots, you shoot back, even if you don't know where they're shooting from, you just empty the magazine. If you're lucky, you hit someone, if not, you make them duck and give you time to get into cover, that's what Deon was doing, protecting the team."

"What's your name?" Dylan asked.

"It's Piet Botha," Piet replied, "not that it makes any difference." There was defiance in his voice. "What's yours?"

"Dylan Williams," Dylan told him, and said, "we've got a bit of an impasse here, Piet. I'm pretty sure you are not going to give up this vengeance, and I really don't want to kill you. You see, I only kill when I'm paid to do so, and I don't think there's a price on your head, so I'll tell you what I'll do; I'll let you walk away now and go your own way, but I'm going to point you out to my friends in the local police, and they'll be looking for you. Also, I'm going to put a price on your head so next time I see you, I'll feel justified in killing you, and you can be sure I will do that, so you've got thirty minutes before I call the police, can you live with that?"

Piet thought for a minute. "Yes, I can live with it, but remember I'm still on your tail, I'm not giving up."

"Okay," Dylan replied, "we have an understanding; nothing will happen for thirty minutes, then all bets are off, but don't think of turning back in those thirty minutes. I'll be watching. Okay, pick up the gun, two fingers only and put it away."

Piet put the gun in his belt, closed his coat, then turned and walked off down the street. He had to admit, even if only to himself, that Williams was right. Deon was the one who caused it all; he knew he could never have hit anything that far off, not with an Uzi, now all the team were dead, and he was going to have to try and kill one very competent marksman.

"Deon, if you weren't already dead, I would kill you myself," he said in a quiet voice, then smiled at the thought of what he'd said.

Dylan went into the house and watched Piet walk away on the security screen until he turned out of sight.

"I've got to admire him," Dylan thought. "He knows it was a mistake on his side, but he was still seeking revenge for his fallen men, to the extent that he is not going to give it up. Now I'll have to watch my back more closely, and be ready to kill him as soon as I see him, and at the same time finish my contract. This is getting more and more complicated all the time. I've now got one man I'm contracted to find and kill, one man who will try and find me who I will have to watch for and kill, and one woman I can't stop thinking of."

Unloading and putting away the target pistol in the gun cabinet, he opened the cabinet from the wall to reveal the secret gun safe; he took out the Glock 17 he'd only put away when he got home yesterday.

"I don't think you, my friend," he said, talking to the pistol, "will be going back to bed any time soon."

Chapter 36

When Rory had arrived at John Carter's house, he was in a bad way, with his moods swinging from anger and wanting revenge, to sorrow and mourning, for the now dead brother, whom he had never been away from in all his life. John and his wife eventually managed to get him to bed, having finally induced him to take a sleeping pill. The pill when it mixed with the alcohol he'd drunk that evening, made him pass out as soon as he laid down.

Once Phillip had finally got away from the police, leaving them at the penthouse, he went to John Carter's house. Between the two of them and with a little help from Mrs Carter, they agreed something had to be done with Rory, until he could be considered to be back and thinking rationally. The most important thing though was to keep him away from the police.

"Could we get his doctor to say he's too unwell to answer questions?" John asked.

"I wouldn't think so," Phillip replied. "Old Mathias is pretty straight where his practice is concerned."

"That's true," Mrs Carter said, joining in with the deliberations, "but if you told the police Rory had wandered off before we could get him to the doctor, then he'd have to agree it was possible for him to have done so."

They were in agreement that they couldn't instigate any action against the other gangs in the city, for a start, they couldn't be sure who would have put out the contract on the brothers or who the shooter might have been. Most likely, it would be someone who has been brought in, maybe from the States, someone unknown to the London underworld. That thought gave birth to the idea that maybe this was the New York syndicate, finally catching up on the O'Brians; they all knew the story, both the brothers were always happy to tell how they'd got one over on the NY syndicate.

"That could be true," John said, "even after all these years, those people never forget, and it is probably more likely than one of the London gangs would try it. But I'll put some feelers out anyway; we'll have to get in touch with our friends in immigration, see if they know if some hitman has entered the country."

"But that doesn't solve the problem of Rory, what'll we do with him?"

"Wales," another interjection by Mrs Carter again entering the conversation, "they've got that big place out in Wales, and they never really use it; he could lay up there for a while. It'll take time for the police to catch on; especially if we tell them he wouldn't leave London, not with his brother newly dead." This idea made sense to all, and they agreed to put it to Rory, when he wakes.

It was late morning before Rory did awake. Mrs Carter forced him to come to the kitchen table and eat breakfast. Phillip Braithwaite had had to return to the penthouse then the police station, but the Carters and the Callaghans were still there to look after Rory.

They all sat around the breakfast table, allowed time for Rory to eat some toast, then John laid out the ideas they had been discussing while he slept. For himself, Rory was in a calmer but still Maudling frame of mind; he wanted to be doing something to avenge his brother and started to become angry again. John pointed out that they didn't have any idea yet as to who was responsible, he had put the word out to all their contacts but didn't expect to get any answers for days.

"These things take time," he told him, "we'll get him, sooner or later. We'll get him," he assured Rory, but it was more of a comforter than a certainty.

"What about you?" he asked Rory who looked up not understanding. "You and Patrick have always been inseparable, and they shot Patrick at a time when you would be together, in the open, so to speak. Was the shooter supposed to shoot you as well?" This observation made Rory sit up. "I mean," John continued, "when did Patrick do anything that you weren't involved in? I think we've got to consider that you must also be a target as well." The room again went silent, each member thinking his own thoughts.

"I think you've got to see that," John stated. "The way I see it, we've got no option but for you to get out of the city."

"No!" Rory shouted. "Not until we've done something about finding who was responsible."

"Look at it practically," John said, "as things are at present, you can't go out in the open; you can't even stand by a window; you just don't know the who or the where, and the police still want to talk to you. We've got enough contacts; it's time to use them. They're the ones who will go and find out; they'll track down those responsible, and once we know who, you could come back and finish it, or better still, we could bring him to Wales, and you could see to him yourself, in your own way."

They could see Rory was thinking; he liked the idea of taking revenge himself.

"But," he said, "the police will insist I stay available for any time they want to see me; I can't do that from elsewhere, can I?"

"That won't be a problem. Phillip can handle the police; he'll tell them you've wandered off, and we don't know where. Anyway, once again, we can use our contacts; we pay them enough and one of them can stop the police looking for you.

"The best bet would be for you to go to the place in Wales, take four or six of the guys and that maid from the penthouse; she's in a bit of a state as well. It'll give her something to do looking after the eight of you, and it'll keep her away from the police as well. She probably can't tell them anything, but servants hear and see things, so you never know."

It took a bit more reasoning, but finally, Rory was convinced; he didn't like it and felt they didn't trust him to keep quiet about the O'Brian's business, surprisingly, this was unusually astute of Rory, but at least, they had managed to achieve the right result without upsetting Rory too much.

At 6:00 that evening, two Range Rovers, with six very hard looking men, Rory, and one maidservant, set off for Wales and a small town called Knighton.

Chapter 37

As soon as he heard of the shooting, John Wilcox had gone to the O'Brian penthouse. He'd been staying close by already, waiting for Dylan to carry out the shooting; he hadn't thought it would be long after he'd accepted the job that he'd carry it out. The visit to the apartment had not been necessary, but he did want to know which brother was dead and that Dylan had left the scene tidy. The two ineffective constables, who accepted his identification without question, informed him.

"We've allowed the other brother" – the constable consulted his notebook – "a Mr Rory O'Brian to leave. He really needed to see his doctor, and the solicitor was making all sorts of legal noises. The maid" – again a glance at the notebook – "a Miss Susan Henderson, had gone with him, at the same time that is."

This Wilcox knew, letting material witnesses leave the scene was definitely against normal procedure, but that was the CID's problem, his requirement was to see that the blame, for the shooting, could be attributed to some other member of the London Underworld. Considering the investigating detectives still hadn't yet arrived, Wilcox could understand the dilemma the two constables had found themselves in; he sympathised with them and knew the trouble they were going to find themselves in; it was well deserved, but with Rory on the loose, Dylan could have another chance at him.

There was nothing unexpected to see, one very dead body, some furniture upset and broken glasses. He did, however, get the feeling someone was watching him, one of them sixth senses that he always took notice of. He carefully studied the surrounding area; it made him feel sure Dylan was still in place, and that place almost certainly was across the river, in the unfinished building. The feeling was so strong he decided to put on a little show for Dylan's benefit. If Dylan was there, then he would understand, if not, then no one would see or understand, so it wouldn't matter.

Now having clarified that Patrick was the dead body, and with the eventual arrival of the CID, he had to wait until after the inspector had finished lambasting the two constables, before he could set about placing a misleading thought of who might have been responsible.

"Tell me, Inspector," Wilcox asked, "do we know of any snipers amongst the local underworld?"

"Not that I know of, sir." The inspector gave the honorific because the Wilcox ID showed him to be senior. "One or two know how to use a rifle, but this is a much higher standard than I would have thought they could manage."

"What's your first thought then, someone brought in to do the shooting?"

"Yes, but don't quote me, I would think that would be about right, possibly an American, they're used to this type of thing over there, and the locals are starting to make contacts in that direction."

"Well, that's something to think about," Wilcox suggested. "Now I'll get out of your way, and let you get on, I'm sure you've got a long night ahead of you." Wilcox now took his leave feeling the seeds had been well sown.

Ω

For the next three days, Dylan occupied himself with work around the shop and helping Rick in the workshop. Everything there was fine; Rick had settled in well; he'd found a place of his own to live in, in the town, and with little social life as yet he was happy to work any and all hours, as Dylan used to, and drive around the county whenever the need arose. He'd soon learned that the little sports car he had owned was not suited to the job and like Dylan had traded it in for a vintage but road worthy Land Rover.

With this time on his hands, Dylan took a trip to Birmingham to buy yet another rifle, legally this time, not for himself but as a present. He'd managed to find online a second-hand Howa M1500, with a 24-inch barrel bored for a 7mm magnum round. Once again, he spent a day in the workshop, much to the consternation of Rick, who thought he had enough rifles by now, fully servicing the weapon, then he took it home and put it in the gun safe. He didn't know if he would ever give it to the person he'd bought it for, but time would tell, and he would take it to every competition in the coming year, as a memory if nothing else.

It was on the fourth day after the shooting of Patrick O'Brian that Dylan received the not unexpected visit, from the man called John, as he still thought of him. Although it had always been understood that Dylan might not be able to take out both brothers at one go, he expected there would be questions asked.

"Just a friendly visit," Wilcox said, "to keep you in touch with what's going on."

"In that case, it's nice to see you," Dylan replied leading John into the kitchen. "Tea or coffee?" he asked. Dylan made the tea and they sat at the table to drink it.

"That was a nice job at the penthouse," John said, "clean and tidy, exactly what I was hoping for. You'll be pleased to know the police haven't got a clue, they're leaning towards it having been a rival gang or even an American Mafia hit. I like to be helpful, so I might have said something like that to the CID when I visited, well, they're happy to have some idea to follow."

"That's good," Dylan replied, "I was thinking you wouldn't be too happy that I only got Patrick and wasn't quick enough to get Rory."

"No, none of it," John appeased, "there you had some bad luck. You see, when Patrick went down, someone exclaimed something, god knows what, but Rory heard and turned sharply to see what it was about and tripped over a coffee table, so he probably fell out of your view. By the time he got up again, everyone else had got on to what had happened, the chaos started and panic took over, and Rory was dragged along with the crowd. If he hadn't tripped, you would have had three or four seconds to get your second shot in, just bad luck."

"So that was it," Dylan responded. "I couldn't understand how Rory had made a move so soon after the shot, never mind, I'll get him next time. Oh, and thanks for your little pantomime, I had remembered, but it never hurts to check. I'd like to know how you knew where I was though. I'm damn sure you couldn't see me."

"Well," John smiled as he replied, "it was the best place; a quick look around and it was easy to see, so easy that it took the scene or crimes people a day to spot it, and even then, you'd left it so clean they weren't sure. So, as I said a good clean job with no problems, then or now."

"Ah," Dylan said, "don't speak too soon; there might be a small problem" – a frown and quizzical look crossed John's face – "nothing to do with this shot," Dylan hastened to explain, "but with the shot in Afghanistan." Now Dylan could see confusion on John's face.

"The security team that was with the targets, it seems I didn't get them all. The leader, a Piet Botha, came around to seek revenge about a week ago." John now looked interested. "As you see, he wasn't successful. I didn't want to kill him there in my front doorstep, so we had a bit of a standoff, which finished with the understanding that one of us would kill the other next time we got the chance. I let him leave, told the local police there was a man with a gun wandering about the neighbourhood and haven't seen him since. I don't know if he'll take the hint or not, but I'm definitely going to keep my eyes open."

John sat quietly for some time; he now had to consider if this information was going to compromise the ongoing work, that was his job. Dylan still had to dispose of Rory O'Brian, and personal feuds couldn't be allowed to interfere.

"Will you still be able to operate with him about, or do you need someone to cover your back?" Dylan was quick to reply.

"No, I can't operate with a nursemaid covering me. I do my own reconnaissance and make my own dispositions; anyone trying to cover me would only get in the way and probably cause me to be seen, no, I can handle the problem. I just wanted you to know what was going on."

"Okay then, what are your plans now?"

"Well," Dylan replied, "I reckon, Rory is going to take a couple of days to get himself sorted out, then he'll realise he's a target, and then, finally, he'll run and hide, and the most obvious place that he knows to hide in is their farm in Wales, throw in a few heavies for protection, and it would probably be a good choice, that is if it was some London gangsters after him, but it's not, it's me, and he doesn't know this. I would think he should be there by now, so tomorrow will be soon enough to go down and have a look. I could do with today off anyway."

John agreed the plan sounded good, he didn't like the idea of this Piet Botha being on the scene, but it was Dylan's call, and he'd seen what he could do, either at long range or close, he didn't want back-up, so be it.

Chapter 38

Piet Botha had not gone to all the trouble of finding Williams to turn and run away, giving up without a fight, even if it looked that way, this was the second time Williams had made him run, and he wasn't happy about it, but at the same time, he wasn't stupid. After his talk with Williams, he realised that as things stood, he couldn't win. Quickly collecting his things from the hotel, he left town, maybe he had to run now, but he'd be back.

When Piet left Dereham, he drove to Peterborough; it was farther than he wanted to go, but it did get him out of the county and therefore out of the Norfolk police area. He didn't know if Williams had put the police on him, but he couldn't take the chance. At least the drive gave him time to consider how he would make his next, and hopefully his last, attack on Williams.

Booking into the Premier Inn, he got a good night's sleep and in the morning was up and ready when the shops opened. Piet's problem now was not to be recognised; this shouldn't be too much of a problem providing he didn't give anyone the chance to study him. When you ask someone to identify something or someone, at first, they will see, what they expect to see, only after a time of looking will they see through a disguise, a small change in appearance can confuse the senses enough, so that someone can hide in plain sight.

By the time Piet had spent some hours in Marks & Spenser's, selecting new very different set of clothes, at a barber's for a haircut and shave, and had returned to the hotel to shower and change, he would never have been seen as the slightly dishevelled, long-haired beardy in an Italian suit he had previously been, at least not at a casual glance.

Leaving Peterborough, he now drove back into Norfolk, not to Dereham but to Norwich where he booked into the Travel Lodge. The receptionist who made his booking saw a smart middle-aged man in a suit and tie; she took him to be a salesman, the same as most of the hotel guests.

Leaving his car in a long term parking lot, he hired a very nondescript dark blue Ford Mondeo; it was probable Williams had not seen his car, but he did have his name, and if the police took the report seriously, he could be traced, so a change of hire car seemed sensible and in the event of a search would cause delay, and by the time they could find where he had hired another car, he would have changed to yet another hire company. Identification was not a problem as his driving licence and passport were not in his own name, as had been the case since he arrived in Italy from Afghanistan.

By midday the next day, Piet was back watching Williams' front garden. Fortunately, Williams never parked his Land Rover in the garage, so it was easy to see if he was home, even at the long distance from the supermarket carpark.

Each morning, Piet would be in position in the carpark by six o'clock and stay there till 9:00 in the evening; the night would have been a better time to lay an ambush, but he had the feeling if Williams was going anywhere, it would be in the morning. Each day, Williams drove off; Piet saw him go and was easily able to follow, but Williams only went into town to the sporting goods shop, where he stayed all day, returning home in the evening when the shop closed.

Friday morning it all changed, as Piet was parking, as usual at 6:00, this time driving a silver-grey BMW Z3, he saw Williams come out of his house and load some bags and a box into his Land Rover. To Piet, who hadn't even had time to buy his morning coffee, it seemed too early for Williams to be going to the shop again, and the bags he'd put in the vehicle said he was going somewhere further afield. Piet waited for Williams to set off and then followed; Williams turned on to the A47 and headed west at a steady speed. Piet staying back as far as he could while keeping the Land Rover in sight followed.

Ω

Dylan anticipated a long day traveling, it would be almost all the way across the country, but that didn't bother him; it was a bright sunny day, which got him off to a good start. Being an early riser, he'd had time for a leisurely breakfast, and as he loaded his hopefully needed equipment, he took a good look around, and seeing no sign of Botha, he set off.

The roads were not busy when he started out at 6:00, but he knew that wouldn't last, once the daily rush hour got underway, it would all change, but if the bad side was a long trip, the good side was that he was finally getting on with the job in hand.

Joining the A47 at Dereham, he decided to stay on it as far as Leicester, for no better reason that his not being in a hurry, besides, the Land Rover was smoother and quieter at around the fifty miles an hour mark, so was better suited to the lesser roads rather than the faster A14. There was also the benefit of finding a café or pub in the small towns he would pass through, so he could take a break whenever he felt like it, rather than have to wait until he reached the services.

His first stop was at Market Harbour, where he found a pleasant little café, where he enjoyed a coffee break and a stretch of his legs. Sitting at a window table, he was able to survey the passing traffic both vehicular and pedestrian, a visit to the restroom then back on the road to Leicester.

Upon reaching Leicester, he now had to navigate his way through the town, leaving the A47, and after some time got on the A511 to Uttoxeter, there he changed on to the A50 to Newcastle under Lyme and finally the A53 to Shrewsbury, where considering it was now nearly twelve o'clock and that Dylan considered he deserved to stop for lunch.

One of the many problems of being in a city was that although there were always lots of places to eat, there was rarely a suitable carpark close by. So Dylan, who didn't want to be separated from his vehicle for too long, or even out of sight of it if possible, searched out and found a Morrisons supermarket, certainly not what would be called a restaurant for the Michelin guide but acceptable food and a large carpark.

It had taken a few circuits of the carpark to find a suitable parking spot, not it seemed an unusual occupation, as he noticed a BMW almost copying his efforts. As he walked into the store, he again saw the BMW, and although he wasn't sure about it, he had the feeling he had seen it before, but he couldn't say where, but there again the BMW Z3 wasn't uncommon, so he let the feeling pass and set about ordering his lunch.

Dylan managed to once again get a window table, where he ate his meal, and at the same time, he was able to watch the traffic, people and vehicles, as they arrived and left with their trolleys loaded with their groceries. He again saw nothing that brought itself to his attention during this break, but the feeling that he was missing something kept rubbing at his subconscious. There was something that was out of place, and there was nothing he could pinpoint, but a life of hunting had taught him not to discount the feeling, not until he had an answer as to what had caused it.

After his lunch, and walking a few laps of the carpark to loosen his leg muscles, Dylan set off into the English Marches that bordered Wales. He left the city and set off down the A49 to Leominster, where he picked up his final road change turning on to the A44, which took him to his destination of Knighton, a small Welsh town, with the main point of interest for Dylan was that it was near to the manor house owned by the brothers O'Brian. *Amend that to brother*, he thought.

It was with great pleasure that Dylan finally pulled in to the carpark of the Knighton Hotel, where he had booked a room for two weeks. As he was retrieving his bag from the Land Rover, he noticed a car pass, a silver-grey BMW and immediately knew what had bothered him in Shrewsbury; he had seen that car two or three times since he had started out.

Dylan knew coincidences did happen, but the chance of two vehicles, one traveling at a medium speed, the other that would usually be traveling at least at the official limit, both traveling the same route, to go to the same small town, that was over two hundred miles from the start, that was too much to believe. He had been followed, that was now for sure, but by whom?

After booking in, he sat in his room and considered the possibilities. Question: has John ignored him and sent protection anyway? Answer: not likely but checkable, or, question: was Piet Botha on to him again, looking for an opportunity to finish their association? Answer: very possible, even likely, or, question: was there someone in the O'Brian camp who knew him to be after Rory? Answer: not possible. Conclusion: it had to be Piet Botha.

Now, Dylan considered, what he had thought would be a simple assignment had been complicated, and he was going to have to keep his eyes open and watch his back, at the same time as he carried out his work.

Ω

Piet had had a bad day; it was his own fault. He had fallen into a routine, always an easy thing to do, especially when doing a long surveillance; he could kick himself for that to start with, even the newest recruit knows not to let that happen when on a stakeout. It meant that when Williams moved out, he Piet Botha wasn't ready and had nearly lost the trail. He'd been getting out of the car when he saw Williams come out of his house, so had to get back in the car and be ready to follow, this meant he had to do without the breakfast cup of coffee he was used to getting from the McDonald's.

Once on the road, the BMW Z3, a car he thought would never be considered to be a surveillance vehicle, became a liability, distinctive, again, he mentally kicked himself. He'd let his boy racer mentality cloud his judgment. Why did he do it; he knew Williams was in an old Land Rover so there was not going to be a high-speed chase. So now he had had to stay an extra-long way back to avoid being noticed, not too hard when on the main roads, although he had nearly lost the Land Rover a few times when the traffic was heavy, and that meant he had had to move closer. And again, once they were on the winding low roads, it became almost impossible to stay out of view; there were so many side roads Williams could have turned into he'd had to keep him in permanent sight.

When at last they had reached the destination and Williams had gone into the hotel, Piet now knew he would have to change everything. Firstly, he had to change the car, then his clothes; the suit he was now wearing would not suit this country. Again, he'd not been prepared to be staying away for maybe days. He had nothing with him, and Knighton had little to offer of the things he might need, besides, he didn't want to be noticed and shopping here would bring him to people's attention.

The change of location had caused most of his problems. This was a rural county, and if things went the way they had so far, then he was going to need a lot more items.

He turned the car around and headed back to Leominster; he would have to hope Williams stayed in the hotel tonight. Only in a larger town would he be able to find a military surplus shop, where he might kit himself out, with the camouflage clothing, boots, water bottle and a flask for hot drinks, a compass, a hunting knife, a waterproof cape, and a backpack to put it all in, but surprisingly, this had turned out to be quite easy to find.

Now he had to do something about the car. There was a Hertz car hire in the town, and it was still open. Fortunately, it was Hertz he had hired the Z3 from. It did take some arguing to change the car, as he had not arranged to dump it away from the place of hire, but with agreeing to pay for a driver to take it to Norwich, they eventually relented, and he was able to arrange the hire of a Nissan four-wheel drive; he thought he might need it in this area.

It was now late in the day and the shops, in general, were closed except for the Tesco supermarket, which was open till late. He was able to get street clothes there, maybe not the colours and styles he would have liked but good enough for the time being. Now at least he was equipped as well as the situation allowed, which should be well enough to at least confuse Williams if he had made him during the day.

Piet decided it was not worth the drive back to Knighton, not knowing if there was another hotel there or not, so he took a room in Leominster; he would still be able to be in position before daylight.

Chapter 39

Knighton in the pre-dawn day felt cool and fresh; the air was invigorating, and the portent was of a fine bright day. Dylan had decided the previous day that he would start his recognisance as early as possible. O'Brian, if he was there, would be defended by at least four men, but he needed to get a good look at the manor house before he could assess what protection it could offer.

Dylan realised he would need a good explanation to be up and about so early, his selected role would have to explain not only the time, but the fact he would be wearing camouflage clothing. After some thought, he'd hit upon the idea of being a birdwatcher, the enlightenment came thanks to the BBC bird watch programme that happened to be on the television that evening; it would be a very good disguise he thought. The avian fraternity, commonly called twitchers, could often be seen moving about the countryside, totally unmolested, that was mainly because most 'non-twitchers' considered the occupation a waste of time, but harmless, and so tended to ignore the practitioners. The disguise also helped to explain to the hotel staff why he wanted a pre-packed breakfast ready to go, so he had no reason to disturb the hotel's routine when going out so early in the day.

A short way outside Knighton was a long earthwork known as Offa's Dyke. It is a large linear earthwork that roughly follows the border between England and Wales. Although it never was the border, it served as such when England and Wales were a collection of kingdoms, and King Offa of England was scared Griffiths, the king of Powys, might attack. It never was a very effective military fortification, but it never needed to be as apart from some cattle raiding across the border King Griffiths never had any designs on attacking.

Currently, the dyke is a footpath that gives nice scenic views out across the English Marches and the Welsh hills and mountains and for Dylan a good chance of getting a close look at the landscape around the O'Brian manor house.

Dylan emerged from the hotel and began his walk, having identified the BMW as a potential enemy, he looked for it but did not find it. He also paid very close attention to all that could be seen in the greying light of false dawn, especially the darker patches and the gateways with overhanging shrubbery, but as he made his way out of town and on to the dyke, he saw nothing of anyone at all. Once clear of the town, he was able to relax a bit but not completely. If it was Piet Botha that was following, then he would know well how to track without being seen, and Dylan was almost certain it was Piet.

Within a few hundred yards of the hotel, the town had given way to rolling hilly countryside, the dyke, and the road to Weston ran almost parallel, sometimes diverging and sometimes almost together, dependent on the nature of the terrain, and to add to the mix, a small river ran twisting and turning around the hills, almost in accompaniment to the other manmade and natural topography that tried to stop it. With some areas of timber, some of grassland and a good amount of gorse, on a nice day, it was a pleasant walk.

Dylan estimated he had been walking for some ten miles when coming over a rise he found himself looking down, on what must be the manor house. It was a moderately large building but not big, certainly not in the sense of aristocratic stately homes, maybe ten rooms up and ten rooms down, with some outbuildings.

It wasn't a fortress but did have a wall around the property, but this would have been more for keeping out bandits or keeping stock in than fighting off soldiers. Being built in the lee of the dyke, it probably had served to house defensive troops at one time or another.

There was only one entrance gate, which through his monocular Dylan could see was chained closed. There were three cars on the courtyard randomly parked and one guard stationed towards the front of the property. There would probably be another around the back he surmised, not that this point was of interest to Dylan, he certainly had no intention of storming the place.

The view from on top of the dyke would be a very good position for taking a shot at the house, but although the angle was perfect, the hillside was almost bare. There was a stand of trees a little farther off; he decided to take a look from there and started to walk towards it. As he walked, he could see the guard in the front of the property was taking an interest in him, enough so that another person came out of the house to join him, and they both stared. Dylan gave a friendly wave and continued on his walk.

Once he had come close to the trees, he stopped and started looking through his monocular at the treetops, to all intense and purposes spotting birds high in the branches, a cursory look at his watchers told him the ploy had worked, and they had lost interest in him, although they didn't move off or stop giving him casual glances; it seemed they had accepted his ploy but still didn't trust him; it looked that they'd learnt from the shooting of Patrick.

Dylan took one more look all around then continued on his way. Passing through the stand of trees, he could see that he was well out of sight of the watching guards but that he wouldn't be able to take a shot from here. The gorse bushes that grew some distance down the hillside would block his line of sight. If he wanted to take a shot from in amongst the trees, he would have to climb a tree and spending a night and probably a day sitting up these trees, which were pines so had no strong limbs and would be very uncomfortable.

Apart from the trees at the top and the gorse halfway down, there was nothing to act as cover. Of course, he could, he supposed, play snake in the grass, the grass was just about long enough. Fully dressed in cams with maybe a cam net over the top, it would be possible; he had done similar before, but then, he'd had back-up, here he would be on his own, and it was very possible some walker might see him; he wouldn't want that. He was only going to get one chance at this shot so wouldn't be able to return even if Rory stayed.

The only piece of terrain left that he could hide in was the gorse; it looked pretty substantial, with plenty of leaf, maybe there would be room to stretch out under it. It did seem to be the only option, not one he favoured, gorse was nasty prickly stuff; he would have to examine the bushes more carefully, but it would have to be after dark, it would be too easy for someone to see him if he tried to move down the hill in daylight.

He'd seen all he could for now, so he'd now on such a nice day have a pleasant leisurely walk along the dyke. The watchers, who had seen him enter the trees, would expect to see him emerge on the far side, so he had better not disappoint them. For the rest of the day, he enjoyed the walk, returning to the stand of trees just as dark was falling.

Dylan was well versed in the use of the varying stages of daylight; he'd been caught out a couple of times and used it to catch out others. Twilight was almost as good as dark for confusing the eye, in the same way that mist made a watcher see ghosts, but a watcher whose eyesight served him well during the day, or might use an image intensifier at night, would find both could let him down in the twilight world that was half-light/half dark.

In the darkening light, it became possible for Dylan to move down the hillside unobserved, his cams helped him to blend with the background, so moving slowly, he had no worries that he might be seen, his slow place was also important. Someone who didn't understand how to use the light would move down the slope as quickly as possible, thinking there was less chance of being seen. However, the truth is the opposite, movement is the observer's greatest friend, even in lowlight levels something moving would register on the peripheral vision attracting the watcher's attention, so keeping low and moving slow was Dylan's best method of approach, as it would be very unlikely the guards would see him, and this proved to be the case.

Once he had reached the gorse bushes, Dylan set about searching about their stems. Gorse always looks as though it is impenetrable, but close to the ground, the growth often leaves tunnels, small animals know this and so do trappers. These tunnels are caused because the light cannot get in to the tangled centre of the bush; the outer growth is too dense. It was one of these tunnels that Dylan was looking for, and the reason he had to chance the approach in twilight, rather than wait for full dark, but it didn't take long for him to find what he was looking for.

Moving a branch aside, he could see a tunnel that looked right; it was about fifteen inches high and two feet wide; he took off his pack and crawled in. The tunnel was a good ten feet long with three turns along the route, but when he reached the end, he had an excellent view of the manor house with the added bonus that like the entrance the outer foliage covered the exit so giving him complete cover. This he decided was the place; of course, he would have to take up position before dawn and wouldn't be able to leave until after dark, but that would be no trouble, he had been in the same position many times.

When it was finally totally dark, Dylan wormed his way backwards out of the tunnel, collected his pack and set off back up the hill, again keeping slow and low, by now, if they had them, their night vision goggles would be effective, but still a fully camouflaged slow low shape would be difficult to see. Once in the stand of trees, he moved well back from the treeline before rising, this careful action was because the dark gave night vision goggles the added advantage of being able to differentiate between hot and cold as well as moving and stationary. Coming out of the trees to the side away from the house, he went a little way down the slope then set off for the hotel pleased with his day's effort. Now he was confident that O'Brian was in residence, and that he had found a good hide; all that was left for him to do was get into place and wait for Rory to come out in the open.

Ω

After entering the town but still on the dark pathway, he caught the flare of a match, or maybe a lighter; it was only for a second and reasonably well shielded, and it was only because his eyes had become used to the dark over the past two hours that he noticed it. Stopping where he was, in the sheltering dark, he studded the car that the flare had come from. It was a dark coloured Nissan, the night having taken all of the colour from it; there was obviously someone sitting in it who had probably lit a cigarette, or such like. There could be any amount of reasons why someone would be sitting, waiting, at this time of night, maybe waiting for someone who was in the hotel, but the fact that the car was positioned where the occupant could see the approaches to the hotel, rather than in the hotel carpark made it look suspicious.

Piet Botha, Dylan thought, could it be? How would he have been able to track me here? Then he remembered the BMW from his trip down yesterday. So, he was back on my trail. Dylan did have the Glock pistol on him, and he probably could work his way to the car unseen. It would be nice to be rid of Piet once and for all, but if he did it now, he'd be stuck with trying to find somewhere to get rid of the car and the body inside it, which wouldn't be easy as he didn't know the area and if found would cause the police to become involved, as well as causing alarm in the town, and they'd be checking out all the strangers in the town and worst of all it would become known at the manor house. No, he would have to leave him alive for now, but at least he knew he was there, and he would settle it once and for all as soon as he had finished with Rory O'Brian. Dylan walked to the hotel and entered all the time feeling he had a target pinned to his back.

Ω

Piet had parked within sight of Dylan's hotel at six o'clock; this time he was ready to go anywhere that Williams went. He'd stopped to get a breakfast burger and large coffee at the McDonald's in Leominster, and now sat enjoying both; he was fully relaxed and ready for the final confrontation with Williams. Common sense agreed with Williams when he said he should accept what happened and get on with his life, but he just couldn't do it, to him it was unfinished business, and Piet Botha didn't leave things undone.

By nine o'clock, Piet considered something was wrong. Williams was an early bird so would always be out and about by this time. By 11:00, he knew he'd missed him, six o'clock had been too late wherever he was going he'd gone, but the Land Rover was still there in the hotel carpark so he was going to return, unless he didn't intend to go out till tonight. Maybe he was resting for the day and would go out this evening; either way, Piet was stuck until Williams re-appeared.

It was after 9:00 in the evening when Piet saw Williams walk along the road to the hotel; he'd given up hope of seeing him by then and so it took him totally by surprise when Williams came along the street, all day watching and he wasn't even there. Piet wondered where Williams might have been all day. At least by the way he had walked past and in to the hotel, Williams couldn't have seen him. Considering he'd been out all day, Piet decided there was little likelihood that he would be going out again tonight, so he might as well go back to his own hotel and tomorrow he was determined to be here early enough to be ahead of Williams. It was a pity though if he'd seen him return only five minutes earlier, this fight would have been over, and he would be on his way back to London.

Ω

When Dylan got to his room, he left the light off. Looking out of his window, he saw Piet pull away from his parking place and take the road back to Leominster. He couldn't hide a smile as he thought of Piet having probably sat there all day waiting for him, only to miss any chance of taking a shot at him. If he hadn't seen him as he returned, Piet might have got his shot in and left. And he thought, *if I hadn't wanted to stay around, I would have shot him and left.* Considering what he had to do tomorrow, he had to make sure he left before Piet could arrive. Dylan went to the front desk of the hotel and booked out letting them know he would be leaving very early.

Chapter 40

It was early, very early even by Dylan's standards; there had been no one else about in the hotel as he left, just a packet of sandwiches and his flask of coffee left on the reception desk. Letting himself out, he loaded his bags into the Land Rover then set off along the road to Weston, as he drove out of the hotel carpark onto the road, there was only one other car to be seen, and it was traveling in the other direction; he paid it no notice.

The trip that had taken nearly two hours to walk, now only took twenty minutes to drive, so it was still dark when he arrived at the same stand of trees. With the trees close together, it was difficult to manoeuvre between them, but with a bit of effort and a few scuffs on the Land Rover wings, he managed to get in amongst them. He'd spotted the gaps the previous night as he'd left here to return to the hotel and decided it would be a good place to hide the car through the day or two he thought he might be here. With careful manoeuvring, he navigated the Land Rover far enough in so it could not be seen, from either the road or dyke.

Getting out, he surveyed the area or as much of it as he could see; there was nothing to disturb the peace of the place or of his thoughts. Opening the rear of the vehicle, he took out the gun case and assembled the AI rifle. As he handled the weapon, with an almost loving touch, he contemplated how it had changed his life, first in his job whilst still in the army, then the personal revenge on Sir Peter, and now the O'Brian brothers. Now he had money in the bank and a lot of it was a businessman with a partnership in a thriving business, and he was a contract killer, with two kills to his credit, and hopefully, in the next few hours a third and maybe even a fourth.

Pulling out his backpack, he locked the Land Rover, hefted the rifle, and with it cradled in his arm, he set off through the wood. Five minutes of very careful walking through the pitch darkness of the wood brought him to where he could look down on the manor house; all was quiet. In the starlight, he could just make

227

out one man patrolling the walls of the estate, moving in a slow almost dreamlike state, although Dylan was willing to bet, he would notice any approach to the house or grounds.

With only starlight to show him the way, he carefully and slowly descended the hill and located the same tunnel in the gorse that he had tested the day before. Taking his backpack off, he entered the tunnel, but this time, he dragged the pack behind him; he was probably going to need the food and drink in it, for only exceptional luck would see him out of here any time soon.

Having arrived at his position, he unrolled his mattress and with great difficulty because of the limited space, managed to get it laid out with him on it. Having got himself comfortable, he now looked at the manor house; it was still too dark to see any clear detail even through the monocular. He did, however, see some movement around by the gate thanks to the cigarette the guard was smoking, but that was all. Resting the rifle down, he took a sandwich and a bottle of water out of his pack and settled back to have his breakfast.

Ω

Having given up on a night's sleep, that is he'd laid down for a couple of hours, but he'd not found sleep during that time. Piet had decided he would rather be sitting in the car watching for Williams, so at midnight had got up and driven to Knighton. He had made the car wobble as he saw Williams' Land Rover coming towards him, on the other side of the road. They passed only a few feet apart, but there was no sign of recognition from Williams.

Piet used the hotel carpark to turn round and set off in pursuit first switching off the car's lights; he didn't want Williams to know he was there, and as there was no other traffic, he could hardly not see him, but without the lights, it was quite difficult not to run off the road so Piet hoped they weren't going too far and settled down about four hundred yards behind. Now he was thanking whatever gods had stopped him sleeping, if he'd left it to leave early, no matter how early, he'd have missed him again, but now, he had him in his sights.

It was only another twenty minutes or so before Williams' lights suddenly disappeared; Piet stopped. 'He's spotted me' was his first thought. *No, that's not possible; he's two–three hundred yards ahead; he can't see me, so he's turned off on to a side road, possible, the only other reason is that he'd arrived where he wants to be and has parked.* Piet crept the car along the road. With the engine only idling, it wouldn't be heard at least not at more than twenty or thirty feet. Reaching the position, he'd estimated Williams' lights had vanished. There was no turning, he let the car move on for another half mile and still didn't find any turning. He knew he had missed the place that Williams had gone; he turned the car and retraced his steps. It was no good, he'd have to walk it, so where to leave the car; it was time to get out.

It took some time until Piet had found a track that wound off the road and behind some bushes; it wasn't the best of parking places, but it was hidden from the road, so no helpful passer-by would stop and question why it was there. He locked the car and stealthily moved along the road passing the small stand of trees looking for the opening Williams must have taken; he walked for about half a mile again without finding a gap in the trees. As he did when in the car he turned around and started back, he knew it was here somewhere, but where. He arrived back at his vehicle and stopped for a smoke.

He's in there somewhere, so there must be a way in, he was only two hundred yards ahead so he's got to be in these woods; it's the only option. It's the darkness, I can't see where he left the road because it's just too dark. I'll have to wait for dawn then look again; I know he's here.

Ω

As false dawn and then dawn itself arrived, it found Dylan resting comfortably in his hide, at least it would have found him if it hadn't been so dark in the gorse bush. Dylan was glad of the dark, if there had been room, he could have jumped up and down and the guards wouldn't have seen him, but there wasn't room, and he never jumped up and down; he did scratch his nose twice though.

Down at the manor house, the only sign of movement was the guards moving around the perimeter, more to keep warm in the early morning chill than to patrol the grounds. A woman in a maid's uniform came to the door and called the guard over, to give him the cups she was holding, and he wasted no time in going to get them, then he went around the house probably to pass one of the cups to the other guard before returning, drinking from his own cup and returning to his post.

Ω

Once more walking along the road, Piet could now give more than a casual glance at the copse of trees.

Williams had to be hiding in there, he thought again, it was almost a mantra to him, *but why was he here?* The problem kept going around in his head, then he spotted the opening in the barrier of trees; it wasn't an opening as such, but a place where the trees were far enough apart to allow a vehicle through. The overhanging branches did a good job of concealing the gap, no wonder he hadn't seen it in the night, if he hadn't been looking for some such, then he would have missed it now, even in daylight.

Checking each way along the road and seeing nothing, he ducked into the gap and among the trees, now he could see the places where the Land Rover had scored the trees. He took the SIG pistol from his pocket, knowing how dangerous Williams could be, he wished he had a weapon with greater power, but he hadn't had time to find one. Everyone said Britain was awash with guns of all sorts, but that was if you knew where to look. Piet didn't know where to look, so he had to rely on the SIG he'd smuggled in.

After standing for ten minutes getting a feel for the smells, sights, and sounds of the copse, listening for anything that might be alien to the area, he started to move slowly through the wood, constantly looking where he put his feet, stepping on an old dry stick would sound like a pistol shot in the silence of the wood.

It took Piet nearly two hours to warily move around the whole of the perimeter without hearing or seeing anything of Williams, or anywhere he might have been. He now started quartering between the trees and only after another hour, did he find a sign, some snapped branches showing something had forced its way through, between two trees. Now knowing the approximate direction the something, which he was sure was Williams, had taken, he began to see other slight signs, a boot mark in a damp piece of ground and some bark scraped off a trunk; finally, he found the Land Rover.

Looking through the vehicle's windows, he could see nothing of any interest, only an old blue box of some sort; he tried the doors, but they were locked, and he didn't want to make any noise so he left it.

It was obvious to Piet that Williams was not being unduly careful; it was clear he didn't expect to be followed by someone who could track; he smiled at the thought. However as he again reached the edge of the wood, he still hadn't found where Williams had gone. The signs had all stopped; it looked as though he had come this far then disappeared. There were no tracks leading back or along the edge of the woods. The grass on the hillside was hard and dry, and if anyone, had, walked over it, the grass where they had stepped was now back to its proper level.

Stepping back into the concealment of the trees, Piet lit a cigarette and pondered, Williams had to be here, the Land Rover showed that, but he wasn't in the woods he was sure of that, so where had he gone. The hillside was bare all the way down to the old house and up the other side; he hadn't come out of the front of the wood so the only option was that he was at the old house or had gone further along the road after the wood had finished. Well, at least he knew where the Land Rover was parked, and Williams would have to come back for that, sooner or later.

It was at this point in his musings that he heard the shot.

Ω

It was nearly ten o'clock before Dylan saw any sign of Rory O'Brian. He came around from the back of the house accompanied by another guard; they were ambling looking deep in conversation and heading for where the duty guard was waiting, while still some ten yards apart, Rory looked up and called out something to the other man.

Dylan had no way of knowing if he had successfully passed whatever message he had started to say, as the expected hole appeared in the middle of his face and a spray of blood, brain, bone, and hair flew from the rear of his head. Dylan chambered another round by pure instinct, without allowing Rory's face out of the centre of his sights; only after this natural reaction did he allow himself to consider what the first round had accomplished and accept that a second shot would not be necessary. He lowered his weapon just as Rory collapsed to the ground. Task completed, he thought as he picked up the spent cartridge case.

Ω

The guards that were still in the compound headed for cover. After the killing of Patrick, they knew this would be the end of it and if they tried to peruse the sniper; it would be the end of them also, so showing due care they retreated to the house and inside.

231

Ω

Although it was still daylight, Dylan considered he could safely move out, besides after they had disposed of their weapons, the guards would have to call the police, so he would prefer to be a long way away by then. Not minding what noise he made, and with not a little effort, Dylan managed to pack up his equipment and turn to face the way back to the woods. His natural caution made him consider the hillside and treeline before he emerged. There was nothing visible to worry him so he moved into the open and started his way up to the trees.

Ω

It had not been a loud noise and another uninformed person would have thought a branch had snapped, but Piet had spent many years on the battlefield where knowing what every sound meant his living or dying; it was the sound of a rifle, one fitted with a suppressor, but where had it come from? It had to be close or he wouldn't have heard it, but there was nowhere for a rifleman to hide. Keeping inside the treeline, Piet surveyed the hillside. He saw nothing, but when he looked at the house, he could see a figure lying prostrate and two other men crawling back towards the house finally reaching it and disappearing inside, Assessing the way the body had fallen retracing the path that the bullet must have taken, he gave a low whistle. "He's in the gorse," Piet said aloud, with some disbelief and admiration, "it doesn't look possible." He continued to watch the bushes and finally was rewarded with the sight of Williams scrambling out of them.

Williams was coming almost straight at him; this was too good to be true. Releasing the safety from the SIG, Piet took aim; he would have liked to let Williams get a lot closer before shooting him, but he was still carrying the rifle, and Piet knew just too well how good he was with it, so from the shelter of a large tree trunk, he took careful aim and fired.

Ω

Dylan had now climbed half of the hill back to the safety of the trees; he didn't need to be in the crouched walk he was using, but it was the way he usually

232

moved out of a danger zone. He felt the tug on his sleeve at the same time as he heard the crack of the pistol that had shot at him. The sound and the tug on his coat sleeve told him the shot had come from just off to the right; the sound said it was from a small pistol, and it had to be from between the trees. With hardly any thought, he swung the rifle in the approximate direction and fired, then jumped to his feet and ran.

Angling to the left to increase the distance from the shooter before he fired again. He was only yards from the trees when the second shot came; it was close enough for him to hear the passing of the bullet, but again without it hitting him, he entered the treeline before the third shot came missing him completely. Carefully, Dylan put down the rifle and took out the Glock, now it had become a close-range fight, and he knew it had to be Piet Botha who was shooting, so now the finale of their revenge duel, he felt, was more evenly balanced.

Ω

Piet was cursing; he'd missed; he never missed at this range; it was the gun; it didn't fire true, but it was his own fault, he hadn't properly practised with it. It was second-hand when he'd bought it in Italy, and he'd only fired one clip of ammo and that on a short range, the one at Williams hadn't been long, not more than thirty yards, and he had tried the gun at that, but it had fired wide even then. Why hadn't he waited a few seconds more? He was also amazed at how fast Williams had been at returning the fire; he would have had hardly any time to think or aim, but he hit the trunk of the tree Piet was behind. Well, no use crying, he won't be able to do much with the bloody great rifle, not with these trees being so close together. Piet had seen where Dylan had entered the wood and now carefully set off in that direction.

Ω

Leaving the rifle where it was, Dylan slowly moved towards the point where the pistol shots had come from, at the same time angling to the left, he was sure Piet would be doing much the same from the other direction, and it would become a matter of who saw whom first. After twenty paces, Dylan squatted down close to a large tree and waited; no point in both of them moving, besides, it's only in the movies that the two protagonists would meet and start throwing lead about. As a hunter, Piet would be able to stalk silently, so there's no point with giving him more information by moving.

When it comes to hiding in a killing ground, the best policy, unlike in the movies, was to remain still. If the hunted was moving, he would probably be seen, but as many animals know if you remain totally still, it is possible for the hunter to stare at the prey and not see it, and if the prey was a man who could fight back, the hunter would lose, or at least he would give the first shot to the stationary man.

Ω

Piet realised that Williams would have moved, but he couldn't have moved far with a rifle that had a thirty-two-inch barrel. The only way to get advantage with the rifle was to line up on a point and wait for the opponent to enter the field of fire; it was the way of the lion, sit and wait, but it was the way of the hunter to anticipate the trap, and Piet had often hunted lion. Moving carefully, not looking for the man, but for the position, a place where a trap could be laid, the place that would have a clear field of fire of maybe five or six yards and enough space to swing the barrel of the rifle.

Ω

Piet had no knowledge of Dylan's history, of all the years of hunting, of setting traps, of swift movement to shoot the snipe before it could jink one way or the other, although the reaction he had shown to the first shot from Piet, should have told him that he knew his way around the hunting ground. So it was that there was a look of pure astonishment as the bullet from the Glock entered, up through Piet's armpit and into his neck, severing the carotid artery, a second shot went between his ribs through the lung and into his heart. Piet had made too many mistakes. First mistake, he was angry and hated Dylan so his mental attitude was wrong. Second mistake, not looking all around before taking a step, the step moved him forward of the tree he had been hiding behind. If he had looked down, he might have seen Dylan, but concealed as he was in his cams, and by the bracken at the base of the tree, it was likely it would not have helped him, for Dylan had taken the first shot before Piet could have looked down.

Dylan stood up and looked down at the fallen Piet.

"Why couldn't you have left it alone, Piet?" he asked of the dead figure. "You and your men must have been so long without a real fight, I suppose you couldn't stop yourselves. I did warn you, but you couldn't leave it, could you? You had to prove yourself, well, I'm sorry it had to happen, and now you won't even get a grave to lie in, as I can't have your dead body telling on me, can I?"

Now Dylan had a problem, he had to lose Piet's body and his car wherever it was, this sounds like a job for 'the man John'. Before returning to the Land Rover, Dylan returned to the point where he had first shot at Piet; he found the two cartridge cases then returned to the car and packed away the rifle, now adding Piet's SIG, then took out his 'special phone' and left a message.

"The task is completed, the second party has departed, and I'm in need of a clean-up." Then he ended the call and set about taking off his cams and putting away the rest of his equipment.

It was five minutes before he had a return call, this time a voice, new to him, asked, "What's the nature of the problem?"

"I have an ex-person who needs to go somewhere," Dylan replied, "and transport somewhere in the area that needs to go home."

"Give me the co-ordinates." Dylan did so.

"Now be somewhere else," the voice told him and hung up. Dylan needed no further telling; he wormed the Land Rover out of the wood and proceeded on his way home.

Epilogue

It was another two days before Wilcox called to see Dylan, he found him with various rifles and pistols spread out on the kitchen table.

"Are you preparing for a war in the near future?" he asked.

"No," Dylan replied, with a slight smile on his face, "but it doesn't hurt to be ready, and all weapons need to be regularly cleaned and serviced even if they haven't been used."

"I don't see the AI amongst them?" Wilcox had a special interest in the Artic International rifle as he had obtained it for Dylan when he wanted him to carry out a very long shot.

"No, you wouldn't," Dylan replied. "If I took that to a shoot, it would certainly cause some comment, but of course, I can't take it anyway because it doesn't exist, does it?" Only the two of them knew the sniper rifle existed, as it had never been registered. "No, this" – he indicated the items spread on the table – "is the usual preparation I do before a competition. I like to know all's well before I leave."

"I was forgetting you had a competitive side to your nature," Wilcox jested, "but that seems a lot of different guns for one shoot. When is the competition?"

"Tomorrow," Dylan informed him. "Why, have you thought of something else for me to do?" he asked with a quizzical look on his face.

"No, you're free to go and shoot your guns."

"Weapons," Dylan corrected him; he really had a great dislike of the diminutive name for his rifles and pistols. To Dylan, a gun was in the nature of being a shotgun or at least a smooth bore sporting breach loader with a single shot per barrel.

"Okay," Wilcox said accepting the correction. "No, I'm only here to let you know that everything has been 'tidied up' down in Wales, and say thanks for a good job." Dylan nodded his acceptance of the praise. "One point though" – Dylan knew it had been a perfect shot so the quizzical look re-appeared on his face – "the tidy up team wanted to know where you took the shot from. They were looking for evidence and couldn't work out how you could get the angle, unless you climbed a tree, and they couldn't see any evidence of that."

This finally made Dylan's face break into the biggest grin Wilcox had ever seen.

"Now that's got to be a professional secret," he said, "all I'll say is they were looking too high." If they hadn't been able to work out he'd been under the gorse bushes, then he wasn't going to tell them. "Just tell them there had been nothing left behind, so they wouldn't have found anything even if they knew where to look."

"Okay, it's a puzzle they'll have to live with, but while I'm here can you tell me what you know about the current terrorist situation?"

Dylan sensed another job possibly coming his way.

"I don't know anything more than what's on the news, why? Is there something I need to know?"

"Not at the moment," Wilcox said in a hesitant thoughtful tone of voice, then he made up his mind; he took a folder out of his briefcase and put it on the table. "There's possibly something brewing; it could be the sort of thing you're good at solving, and I might want to put it your way. This is just some reading material, for now" – he indicated the folder – "but if things go the way it looks like they're going to go, then I'll be back with a work folder."

Dylan was thoughtful for a while after Wilcox had gone, but he decided he couldn't plan anything until he had been tasked so returned to his competition planning.

For this competition he had chosen to enter for three events, so from his selection of weapons he chose the Ruger 21186 .22 rifle, the Walther GSP .32 pistol and his Beretta J24 shotgun with the 28-inch barrel, all weapons he'd used many times. Finally, he packed the Howa 1500 he'd bought and refurbished. He had no intention of using it on this competition; it was a present he'd bought for Jackie, why he didn't know, but he'd just felt like it. He didn't know if he would be able to present it as they hadn't made any arrangement, but he'd told her about the competition and how she should come along if she really had an interest in shooting; he didn't know if she was that interested, but he hoped.

The competition was being held on a private estate south of Cambridge, and as was usual, Dylan was there early wanting to take advantage of some practice before the start. He'd fired off ten rounds from each of the rifle and pistol and was happy with the result. As he was clearing his weapons, he heard the familiar voice. "You seem to be in good form today," Jackie said.

CPSIA information can be obtained
at www.ICGtesting.com
Printed in the USA
BVHW040840290821
615416BV00015B/664